A DREADFUL TRADE

There is a cliff, whose high and bending head looks fearfully in the confined deep ... the crows and choughs that wing the midway air show scarce so gross as beetles; halfway down hangs one that gathers Samphire, dreadful trade.

William Shakespeare *King Lear*

A Dreadful Trade

C. J. Bateman

EHB
Edgehill Books

Also by C. J. Bateman:
If The Cap Fits, Tony Williams Publications, 1993
String Fellows, Matador, 2010

ISBN: 978-1-9998037-0-4

First published in 2017 in the UK by Edgehill Books,
Edgehill House, Hawkhurst Road,
Cranbrook, Kent TN17 3QD
colinjbateman@hotmail.com
(00 44) (0)1580 712366
Reprinted 2018

Design and layout by Amanda Helm
amandahelm@uwclub.net

Printed and bound in Great Britain
by Short Run Press, Exeter EX2 7LW
www.shortrunpress.co.uk

Cover images:
(*front*) Beach at Dungeness © Robert Canis
(www.robertcanis.com);
(*back*) Early Spider Orchid on a Kent cliff © Jon Dunn.
(www.jondunn.com)

Author's Note

Although this is a work of fiction, the research and conservation work undertaken at the Royal Botanic Garden in Edinburgh and on the remote island of Socotra is both real and precious. I have used genuine locations wherever possible although I have taken a few liberties with the Kent geography to include the invented communities of Shoreness and Normanden. All characters are fictitious.

My thanks go to Martin Gardner and Sabina Knees for their infectious enthusiasm for the plant world. Also to my list of guinea-pig readers: Kay and Clive Harry, Steve and Siriol Hunter, David and Hilary Llewellyn and Simon Mann, and the ladies of the St Leonards-on-Sea book club for their thoughtful and encouraging appraisal. To James Essinger for his professional prompting, to Mary Kain for proof reading and to Amanda Helm for her great assistance and expertise in turning my efforts into a book. My thanks also to the two photographers, Robert Canis and Jon Dunn for allowing me to use their images on the book cover.

For Oliver

1

THE black-backed gulls and the herring gulls wheeled and circled gracefully beside the cliff, their incessant cries battling with the wind. I watched their aerobatics with admiration. A few of the birds broke away from the group to swoop towards the sea far below. They landed briefly on the waves and pecked tentatively before lifting off into the pewter grey sky again. Even the great scavengers of the shoreline did not appear to like what they had found.

It was a curious thought: I was standing on the same piece of wind-blown England where William Shakespeare was said to have walked during a visit to Kent. The cliffs now bore his name. Shakespeare had even led the Earl of Gloucester to this precipitous spot for a scene in King Lear.

Down below, however, was land not seen by Shakespeare and not shown on the dog-eared Ordnance Survey map that I had found on a bookcase in the holiday cottage. It was new land. From the North Downs Way above the white cliffs, I looked down on a piece of flat grassland where there should have been just sea. It looked incongruous, like a giant billiard table stuck on to the foot of the rock face poking out into the English Channel. There appeared to be no way down and yet there was a car park beside the water's edge with a handful of vehicles dotted around. The weak late-afternoon March sun had broken through a rare gap in the clouds and glinted off their roofs.

Another ten minutes into my walk provided the answer. The path divided beside a sign pointing down a steep stony slope. It said 'Samphire Hoe' and led through a thicket of conifers to the gaping mouth of a tunnel carrying a single track road through the chalk escarpment. Beside it was a raised path behind a metal barrier for cyclists and pedestrians.

When I emerged at the other end of the tunnel, the cliffs I had been walking along thirty minutes earlier reared up to my right. On my left was a forbidding concrete wall interrupted only by two closed metal gates. They were overlooked by a security camera below which, painted on the wall, was a blue and red circle containing the words 'Euro Tunnel'. In front of me, the vista opened up to reveal rolling grassland, a squat wooden building beside the car park and, beyond that, the vast expanse of heaving grey sea.

The information board in the visitors' centre told me that Samphire Hoe was a 'Countryside Project.' It was created by the millions of tons of chalky spoil dug out of the earth during the building of the Channel Tunnel and dumped off the shoreline. The new land bulged into the English Channel to the west of Dover at the foot of Shakespeare Cliff.

Growing on the crumbling chalky cliffs were the samphire plants that gave the Hoe its name. Until early in the twentieth century, the samphire had been collected by the hardy souls who scraped a dangerous living scrambling over this two-mile stretch of coastline. They dangled their children on ropes from the top of the cliff to harvest the precious fleshy leaves. The samphire, used to garnish plates in expensive London eateries, was pickled in salt water and sent to the capital by the new steam railway from Dover that emerged from tunnels and briefly rattled along the foot of Shakespeare Cliff beside the shoreline.

The railway and a short stony platform of the long-abandoned Shakespeare Halt station were all that remained from that era.

I started to follow the recommended circular route from the visitors' centre around the Hoe, which was criss-crossed with shingle paths. The route led to the sea wall where the waves crashed into the metal piles. The sea seemed angry that some of its shore been taken away by man, the spray flailing onto the wide concrete steps protecting the grasslands. The black-faced sheep, the bells around their necks clanging incessantly in the wind, turned their backs and continued to graze unconcerned behind the stock fence. The salty water thrown over the sea wall tumbled down the slippery barrage steps and through the drainage holes back into the churning waves ten feet below.

Out in the Channel, the red shape of the Varne Lightship stood out from Cap Blanc Nez on the French coastline with its own white cliffs. A sluggish tanker slipped along the horizon barely seeming to move as it headed towards some north European port. A little closer to the shore, a tossed blue stern trawler towed its net while a white cross-channel ferry waited patiently, its stack smoking, for its turn to enter Dover Harbour.

I walked with the wind buffeting my face towards the west, not passing or seeing another soul, only the gulls, circling and crying overhead, kept me company.

At the far tip of Samphire Hoe the flotsam gathered, trapped by the sea wall. Among the blue plastic bags and clumps of khaki seaweed, the discarded netting and wooden planks, bobbed something that was attracting the gulls.

It was the naked, bloated ashen body of a man. A gull landed in the water beside it and pecked at the unyielding flesh on the back before taking off, screeching as it went. It was the first time I had seen a dead body. It was face down. Long strands of black hair floated out in a circle around the crown of the head that was just above the water. A short piece of wood with jagged ends was caught underneath the right foot, which was twisted at an unnatural angle. The arms were stretched out as if reaching for help but touching nothing. It bobbed, its arms and legs moving with the swell of the sea but life had drifted away some time ago.

2

It was eight on a Monday morning, nine hours before my walk along Shakespeare Cliff. I was in my sister's tiny south London flat, a world away from discovering a body floating in the English Channel.

As I squashed my washbag into the space I had left in the suitcase, I contemplated my situation and did not like to imagine what else could go tits up.

The dull throb in my head reminded me of the farewell drinks I had had with well-meaning colleagues the night before. Now it was time to move on. Six months short of my 45th birthday, I was facing either a bleak future or an exciting prospect. My view of it had lurched between the two over the past week since I had lost my wife and my job on the same day.

Packing was something I prided myself in doing swiftly and efficiently, the result of having spent half my working life moving from hotel to hotel, country to country. A suitcase with all the essentials took twenty minutes to pack. And if you forgot anything, you could always buy it when you reached your destination, unless you were camping halfway up Everest or exploring Antarctica, two of the few places I had yet to visit.

Anyway, when your life has taken a drastically bad turn, as I knew mine had, you realise how little possessions actually matter. All those keepsakes, gadgets, and clutter that filled the matrimonial home no longer seemed important. Katie could have the lot for all I cared – apart from my laptop, music and clothes.

Not that she had been totally unreasonable when she had kicked me out a week earlier.

I had taken an early train back to London from Manchester, where I had spent the weekend working. There was the usual Monday morning editorial conference to attend at work but first I wanted to dump my overnight bag off at our home in Blackheath.

It was just after nine when I walked in. I was surprised to see Katie there. She usually went to the gym after doing the school run with our thirteen-year-old daughter Alice. She had clearly been waiting. Perched on a stool at the granite-topped kitchen bar, she was wearing her favourite black Burberry coat that her wealthy grandmother had bought her for her fortieth birthday. Her handbag was sitting on top of the two suitcases beside her.

She stood up and folded her arms across her chest. 'I want a divorce, Tom. And it's not open to debate.' The words sounded emotionless, as if she had been rehearsing them.

'I've been thinking about it for some time and this – our marriage – isn't working, although I don't suppose you've noticed.' She paused. 'You don't notice much around here.' Her voice sounded so cold, so hard.

'Katie. What? Why?' I could hear my voice rise in a crescendo until I shouted the final word.

She almost laughed. 'Oh come on, Tom. You know why. Or have you been that wrapped up with your work to not see it?

'Alice?' I looked around to see if our daughter was there.

'She's at school, of course. Do you think I wouldn't take her just because of this? Her life needs to stay as normal as possible. I've told her all she needs to know for now. We're going to stay with my parents for the week. You can take what you want but I'd like you out by the weekend. Alice needs a settled life and this is her home.'

'Katie, what the hell's going on?' I felt a mixture of panic, anger and despair rising inside me. 'I can't believe I'm hearing this. What the fuck's happened?'

'Nothing's happened, Tom. That's the trouble: nothing ever happens between us.' She started to sound angry. 'Can't you see the marriage isn't working?'

'What do you mean, isn't working? Look Katie, let's talk about this. Please.' I had started to plead. 'We can't trash fifteen years of marriage just like that. And what about Alice?'

'Alice will cope just fine – she's seen enough of her friends deal with their parents splitting up. She's not a kid anymore, Tom. Or haven't you noticed that either?'

'I really can't believe this.' I took a step towards the woman I thought I had loved for more than twenty years but decided against going any further. 'Ok – look, I know I'm away quite a bit with work but I do my job for us and it's well paid. It pays for this house, our nice lifestyle, Alice's school.'

I paused, searching to find reason. 'You've got your tennis, the am-dram society, your circle of friends. I thought that's what you wanted, for Christ's sake.'

Katie gave me one of her withering looks that she did

so well. 'It's not the "lifestyle" as you call it, Tom. It's us. When did we last have a proper holiday just the three of us? You cancelled the skiing trip in January because of your damn work. You didn't turn up for my parents' golden wedding anniversary. We don't have any fun anymore, we barely go out. There's no spark. Do I have to spell it out?'

We were now shouting at each other.

'What do you mean? I took you to the theatre two weeks ago. And last week we went to that party at the Baldwins … we had a laugh, didn't we – and when we got back. Well I thought it was good.'

'Yes, we screwed. Fuelled by red wine, we had our monthly fuck. And that's all it was. A quick fuck.'

I was stunned to hear her be so crude. She rarely swore unless it was at traffic wardens, and never in the house. We bickered, yes, but didn't all couples after fifteen years of marriage? There had never been any fighting or crockery throwing, though. After the arrival of our daughter, Katie seemed to lose some interest in sex, and she made it clear she did not want another child. She did not seem to be inclined to go back to her work as a primary school teacher either, so I had assumed she was happy with her routine.

I was desperately looking for some straws to clutch at. I sensed my well-structured life was falling apart in front of my eyes.

'I'll change, Katie. Change job so I'm not away so much if you like. Please, let's give this another chance. I need you and Alice. You're my life.'

The face that had once beguiled me showed no

emotion. She picked up the car keys from the kitchen counter and slipped them into her coat pocket as if the conversation was at an end.

Pushing its way through the crowd of questions in my head demanding to be asked was the most clichéd one of all.

'Is there someone else?' I blurted it out.

She looked straight back at me and said indignantly: 'No. Of course not.'

But I was sure she was lying. My work as a journalist forever asking questions had given me a sixth sense as to when someone was avoiding the truth.

One tell-tale sign was if the interviewee started playing with their hands. Katie was stroking her well-manicured fingers up and down the empty mug on the counter beside her. She was wearing bright mauve nail varnish, something I had not noticed before. I remember wondering then if she was made up to meet someone else.

'It will be better for both of us, but especially for Alice, if we keep this civilised,' she said.

With that, she hoisted her handbag over her shoulder, picked up her suitcases and headed down the hall. I remember that she made a point of slamming the door behind her like a loud emphatic full stop.

A week into my life as a single man heading for a divorce, I found myself gloomily replaying the scene again as I stared out of the grimy window of my sister's London flat. I had done this a lot over the past seven days and, to my surprise, Katie's words no longer cut through me. I was almost ambivalent to the situation. Perhaps she had been right all along: the love had gone cold and congealed. There was even a certain *frisson* about having an unchartered future. My only gnawing concern was how it would affect our daughter Alice.

The capital was busily going about its business as usual on an overcast March Monday morning. I watched a commuter train creep into Loughborough Junction. Its doors slid open for the passengers on the platform to elbow themselves into already packed carriages.

I had never been part of the daily commute and thanked my lucky stars for that as my eyes followed the train out of the station. My life as a newspaper journalist had involved irregular hours, often in unpredictable places. I rarely had to wear a suit, lived more than half my life in hotels and had spent more evenings sitting in a bar than a restaurant. I could not imagine life any other way, but I was beginning to wonder if I might have to.

The flat I had been staying in for the past week was not really meant for living in. It was more just a place to sleep. It was my sister's bolthole in London. Fleur had kept it on from her student days and used it for visits to London – for conferences, weekends out, even, possibly, romantic assignations – although I did not know much about that side of her life. She seemed too engrossed in her work in Edinburgh to bother with men. Probably we were similar in that respect: both putting our professions ahead of our personal life.

I was grateful to have been able to make use of the second-floor flat with its double bedroom and kitchen-diner, which also served as a living room, but in the past week I had seen too much of its four off-white walls hung with botanical prints.

I had studied every crack and cobweb idly wondering why life had dumped on me in such a spectacular fashion – and concluded I did not really care.

After Katie had left me standing alone in the kitchen of our elegant Victorian house, I had had no idea what to do. What do you do when your wife tells you she wants a divorce? So I went to work at the *Herald* newspaper as planned.

Being a Monday morning, all the staff from the sports department who were in the country were expected to attend the weekly conference to discuss the diary and plans for the coming week. But I never did attend that meeting. When I got to the newspaper's tall black-glass building in Canary Wharf, I was given the same message as I had received from my wife just two hours earlier: 'Sorry, but you are no use to us anymore.' Or words to that effect.

An embarrassed-looking sports desk secretary handed me my mail, on top of which was a brown A4 envelope with just my name typed on it: Tom Kidd.

The sheet of headed paper inside had the managing editor's name at the top and informed me that due to a 'reassessment of resources' I was being 'offered' redundancy. My role as the *Herald's* sports news reporter – the jack of all trades who turned up at big events to cover the rows, scandals, intrigue and hooliganism that surrounded sport – was being scaled back, said the letter. I was offered six months' salary as a redundancy pay off, and if I objected to that, I knew from the experiences of other journalists who had suffered the same fate, they would probably offer me three months instead.

It was a double whammy, to use the parlance of my profession. 'Kidd on the block' or 'Kidd on the skids' the headline would have read if the story had been worth writing. I was just another victim of an industry on the retreat.

I had lost my wife and my job on the same day. Careless some might say. A God-sent opportunity some of my more cynical colleagues suggested in the pub that evening with a wink, wink, nudge, nudge that would have done Eric Idle proud.

That was a week ago – a week of farewell drinks and handshakes with colleagues and friends. At the empty matrimonial home I had collected a case of clothes, a cardboard box filled with my favourite CDs and a few books, my personal laptop and passport, and decamped to Loughborough Junction. I was now packing again. As I zipped the lid shut, I looked out at the next packed train full of tired-looking commuters.

I wondered. They say troubles come in threes, but even if they do I was pretty damn certain I was still better off than the workers on their daily grind into London's money-making sweatshops.

3

For the first time I could remember, my life was not in a rush. No deadline to meet, no appointment to keep. Not even a dinner to get home for. As I eased my ageing Audi through London's choked traffic heading south on the A21, the rasping of Tom Waits seemed a suitable soundtrack to life. I slipped 'Heartattack and Vine' into the CD player.

On the leather seat next to me was my trusty map book and a pamphlet for Lighthouse View Cottage, a holiday let in Kent that my sister Fleur had fixed up for me when I had told her I needed to get away. It belonged to a colleague of hers, Gideon Squires, who worked at Kew Gardens. He had told Fleur that he was more than happy to have someone use it at this time of year and I could stay there without charge until the Easter school holidays, which were a month away.

Since Katie had delivered her vitriolic verdict on our marriage, I had tried, with some success, to convince myself that a change of direction in life was not such a bad thing. The *Herald* had also done me a favour by making me redundant, I reasoned. I would write that novel I had always believed lurked somewhere inside me.

In the seven days since life had been turned on its head by my wife and my editor, the toughest moment had been that first phone call from our tearful daughter Alice.

'Dad, I don't want you and Mum to split up.'

'Neither do I, Ali, but Mum has her reasons.'

'She told me you and her had grown apart over the years and both wanted to do your own thing. Isn't that right?'

'Not totally. But I think she became fed up with me being away so much working, although that's all changed now.' I told Alice about my redundancy from the *Herald*, which had taken immediate effect.

She brightened up. 'Give it a few weeks, Dad. You and Mum could get back together, especially when she hears about your job and knows you won't be going away all the time working.'

I had felt like replying 'fat chance' but said simply: 'We'll see Ali, I don't know. I think your mother may have other plans. Whatever happens, I won't be far away. We'll still see a lot of each other and you can always ring. It won't affect us.' I put the emphasis on the last word.

'What are you going to do?'

'I think I'll take a few weeks holiday. Probably in Kent, so not far away. I'll be back for the parents' evening – if that's OK with Mum. I'll see you then. I'll be OK, don't worry.' I was beginning to choke up and abruptly called a halt to the conversation. 'Bye love. Hugs and kisses.'

The memory of the call made me feel tearful. I increased the volume on the CD player a few notches, pushed the Audi up to eighty miles-per-hour and whistled down the dual carriageway of the A21 not caring whether there were speed cameras or cops waiting around the next bend.

My foot eased off the pedal as the dual carriageway

gave way to narrower roads and familiar farmland. The Audi hugged the corners that I knew well, and I started to get excited about the prospect of penning the novel, which I had attempted to start in Fleur's flat last week without any success. I had done the laptop equivalent of ripping the paper out of a typewriter, screwing it into a ball and tossing it into a bin countless times. The 'del' lettering on the delete button was beginning to fade.

Since childhood days staying with my grandparents in the Weald of Kent, I had loved the stories of the eighteenth-century smugglers who shipped live sheep across the Channel at night and brought back barrels of brandy and chests of tea in return. From time to time, fights would break out between the gangs, such was the rivalry, and herein lay the seed of my plot for a novel. Unapologetically ripping off an original idea from William Shakespeare, who was hardly likely to sue, I was going to weave the story around two star-crossed lovers from the rival village clans who met in secret and were determined to break away from the lawless ways of their families.

'Sounds like a great bodice ripper,' one of my rather leery colleagues had commented over a pint one evening a few months earlier when I had outlined the idea of one day writing a book. 'Already playing out the steamy scenes with Katie, are you? Making sure they're authentic?'

The fellow reporter had smirked at the idea. If only he had known my love life with Katie even then was not so much steamy as freeze-dried.

I jabbed the eject button and swapped Tom Waits for a Squeeze CD to lighten the mood, but it did not really work. I still felt Up the Junction. Having had a partner for almost half my life, it was disconcerting to be single again.

'Thirst things first,' I muttered to myself, pleased with the twist on a well-worn cliché as the Audi pulled into a pub car park, almost with a mind of its own. I could now afford these little stops with no pressure of deadline time to hurry me along. The pub, appropriately called 'The Smugglers Retreat,' looked welcoming enough with its blackboard menu propped up against a flower tub by the front door. I switched off my mobile phone, picked up the newspaper I had bought that morning and headed inside.

Halfway down a pint of Shepherd Neame, I scanned the paraphernalia decorating the bar. I was the only customer as yet this Monday lunchtime. On the walls beneath the black and white beamed ceiling were pinned corny reproductions of wanted posters for 'Ye Smugglers of Kent County' and a gruesome account of the hanging of one Thomas Kingsmill in 1748 for the murder of two dragoons who were escorting a shipment of tea from the Rye Customs House to London.

'And they say these are dangerous times.' The young lad from behind the bar who had served me cut through my train of thought. 'There's always been bad 'uns, I reckon.'

'Yes indeed. You're right there. Same again please, and I'll go for the soup of the day.'

He offered me the fresh pint adding: 'I'll bring the soup over.'

'Does smuggling still go on along the Kent coast?'

'Think so,' he said. 'Only these days it's for fags and drugs – and, of course, those immigrants holed up in Calais. People smuggling's often in the news.'

'Yes, of course. I've read about it,' I retreated to a corner table with my newspaper and turned my attention to the crossword.

1 across: *Lunch for a cowardly balloonist (7,2,1,6).* 'That's easy', I thought filling in the little squares: *Chicken in a basket.*

Two pints of Best at lunch time may not have been advisable but had made life seem so much more acceptable as I slipped back into the creased leather seat of the Audi. I had thought about replacing the A4 several times and it was not the cost that had deterred me. I had grown very fond of the old girl. We suited each other, unlike some other relationships in my life – and, unlike those other relationships, I could not be accused of neglect in this case. The leather seats were literally squeaky clean and gave off the rich smell of hide cream. I was scrupulous about having the car serviced and repaired, and was very pleased with the latest installation, a hands-free Bluetooth telephone kit.

I found the number I wanted and pressed the 'call' button as I eased out of the pub car park. After a couple of rings, a hearty voice crackled over the speaker system in the Audi.

'Billy, you old bugger. Howya doing?'

Larry Lander was one of the few colleagues who still used my nickname – Billy the Kidd – from my days as a cub journalist in Nottingham. We had joined the local evening paper at about the same time, learned our trade together, got drunk together and chatted up girls together. It was a deep, unshakeable friendship that could be picked up at any time even though we saw each other probably only once a year, and never exchanged Christmas cards.

'I'm good Larry, and you?'

'Fine. More to the point, what about you? Read about your redundo in the *Guardian Media Supplement*.'

'To be honest, I'm OK about it, the *Herald* was becoming a joke with all the cut-backs. I'm not sorry to be out. But there have been a few other things in my life too that aren't public knowledge. I've split from Katie for one thing, or rather, she's split from me.'

'Wow. That is big news. Sorry to hear it,' said Larry. 'Although, she was always too good for you. She should have chosen me that night at the barn dance.'

The barn dance. I remembered it well and felt a pang of sadness. Katie, who was dark haired, slim and striking, and her shorter, plumper blonde friend, whose name I could not recall, had come over to the Lander–Kidd axis at the bar that evening to ask for a light. Lander had pointed to the straw bales all around the barn and the large 'Strictly No Smoking' sign over the bar. The result was the four of us had retired outside to fan the flames of our youthful passion. As far as I could remember, Lander and the blonde had lasted a couple of energetic weeks, but I was infatuated by Katie from day one.

Lander and I had run a racy and profitable little newspaper agency business in the Midlands before going our different ways in the trade. The success of the agency and the stories we sold to the national newspapers had got me noticed and led to the offer of a staff job in London. Lander had had his offers too, but said he did not fancy the big city life. Instead he had stayed on the provincial circuit, moving on to become the editor of various local papers, ending up at his present cosy number in charge of the *South Coast Gazette*, a weekly that served the south coast from Dover to Brighton. Despite our different career moves, we were about to end up as neighbours again.

'Larry, I've got a favour to ask and it's to do with my new life as a poor unemployed writer making a fresh beginning,' I said, turning the Audi off the main road and heading along deserted lanes that were alive with the white blooms of wood anemones in the coppiced woodland on either side. The coast was not far away now and the sun appeared as if on cue.

'Aw, my heart bleeds,' said Lander. 'What is it, wanna job on the *SCG*?'

'No, nothing like that, but I do want to use the *South Coast Gazette*. Look, I'm on my way to Shoreness for a few weeks in a holiday cottage. It's not far from you, so how about meeting up? I'll explain then.'

'It'll be good to see you again. Lunch tomorrow? I think I can squeeze you into my busy diary,' said Lander with a hint of self-mockery.

'Perfect. I'll ring in the morning when I'm settled in. How's Sue, by the way?'

'Uhh-uh. Long story. Tell you tomorrow.' With that Lander hung up. Either that or the signal on the mobile had cut out as I drove towards the desolate flat marshlands that stretched to the coast in this corner of southern England.

I pulled into a muddy farm gateway and a few sheep wandered over to peer through the five-bar gate, their bleating lambs not far behind. I picked up the directions for Lighthouse View Cottage that I had printed off the internet to make sure I was still on the right road. I was.

'The perfect secluded holiday getaway on one of the most unspoilt stretches of coast in Kent. Lighthouse View Cottage is ideally located for walkers, nature lovers, artists or those who just want to get away from their hectic everyday life. Conveniently situated with a local store, pubs and Shoreness Wildlife Centre nearby. Two bedrooms, central heating. Dog owners welcome. Weekly rates on application.'

I read the blurb on the printout again. I was sure it would do the trick, and I liked the sound of 'pubs' plural. I glanced at the map book and pulled out on to the lane just as a tractor started to fill the rear-view mirror. It was indicating to turn into the gateway where I had been parked. Do not want to upset the locals just yet, I thought, holding up a hand of apology to the farmer as I floored the accelerator.

Five miles to go and then I could settle into the holiday cottage. I planned to take a walk before it got dark to clear away the cobwebs, then I would get stuck into tales of smuggling, dirty deeds and plenty of bodice ripping.

4

I never did get round to heaving bosoms and ribald smugglers on that first evening in Shoreness. Events seemed to overtake me as much of it was it was spent at Dover Police Station explaining how I had come to discover the body floating among the flotsam in the water at Samphire Hoe.

'A walk, Mr Kidd? From where?'

'From Shoreness, along the cliff path originally, then to the Hoe.'

'Shoreness? That must be at least five miles from Samphire Hoe.' The young male constable sounded incredulous as he looked up from his note-taking. 'Do you often take such long walks?' Trying not to sound condescending, I told him I did.

The police had arrived in two marked cars at the Hoe within ten minutes of me reporting my find to a warden in the visitors' centre. I took them to where the body was bobbing with the rest of the debris trapped by the sea wall. Two divers in wetsuits attached to ropes were climbing down the metal rungs of a ladder into the icy waves.

I did not wait to see them fish the cadaver out. The macabre held no fascination for me.

Back in Lighthouse View Cottage, having been given a lift to my latest temporary home by an officer just finishing his shift, I decided the world of fiction could wait. Instead I opened the bottle of Rioja I had bought before leaving London that morning along with other essential provisions, and settled on the sofa to map out my week ahead.

The cottage was quite perfect although Shoreness was not how I had imagined. When I had arrived in mid-afternoon, the keys were, as promised, waiting for me under an upturned flower pot behind the wheelie bins at the rear.

To the front of the cottage was a vast, bleak expanse of pebbles and scrubby vegetation beyond the single track road that ran past the small front garden. The flat landscape melted into the grey seascape of the English Channel which met a grey hazy horizon, but even the greyness of the surroundings had not diminished my determination to be positive about my new status as an unemployed estranged husband.

The last part of the journey that afternoon had been one through places whose names resonated with history. The Isle of Oxney had taken me to Peening Quarter. I had taken a wrong turn in Rye Foreign and passed signs for Snave and Brenzett before driving across the eerie Romney Marsh. Its dark reed-filled drainage ditches on either side of the road looked ready to swallow up any careless passer-by. The flatlands, once a flood plain for the sea, gave way to the stubble and stones of Shoreness, that jutted into the Channel like a giant nose.

The vista was barren and bleak yet had a curious attraction. It seemed that no-one bothered with planning regulations, judging by the shacks and huts propped up on brick footings alongside the beach road. Some were cared for, painted in bright reds, blues and greens with neat rockery gardens and benches outside the front door. Others were neglected and ugly. One blast from a winter gale and they looked as though they would be reduced to a pile of firewood.

Before I had reached the beach road and the nearby Lighthouse Inn, I had driven past the 'Welcome to Shoreness' sign. I also noticed a less official message to motorists daubed in white on the side of an abandoned farm wagon in a field beside the road.

FUCK OFF OFF.

A little further on, painted in green lettering on the road in much the same way as cycling fans write the names of their Tour de France heroes on the mountain climbs in the Alps and Pyrenees, there was more graffiti, although this message had a little more decorum about it.

SOS.

Green ribbons flapping in the wind were tied to a ten-foot high fence topped with twisted razor wire that had appeared on the right beside the road. With no other traffic in sight, I had pulled on to the stony verge. Behind the wire on a metal post was an altogether more menacing official sign that brooked no argument.

'Keep Out. Danger Area. Ministry of Defence'

I followed the MoD fence for at least a mile before it cut away from the road at right angles and headed towards what I assumed was the distant shoreline. What lay behind it was barren land and a few seemingly unoccupied Nissen huts with blackened windows and smokeless metal flues sticking out of their corrugated roofs.

As the road swung to the east, I saw the square bulk of the Shoreness Nuclear Power Station lit up like a twinkling Orwellian installation ahead. The Audi's ten-year-old suspension complained as it bounced over a single line rail track that curved through shut gates in the perimeter fence of the power station. Beside a gorse bush next to the track was a battered old Chesterfield sofa that someone appeared to have fly-tipped.

I passed the road entrance to the plant, the junction illuminated by floodlights burning brightly even though it was not dark.

'You are now entering a Nuclear Licenced Site. No unauthorised vehicles' said the signs on the verges on either side of the long straight side road that led towards the power station. In the distance, there was a check point, red lights and a barrier. I could almost feel the security cameras on top of poles either side of the road following me as I passed, watching me with a sinister electronic eye.

I was expecting a few calls that first morning in the holiday cottage so I took my recharged phone into the little bathroom as I prepared to face the day. In the shaving mirror I was disappointed to see a rather dishevelled saggy face staring back at me. The reflection belonged to that of a man closer to fifty than forty. I rubbed the grey whiskers on my chin. Although I still made a point of trying to jog at least twice a week and had virtually cut red meat out of my diet, there was no denying the march of years. No wonder Katie, who still looked spectacularly good to me, was keen on a newer model. I was attacking the four-day stubble when the phone started chirping merrily.

'Hi Sis,' I had seen Fleur's name on the screen.

'Hello Tom. You settling in at the cottage?'

'Yes, it's perfect. How's Edinburgh?'

'Edinburgh's lovely as usual, except the debate about independence is still hanging around like a bad smell. It won't go away I fear until the SNP get their way. Anyway, important matters – you still on for this weekend? Hope your writing sojourn will not get in the way of that.'

'Definitely not.' It had been almost three months since I had last seen Fleur over Christmas at our parents' home in the Midlands. I liked and admired my younger, brighter sister enormously but we did not see nearly enough of each other, she with her work at the Royal Botanic Garden in Edinburgh, and I with a job that took me around the world. Well, that could all change now. The Edinburgh visit had been a long-standing arrangement and, although it had become a solo trip instead of being a family one, I was in no mood to cancel.

'I'm planning to come up on the Friday sleeper. Should arrive about eight Saturday morning. Is that OK?'

'It is and it isn't,' said Fleur, whose middle-England accent was taking on a slight Scottish burr. 'It's fine for the weekend but I can't pick you up at Waverley Station. Got an important visitation from the wee men of Japan. It's a VIP delegation as they sponsor us so heavily, and I'm under a three-line whip from the bosses to be there for a working breakfast at the Garden and to give them a chat in the lecture theatre afterwards.'

'No problem. I'll have breakfast in town and get a bus to the Garden. Meet you there late morning. I'll text when I arrive.'

'Perfect,' said Fleur. 'And I'm taking you out for dinner to a super new place in Leith Docks on Saturday night with my partner Chris. I want you two to meet, I think this is pretty serious this time … but not a word to Mum and Dad yet.'

'Intriguing. See you Saturday, and I'll bring my best kilt.'

'No you won't. Bye, take care.'

Fleur hung up. She had sounded excited, a bit like a teenager on a date with the classroom heart-throb. As far as I knew, my sister, five years my junior, had never had a serious romance. I had always assumed it was because she was so in love with her preservation work trying to save some of the world's rarest plants that she brought back to Edinburgh from her trips overseas and nurtured in the acres of greenhouses that the public visiting the Garden never saw. She had climbed the ladder in the botanical world, so much so that Kew had tried to lure her down to London more than once. But she loved Edinburgh and its pioneering work too much to move, even to the most famous gardens in the world. She was now Dr Kidd and most of the men she worked with were under her supervision. Perhaps they found Fleur, who had been perfectly named for her vocation by our far-sighted parents, too intimidating. Like most big brothers, I felt protective towards my little sister, and I looked forward to giving Chris the once over. Not that I was an expert in choosing the right partner, I thought to myself as I returned to the shaving mirror.

Breakfast done, I cradled a third mug of strong black coffee as I sat on the sofa and flicked through a copy of last week's *South Coast Gazette* that had been left on the kitchen dresser. I thought I had better give the paper the once over before ringing its editor Larry Lander as arranged.

The front page story was about a suspected increase in people smuggling across the Channel and heightened customs patrols along the Kent coast. Otherwise the paper was full of the regular diet that sustained a local rag: council planning rows, reports from the magistrates' court of minor misdemeanours, local sports, weddings and funerals. The letters page was a collection of robust views, many of them, no doubt, penned by the staff of the *South Coast Gazette* if they did not have enough genuine correspondence that week to fill.

It was part of journalistic folklore that 'Disgusted of Tunbridge Wells' had been born when a reporter on the town's paper invented a particularly indignant letter about a local issue and signed it with the now famous pseudonym.

I dropped the paper on the sofa, picked up my phone and dialled Lander's mobile number.

'*SCG*, good morning,' said a bored sounding female voice.

'Oh, sorry. Have I got Mr Lander's phone?'

'Yes. I'll see if he's free. Who's calling?'

'Tom Kidd.'

'Ah yes, Mr Kidd. Larry mentioned you might call,' she suddenly sounded more alert. 'I'll get him, he's just on the landline to the police. Morning calls as usual.'

Before I could say I would call back if it was more convenient, I heard the phone at the other end being put down and muffled voices in the background.

'Morning calls'. That took me back to my days on local newspapers. Morning calls were the staple diet of a district reporter, checking with a round of contacts for anything that might be happening. The local police always had a duty officer ready to fill in the media about any stories they wanted out in the public domain, such as seeking witnesses to the vandalism at the bus shelter by the village green or an appeal for rubberneckers to keep away from the suspicious fire that had engulfed the cricket club pavilion. Sometimes it was even more serious than that.

'Billy. Sorry to keep you waiting,' Lander broke into the reminiscences. 'Needed a long chat with the cop shop, there's a lot going on in your neck of the woods.'

'My neck of the woods?'

'Yes. Shoreness. There are a couple of protest groups hovering around making news, but now there's something more interesting – a body has turned up. It's too long-winded to go into over the blower, is lunch still on?'

'Certainly is. How about my local, the Lighthouse? It looked OK when I passed it yesterday.'

'That's fine by me, I want to do a bit of sniffing around there anyway. You seen the "Fuck Off Off" protests?'

'Yep, what's that all about?'

'Patience dear boy. My secretary's waving at me, I

think I have another call on the landline. See you about twelve thirty.' The line went dead.

It was time to get to know more about my new surroundings, the parts of Shoreness that I had not taken in on my walk out of the village to the North Downs Way yesterday.

My cottage was a well-maintained wooden chalet among a rather decrepit series of homes along the beach road that ran through the shingle landscape that in turn gave way to the sea, some two hundred yards away across a rotting boardwalk. The cottage was painted green and white under a red corrugated iron roof. The little porch led to the pebble garden with no borders save for four flower tubs sprouting early daffodils, their yellow trumpets swaying wildly in the wind. Beyond the tubs was the verge of the road.

As soon as I opened the porch door I was thankful to be in my fully lined all-weather jacket, a must for journalists who had to spend hours standing outside hotels in car parks waiting for a chance interview, or for those evenings spent in freezing football grounds. The wind off the English Channel was biting, and the solid banks of clouds raced across the sky, chasing each other. I zipped up the jacket so that even my chin was nestled in its warm soft liner.

My new neighbourhood could never be called 'touristy'. The pebble dunes stretched out ahead until they ran into the high fence that surrounded the looming bulk of the nuclear power station, its vast pylons standing like sentries on one side and marching into the distance. I had learned over breakfast from a pamphlet in the cottage that English Heritage had designated the area a desert as it was one of the driest and most unusual habitats for flora and fauna in the country.

I started walking towards the power station with the sea to my left. I could not see it but I could smell its salty freshness and hear its rhythmic waves rolling pebbles up and down the beach behind the stony dunes. Along the land side of the road were dwellings, a few well-kept, others neglected and seemingly empty. Many were painted black or were simply stained wood. There was not a brick in sight apart from those used to build the pillars on which the shacks were perched above the stony ground.

Some of the homes were long narrow huts with rounded roofs that looked vaguely familiar. Railway carriages. I realised that was what they were. Old carriages that had been dragged here somehow and propped up on bricks, painted and turned into quaint homes with net curtains and a flue stack. Some of the residents had added porches at the front and extensions at one end, but the distinct shape of old railway rolling stock was still obvious.

On the sea side of the road there were fewer homes but there was the 'Shoreness Fish Shack' which was clearly not open for business on this gloomy March morning. Another boarded up caravan, its tyres flat and windows grubby, had a sign propped up outside offering fishing trips and live bait, while another promised 'diving trips to the wrecks – fully licenced.' These businesses appeared to be in hibernation for the winter. There was little sign of life apart from some movement further out across the pebbles nearer the shoreline. There, some half-a-dozen four-wheel drive vehicles were parked and figures moved around, disappearing over the last ridge of stones towards the water. Two abandoned fishing boats, their planked hulls full of holes, masts broken, stood at drunken angles on the pebble bank, as did a more modern small red trawler next to a tractor that was puffing diesel fumes, its engine noise indiscernible, blown away on the wind. A narrow-gauge rail track on rotten sleepers, once used to haul boats up the beach, snaked across the stones to the shore.

With gusts of the westerly slapping into my face furiously, my earlier sense of anticipation started to fade. I was slightly dismayed that the surroundings were not more inspiring. If the muse of creative writing was going to settle on my shoulder over the coming two weeks, I had imagined it happening while I sat at my laptop as I looked out of the cottage window at a glorious seascape seeking inspiration. Instead, all I could see were mounds of stones, grey skies and a tractor.

The image of the swollen body floating in the water, came drifting back into my consciousness. What possessed anyone to go swimming in the English Channel at this time of year? I shuddered. The policeman who had given me a lift back the previous evening had suggested these were the most likely circumstances surrounding the drowning. 'Poor sod, what a way to go,' he had said.

The lighthouse was the only other notable feature on the beach road, set a mile from my holiday cottage down a crumbling tarmac track nearer the tip of Shoreness and just outside the power station fence. Opposite the lighthouse track on the other side of the road was the pub of the same name. The Lighthouse Inn did not need a car park. It was surrounded by densely crushed stones. It made the sign that told visitors that there was overflow parking at the rear seem superfluous. Outside were two more four-wheel drive vehicles and a red MGB roadster with its roof down and chrome bumpers shining. It was a fine example of a classic car I had once driven in my youth.

The Inn was another single-storey wooden building. The pub sprawled this way and that as if extensions had been added over the years. At the front was a conservatory full of dining tables that were probably packed in the high season, but today a ginger cat was the only occupant, curled up on the table nearest the window, luxuriating in a fleeting appearance of the sun finding a gap in the clouds and shining through the glass. The cat did not even bother to look up when I opened the door and let in a gust of March wind.

Beyond the conservatory was the low-ceilinged bar, dining tables at one end, pool table at the other, with a small area in the middle for drinkers. The place had that heady aroma of polish and disinfectant that all pubs seemed to have after their morning clean.

Car number plates from around the world, many battered and rusty, festooned the walls. Among the plates were old black and white photographs of ships. There was a shipping map of the local coastline with contours showing the depth of the sea as it sloped away from the shore.

'Can I help?'

I turned to see a young woman with a pleasant beaming smile. She was wearing a tee shirt at least two sizes too small for her ample proportions which bore the slogan 'I love shucking' beside the picture of a juicy oyster.

'Can I just get a coffee, please?' I made sure I looked her in the eye.

'Of course. Latte, cappuccino?'

'Just plain black please. Americano.'

'Anything to eat?'

'Not just yet, I'm expecting someone. I'm sure we'll have something then.'

'Won't be a moment, take a seat, I'll bring it over,' said the girl, as she disappeared through a door behind the bar.

I did as I was told and while I sat at a table I glanced at my fellow customers. There were four of them. Sitting in the bay window were two ladies who looked to be in their sixties and were clearly dressed for walking with thick boots, rucksacks on the floor and an Ordnance Survey map sprawled across the table which they were studying intently. I guessed the MGB belonged to them. Sitting by an open fire, where logs crackled and threw off a fierce heat, was a craggy, white-bearded man sucking on an unlit pipe. He looked like an old fisherman still perplexed by the smoking ban in pubs. At the far end of the bar in the gloom near the vacant pool table was the only other customer, a burly man dressed in denim shirt and jeans who eyed me sullenly. When our eyes met, he drained his pint, picked up a packet of cigarettes and slipped off the stool, calling 'Bye, Eve' as he walked past me to the door.

If Eve was the barmaid, she did not reply, but she did emerge with a coffee and a menu tucked under a plump arm.

'No rush to order, but thought you might just like to see what we're offering,' she said sweetly, handing over a single sheet of typed card. 'Dab is off, they're a bit scarce at the mo, but Mum's doing local sole instead. With or without the caper butter, on or off the bone.'

'Thanks,' I said as one of the four-wheel drive vehicles gunned out of the car park amid a shower of gravel.

'That's Gary,' said Eve, glancing out of the window at the dust swirling in the shafts of sunlight. 'Never did pass his test but likes to think he's a bit of a boy racer.'

I made a start to the crossword I had found in the *South Coast Gazette* that morning. I had decided that, with my 50th birthday on the not-so-distant horizon, a daily mental workout was the best way to stave off the onset of dementia. Whether there was any medical evidence to back up the theory, I had no idea, but I had seen my once articulate and argumentative grandmother deteriorate rapidly in her care home. Now she no longer knew who this man was when I visited. The thought of going down the same dark path terrified me, so I had decided to keep the marbles rolling with the cryptic word puzzles.

Some were easier than others, and the *SCG* clearly did not expect too much of its readers.

4 Down. *Material for building a windscreen (6-6).*

I was about to put pen to paper when Larry Lander puffed in, red-faced, bald as a billiard ball and just as round.

'Christ, is this Brooklands round here? Sodding idiot in a Range Rover almost forced me off the road.'

'You haven't changed.' I grinned, getting to my feet and shaking my head at my old mate. 'Still battling the anorexia, I see.'

'You can talk … a few pounds have been creeping on your waistline since I saw you last summer,' replied Lander, eyeing up the beers on offer as well as Eve's well-filled tee shirt.

'Only a few,' I conceded. 'Haven't been jogging lately but I aim to take it up again while I'm here, it's certainly nice and flat for running if a bit windy.'

'Pint of Clipper, please, m'luv. What about you, Billy?' asked Lander, making a point of sneering at my half-finished coffee.

'Go on then. I'll have the same. And the lady is ready to take our food order when you're ready.'

Over the first pint I told him how I had received my marching orders from the newspaper and my wife on the same day. Lander in return revealed that he was not only in the dog-house but on the end of a very short leash as far as his wife Sue was concerned after she discovered he had been away on a 'working weekend' with Jasmine – the secretary who had answered my call that morning.

'You idiot. Is that the third time Sue's found you out? You're getting too old for all that.'

'Fourth time,' said Lander sheepishly. 'She'll be OK in a few weeks. Trouble is, Jazzy – that's Jasmine – thinks we still have something going on. It's all rather messy.'

'Literally, I should think,' I said as the food arrived cradled by a round rosy middle-aged lady who could only have been the mother of Eve the barmaid.

'One traditional fish and chips,' she said, putting down a mountain of food in front of an appreciative Lander. 'And one grilled sole with side salad instead of chips. Enjoy, gents.'

Lander smothered his chips with salt and created a lake of ketchup beside his fish. 'So Billy, you said this was not just a social get-together. What can I do for you?' he said through a mouthful of cod and batter.

'Your paper goes back a long way, doesn't it? I'm assuming you have archive files stored away somewhere. I want to do a bit of digging to make my novel authentic. Do you have copies going back to the nineteenth century?'

'I'm sure we have. They'll be on microfilm now because all the old newsprint was just falling to bits. Help yourself. When are you thinking of coming?'

'Thanks – tomorrow afternoon if that's ok?'

'Fine,' said Lander. 'You'll get the chance to meet the lovely Jasmine too, and you can admire her secretarial assets.'

He winked and grinned the sort of lascivious grin that once spawned a thousand laughs in the Carry On films. Lander's attitude to the opposite sex would no longer be tolerated in a modern national newspaper office. Perhaps, I thought, that was why he had happily spent his time in journalism's backwaters where political correctness meant voting Tory.

The pub lunch was accompanied by exaggerated tales of our past together and washed down with plenty of laughs. It was the sort of friendship that had been bolted together by youthful escapades that formed a strong and unspoken code between us.

'Now there's something I think you could help me with if you're prepared to put your journo's hat back on for a while,' said Lander, pushing his empty plate away with a degree of satisfaction.

'I'll get another couple of pints and you can try me out. That wasn't the idea of my visit to Shoreness. I've given all that up, Larry. At least for now.'

Through the second pint, Lander told me about the police calls he had been making that morning. The naked body of a young man – aged about twenty – had been spotted in the sea by a walker at a place called Samphire Hoe that weekend, he said.

I held up a hand to stop him. 'I was that walker,' I told him, enjoying the look of shock on his face. 'I was going to get around to telling you about my walk yesterday but we sort of became side tracked with the trip down memory lane. Anyway, there's not much to tell really except I saw the body and the police were called. You probably know more than me.'

'The police haven't officially identified the body,' said Lander. 'But they've told me off the record that they're pretty certain it's that of a young artist-cum-hippy who was living here in Shoreness. Been here for about three months holed up in an old VW Dormobile at the nature reserve. There's no sign of him there now.

He's half Danish on his father's side with a British mother, and the police think the parents, who live in Bristol, are away. They haven't been able to contact them yet to get formal identity of the body. No-one around here knew him that well as far as they can tell, but he hasn't been seen since last week.'

Lander paused while the barmaid collected the plates and gave the table a cursory wipe with a grey dishcloth. 'Can I get you anything else?' she asked. I noticed the smile had gone.

I shook my head and patted my stomach. 'Not for the moment, thanks. It was delicious.'

As she disappeared towards the kitchen, I looked back at Lander. 'Why do you want my help? Isn't it a routine tragedy – if there is such a thing. Swim gone horribly wrong?'

'I expect so,' said Lander, lowering his voice and looking around the bar theatrically. 'But there's a touch of the Wild West about this place. The yokels can be a law unto themselves especially out here on the Ness, and they don't take too kindly to incomers unless they're tourists with fat wallets.

You've probably noticed they don't take too much notice of planning regulations either, and they've never heard of the Highway Code or drink-driving laws. I don't suppose they warmed to a young arty-farty lad moving in. He may have made enemies because he is – or was – involved in the other business going on around here.'

'Fuck off off?' I suggested, keeping my voice down so as not to alarm the lady walkers.

'Yes. You saw the signs, I s'pose? Fuck Off OFF stands for *fuck off Octagon Fossil Fuels*. Octagon have been doing some exploratory drilling on the Ness to see if it's suitable for fracking. It's been big news locally and split feelings among the residents.'

Lander paused to attack his pint and then continued:

'Most around Shoreness are in favour because it will bring jobs and money into the area – and, boy, does it need it. But the locals in Sanctuary Bay, a more up-market settlement about a mile along the coast, are up in arms because they think it will hit house prices – usual thing.'

Lander took another deep swig to lubricate his tonsils. 'Then there's "SOS" which is a different protest. It stands for *Save Our Shoreness* and is a campaign against proposals for the construction of a second nuclear power station here to replace the current one, which is soon to be decommissioned. The Greens are the driving force behind that one but the F-Off OFF mob are opposed to this protest because the power station provides about seventy-five per cent of the jobs in the area.

They don't mind if the nuclear plant expands but are against the fracking. If you ask me, the two protest groups will get nowhere, but they make good copy for the paper.'

Lander broke off again to drain his glass. 'The odd thing is that according to the cops, the lad who has gone missing believed drowned was supportive of each group because his main concern apparently is – or was – the nature reserve. He thought the frackers and the generators might affect that. So he was rubbing plenty of people up the wrong way.'

'What do you expect me to do, Larry?'

'I wondered, with your contacts, whether you might be able to see if you can find out anything about the lad. His name is Jimmi Valgren. You know some crime reporters on the nationals, they might come up with more detail than the local cops are prepared to let me know about. It could make a bit of a scoop for my little paper.'

I reluctantly said I would see what I could do without holding out much hope, and with that Lander checked his watch, swore, and said he had better get going.

I sat there alone again with the last third of my second pint. The two ladies in the window seat had folded up their map and left, while the old boy by the fire had long gone. The bar was now empty and quiet apart from Dolly Parton, who was singing about her 'Hard Candy Christmas' somewhere on an audio system.

I returned to the crossword and filled in the answer to 4 down: *Breeze-blocks.*

'Sorry, Sir,'

I looked up straight into the dripping oyster shell on Eve's tee shirt.

'I wasn't listening to you and your friend but I couldn't help hearing mention of Jimmi's name,' she said in hurried hushed tones.

'Oh, yes?' I said, now distracted from the oyster.

'He's a really nice guy, I know him quite well, but I haven't seen him since last Thursday and I'm a bit worried about him. You see, he'd pissed off quite a few people around here.'

Gideon Squires was not as I had expected. Just what I had expected, I was not sure, but I did not expect a botanist from Kew to have gelled swept-back hair and be wearing a black designer-labelled tracksuit and trainers.

His handshake was warm and enthusiastic. 'Nice to meet you Tom, I've heard a lot about you from Fleur.'

Squires was about my age. Short, slim and urbane. A

colleague of my sister, he was the owner of my holiday cottage in Shoreness. He had arrived, as arranged, on my second evening 'to make sure I was settling in OK.'

I told him I was. 'It's a lovely place, and very kind of you to let me stay, but, please, let me pay something towards the rent.'

He shook his head. 'I wouldn't hear of it. Fleur told me of your tricky situation and I'm only too happy to help out. She's been a very good colleague for a long time now – I just wish I could persuade her that the real future for our science is at Kew and not Edinburgh.'

'Have you had this place long?'

'About five years, I bought it as an investment really. We use it for a few weeks a year for family holidays, but the rest of the time I let it out. I used to come here for holidays with my parents, I've always loved Shoreness. I've got to know the locals pretty well and I live only twenty miles away, so it's handy. I can keep an eye on things.'

'I've hardly met any locals, except the barmaid at the Lighthouse Inn.'

'Decent boozer, it's run by Will Hathaway and his family. Will's a bit rough round the edges but he's OK – and he keeps an eye on this place for me when it's empty. The other boozer is the Lucky Fisherman. Better food there, but it does attract a few too many kids for my liking.'

'I'm sure I'll be trying both of them.'

'I'm sure you will.'

5

The bedside clock-radio said it was almost eight. Time for that morning jog I had been putting off. I could be back, washed and dressed by nine, ready to start the day as a budding author. Not that I had even given my steamy historical novel a working title as yet. Every time I had tried to put my mind to it yesterday afternoon, my thoughts had kept drifting back to the hushed conversation with the barmaid at the Lighthouse Inn about the missing – feared dead – Jimmi Valgren.

Eve and Jimmi, she had explained, had become good friends over the past three months. I was not sure how close. I had not asked and Eve had not volunteered such intimate information. What she had done was paint an affectionate picture of the lad, whose naked body, it seemed, I had found some five miles along the coast, a morbid detail I decided to keep from Eve for the time being until identification had been confirmed. All she knew for now was that he had gone missing.

She said Jimmi had been an art student at the University of Brighton, but he had dropped out mid-way through his second year, bought himself an old blue VW Dormobile and set up home in the nature reserve at Shoreness, where he pursued his love of photographing and sketching the birds on the lake there. His plan, said Eve, was to sell the pictures to tourists in the summer to finance his Bohemian lifestyle.

She had first met Jimmi about a year earlier at the university. She was also studying photography, but was on a part-time evening course when her work at the pub, run by her parents, would allow. Eve had admired his work at a university exhibition, and the friendship had blossomed. He confided in her about his disillusionment with the coursework and when he told her he had decided to walk out to go it alone, Eve suggested he spend some time at Shoreness.

'That was when our relationship started to become more serious,' she had said in a whisper, which seemed odd to me at the time as the bar was otherwise empty.

'He is the kindest, most brilliant person I've ever met. I'd hate to think something bad has happened to him.'

Jogging into what felt like a gale-force westerly on the deserted beach road, I recalled how Eve had started to brim over with tears as she talked about Jimmi, who she described as a gentle soul with a deep love of nature and a loathing of violence.

'He joined some local residents when they set up a twenty-four-hour vigil around Dead Oak Farm, where the fracking company was about to start some exploratory drilling to see if there was shale gas in the area,' said Eve.

'To be honest, I don't think the locals cared much for Jimmi with his dreadlocks and scruffy clothes. He wasn't really one of them. Most of them were toffs from Sanctuary Bay. But they needed numbers there to keep the lorries out, and Jimmi always had a camera with him, which was useful to them. If the police tried to break up the protest, he would take pictures if they or the heavies from OFF started throwing their weight around.'

'Did that happen often?'

'Not often, but a couple of Jimmi's pictures of a scuffle appeared in the local paper, and they were posted online too. The company hated that. I've warned Jimmi to be careful where and when he points his camera.'

I changed direction along the track to the lighthouse, relieved that the wind was now coming over my right shoulder instead of directly into my face. My knees were beginning to complain. I thought I felt a twinge in my left ankle. The best thing for it was to think about something else. I returned to the conversation with Eve.

'So he wasn't popular with the police or this Octagon mob – or even the residents, come to that?' I had asked.

Eve nodded. 'That's about it. And then there are the Greens. He even got himself involved with their sofa protest outside the power station.'

Sofa protest? That sounded a cushy number. I remembered the battered Chesterfield I had seen by the nuclear plant perimeter fence on my way to Shoreness for the first time. 'Explain,' I said.

'Greenpeace are against plans to build a second nuclear plant next to the old one here,' she said. 'As well as lobbying the Government and running a petition against the project, they have an old sofa they put on the railway line and sit on when they know the train carrying the nuclear waste is due to leave. It's a peaceful protest but causes no end of disruption to Genor-X, the power company.'

It struck me that Jimmi Valgren had been making enemies rather too quickly for a bird-loving, tree-hugging photographer who was trying to endear himself to the local community.

'Then there are the bats wings and the smuggling ....' Eve's voice had trailed off as a tall, angular man in black jeans, military boots and red roll-neck sweater had entered the pub.

'You not done yet, Eve?' he had barked as he threw a bunch of keys on the bar.

'Just finishing here, Dad, last customer's just leaving – aren't you sir?' she had said, wiping the table for at least the tenth time with the grubby cloth and collecting my long-emptied pint glass.

Aware of the slight panic in Eve's face, I had nodded and stood up, but the man had already disappeared behind the door marked 'Staff Only'. That had been the end of my conversation with Eve the barmaid.

I was now feeling the benefit of the wind in my back as I headed towards the cottage. On the shoreline I could see figures huddled behind large colourful golfing umbrellas set at angles on the beach, fishing rods propped up in front of them, their invisible lines reaching out into shimmering water. I made a mental note to talk to them about the currents on this stretch of coast and ask whether they saw many people swimming at this time of year. It was a way to dip a metaphorical toe into the water.

Had I had heard Eve correctly the previous lunch time? She had said something about smuggling, but the other phrase had sounded like 'bat swing or bats wing' which made no sense at all, a bit like one of those Chinese whispers that get passed down a line and forever distorted.

When I reached the green door of the cottage panting heavily, my mobile was shouting for attention inside but by the time I had stumbled through the hall into the bedroom where I had left it recharging, the phone had fallen silent.

'Missed call. Katie,' it said on the screen.

'Bollocks,' I muttered – not so much because I had missed the call but because I did not particularly want to speak to my estranged wife right now. The idea of coming to Shoreness had been to get away from all of that but I knew I had better call back, just in case there was a problem. It could, though, wait until I had showered and had the first coffee of the day. Standing there in sweat-soaked running gear, I was beginning to shiver.

As I waited for the coffee to brew, one hand resting on the warm plunger, I contemplated the crossword I had started a couple of days earlier on the journey to Shoreness.

7 Down. *Sammoc (8,6).*

Before I had time to start doodling possible answers, the mobile shrilled into life again. Katie.

'Hello Katie, I was going to ring you back. I've just got out of the shower,' I lied easily, which came as a surprise. Lying to Katie had always been something I had found hard to do, just one of the reasons I had never even considered infidelity during our marriage.

'Two things,' she said, sounding very businesslike as if she was talking to a stranger at the local council to make a complaint about bin collections.

'You should know that I'm using Slaughter &

Slaughter, my parents' solicitors, for the divorce. You'll be getting an email from them this week, I expect. Then they will write a formal letter. As I said last week, I hope we can keep this simple and civilised, for Alice's sake.' She paused, waiting for a response.

'Yes. OK.' It was best to keep it brief if that was the mood she was in.

'And talking of Alice, I just wanted to make sure you have it in your diary for next Tuesday's parents' evening: seven at the school. I'll be there of course, but there's no reason for the teachers to know our situation. I'm hoping we can just play loving parents for the evening. OK'

It was more a demand than a request.

'OK'.

'Good. I'll see you there. Bye.'

For a moment, I thought I detected a touch of sorrow in her voice in those last few words but before I could say anything, she had hung up.

'Got it,' I thought to myself. 'Sammoc: *inverted commas*. Of course. Nice one.' I filled in the little squares with satisfaction to complete the crossword. Chats with Katie had always been good for clearing the mind.

I poured the thick black coffee and sat at the table looking out onto the Ness. 'Let's do this,' I said out loud, lifted the lid of my lap top and I typed capital letters across the top of the blank page on Word: THE BODICE RIPPERS. On the next line, I wrote: Chapter One.

It made the book sound like second-rate soft porn. I did not like it and, lacking enthusiasm for panting lovers and pistol fights, I went instead into the search engine and typed in Genor-X. After first trying to divert me to the children of the Sixties – Generation X – the search list offered what I wanted.

Genor-X. A joint British-Canadian utilities company based in London specialising in electricity generation and supply. See also Nuclear Power.

I clicked on the link to the company's website and, skipping over the promotional make-you-feel-good jargon on the home page, found the list of contacts I wanted in small type at the foot of the page. I clicked on 'media inquiries' and wrote down a name, email address and telephone number.

I looked at the screen. 'Why are you doing this, Tom?' I said out loud again. I knew the answer, of course: the sight of the body in the water had shocked and, I was rather ashamed to admit, excited me. The fact that I had been the one to discover Jimmi Valgren in the waves made me part of his sad story. Eve's plaintive plea for help had touched me too.

Something had tickled my journalistic curiosity and I just had to scratch it.

I went back to Google and typed in bats wing and smuggling. The screen offered directions to the Bats Wing Tearooms in Ventnor on the Isle of Wight and a story about the smuggling of stolen goods taken from the British American Tobacco (BAT) Company. I was none the wiser so I called the number for the head of communications at Genor-X.

Inevitably the call went through to an answering machine telling me to key number one for 'bill enquiries', number two for 'complaints' right through to number eight. I ignored the lot and waited for a human voice to come to the rescue.

'Good morning, Genor-X. How may I direct your call?' said a cheerful mid-Atlantic accent.

'Joanne Etheridge, please. My name is Tom Kidd.'

I was put through and had no hesitation in spinning a yarn to circumvent the minions who stood between me and Ms Etheridge. 'My name's Kidd, a journalist from the *Herald*. We're running a story about your company's plans to build a new reactor at Shoreness, and the safety concerns of the locals there.'

I was told to hang on and within seconds was put through to an Australian accent with an air of authority: 'Jo Etheridge here, Mr Kidd. Head of Comms. How can I help?'

It was an old journalistic trick. Set alarm bells ringing at the other end and you are usually put through to the head honcho. Trick number two was to sound chatty and unthreatening.

'Jo, good of you to speak to me. I'm investigating the disappearance of one of the Greenpeace protestors at your Shoreness plant. There is no suggestion that Genor-X are to blame but he was last seen on a sofa on a railway line outside the power station.'

Another little lie, but Ms Etheridge was hooked.

'Sofa? I don't understand. I have no knowledge of this person, does he or she have a name?'

'Jimmi Valgren, a Shoreness artist, and activist by the sound of it,' I said, convinced her interest was aroused. 'He's not been seen since last week and there are concerns about his safety. He had been involved in the blockade on the railway line just outside the power station.'

'I'll need to make some enquiries with our security people, Tom. Give me a couple of hours. I will call you back or, if your enquiry isn't urgent, I can answer all your questions face to face, which is the way I prefer to work.'

'Me too.'

'You know, we're proud of our safety record at all our facilities and our commitment to being open and honest with the public. How about we discuss this over a coffee and I'll show you around? I'm at Shoreness every Thursday so I could do tomorrow. Bring a photographer if you wish.'

'The photographer won't be necessary, but I'll be there. What time?' I was surprised at how readily she had made herself available. She was clearly keen to keep the media onside with the proposals for a new nuclear plant still generating plenty of heat at Government level.

'How about ten? Give me your car registration for security reasons. At the front gate just mention my name. They'll direct you. Oh yes, bring some photo ID and wear long trousers and solid shoes.'

'Well I wasn't thinking of coming in shorts and flip-flops this weather,' I said, rather puzzled before reciting the car number.

'Good. See you at ten, Tom.'

Like all good PR people she had slipped into the informality of Christian names very quickly to accentuate the mood of trust and friendliness. She also sounded as if she might be rather attractive, if that made sense. Well, I am a single man. Virtually.

Normanden was one of those typical English market

towns found all over the country and much loved by the reasonably well off who wanted to escape city life. At the cobbled hub was the old market cross and church, and even the proliferation of fast-food takeaways and charity shops did not detract from the charm of the High Street. Also there were the main offices of the *South Coast Gazette*.

The front window of Lander's empire proudly presented framed front pages of recent editions. One showed the sofa protestors on the railway line outside the power station under the headline 'Nuclear Plant plans on the wrong track say protestors.' Another edition proclaimed that Spanish trawlers were being blamed for the drop in local fish hauls with the banner headline 'Hands off our soles, senor.' I grinned. Lander had not lost his touch.

Inside, I was greeted by a bottle blonde whom I assumed to be Lander's latest squeeze. And there was plenty to squeeze. Jasmine sat at a desk behind two computer screens with two telephones at her left elbow. One rang and she ignored it.

'Hello.' She flashed a gleaming white smile. 'Is it Tom?' When I nodded, she pointed to the frosted glass door behind her, waved me through and finally picked up the impatient phone.

Lander's office was much the same as I remembered that of our first editor in Nottingham more than twenty years ago except instead of a typewriter, there was a screen and keyboard. The discarded bits of paper, the old coffee cups, biros, paperweights and overflowing ashtray were much the same.

'They've confirmed the body is Jimmi Valgren's,' said Lander. 'No suspicious circumstances.' He sounded almost disappointed. 'At least, that's what they say.'

'How do they explain him being naked?'

'The police think he went for a swim. The pathologist found traces of cannabis in his system. Could have been high as a kite when he hit the water. The cold this time of year would have killed him very quickly if the currents didn't.'

'Any trace of his clothes left on the beach?'

'No. But the tide comes in a fair way, they could have been swept away too.'

My old friend was looking harassed and edgy. Probably more to do with his personal life than the approaching Thursday deadline for the *Gazette*, I concluded.

Lander said: 'One other thing, though. After I left you yesterday, I spoke to the local postie. He told me he'd heard that Valgren's Dormobile had been ransacked last week, but he knew nothing about any drowning.'

'I'll sniff around. Now – the archives?'

I followed Lander up a flight of narrow wooden stairs to a back room where floor to ceiling metal shelves were stacked with what looked like old shoe boxes. Each one was dated in neat writing on a label stuck to the front, the sequence stretching back to 1850. Two boxes covered each year: January – June, July – December. In the boxes was microfilm.

'Might as well start with January 1850,' said Lander, grunting as he stood on a chair and reached for the highest box on the shelf. He took a black plastic reel out of the dusty box, lifted the lid of what looked like an old-fashioned reel-to-reel tape player on the desk and clicked the film on to a pin. He fed one end of the microfilm through a gate and around a spool onto an empty cassette and shut the lid again. With a push of a green button, pages suddenly appeared on a screen next to the microfilm player.

Lander showed me how to roll the film on and how to print off any articles that took my interest. 'The first fifty years are a bit hit-and-miss I'm afraid,' he said. 'When we came to put all the back numbers on microfilm, a few copies were missing or simply falling apart, but it's a reasonable record. I'll send Jasmine up with some coffee. Take as long as you like.'

Just what I was looking for, I was not sure. Smuggling was very different in the mid-nineteenth century to the era of Thomas Kingsmill and the Kent gangs a century earlier, but I thought there might be some court reports of racketeers being hauled up in front of the local magistrate, or stories of thefts from customs warehouses. Instead I found tales of fishermen lost at sea and the building of a new lighthouse at Shoreness, but no smugglers apart from a report of a clipper that had been wrecked in 1853 in the inappropriately named Sanctuary Bay during a storm, in which its contents and crew had mysteriously disappeared.

I noted that the curate's wife had twins in 1854 and then another set in 1856. In 1857 the people of Normanden formed a blockade to keep travellers and tinkers out of the parish. Nothing much changes, I thought.

Three hours, two decades and one pot of coffee later, I looked at my virtually empty notebook. This was hopeless.

I carefully replaced the reels in their boxes and returned them to the shelves. Then I reached for the box nearest the monitor and fed in the microfilm. It contained what I wanted: this year's editions of the *South Coast Gazette*. I found the front page I was looking for and zoomed in on the photograph of the Greenpeace protest group sitting on and around a sofa on the rail track. Staring back at me was an earnest looking young man with wispy dreadlocks. I printed off two copies and put them in my backpack. Inside the previous week's paper was a story of the anti-fracking campaign. There were more pictures, possibly taken by Valgren as he was not in them. They showed burly security men holding back the protestors as a lorry went by, but these were too indistinct to be of any use.

My mobile chirped. It was a text message from Alice.

'Hope the book is coming along. You'll be the next JK Rowling. Ali xx'

I started to feel utterly deflated. I had no job and no family life any more. And my chances of being the next JK Rowling were as likely as Harry Potter running for Parliament, which might not be such a bad idea.

Driving back towards Shoreness with dusk closing in across the lowlands, I came to a grinding halt. Red lights flashed, bells rang and the barrier dropped at a level crossing on the road out of town. There was no sign of life in either direction on the single track line that left Normanden Junction and headed across the flat marshland towards the coast. Although there was nothing but fields, ditches and a few sheep to be seen, the railway was protected on either side by a six-foot wire fence.

At first the noise was a distant rumble but it grew to a deep roar as the train approached from the Shoreness direction. With diesel locomotives at front and rear, it comprised two empty flatbed trucks either side of another truck carrying a ribbed grey metal flask the size of a small shed. The train rattled slowly through and the barriers rose again. As the red light on the rear locomotive disappeared into the mist, I had little doubt what freight was being carried in the flask.

When I opened the door of the cottage, there was a piece of paper on the mat. It was not the usual advertising flyer. It was a neatly written note on a sheet of folded paper.

'Don't talk to me about Jimmi if Dad is around. He doesn't like me seeing him. Eve Hathaway'. She had also written down a mobile telephone number. I had mentioned to Eve where I was staying. Clearly she wanted to keep in touch.

I decided that rather than ring her, I would send a text message. That was no way to tell her that her friend Jimmi Valgren was dead, drowned in the sea and washed up along the coast so I simply typed: 'Got your message. This is my number, ring me when you can. Tom'.

I was peeling back the cover on a steaming chicken Madras fresh from the microwave when the mobile rang. It was Eve. She sounded tearful: 'Mr Kidd, is it true?'

'Yes, I'm terribly sorry, Eve. And please, call me Tom. How did you hear?'

'Postman told me this morning. Word gets around

quickly in Shoreness. How did it happen?'

I hesitated. What Lander had told me from the police was officially off the record at this stage, but there was no harm in telling Eve the little I knew.

'His body was found a few miles down the coast at the weekend. He was naked and had pot in his system. Police think he went for a swim and got swept away. Death by misadventure it seems.'

Eve fell silent apart from a few sniffles. Then she said on a rush of words, 'Something's been going on, Tom. I don't know what but I'm sure Jimmi wouldn't have gone swimming. He hated the sea, wouldn't even paddle in a rock pool.'

'But if he was high on pot?'

'I doubt even that. He smoked a bit, but not much. I never saw him off his senses on the stuff. Do you know he had his Dormobile broken into and searched at the end of last week? Who'd do that and why? He wouldn't harm anyone.' She started sobbing.

I felt embarrassed. Crying women made me feel helpless. I told Eve I would ask around discreetly and get in touch by text again.

'Thank you, Tom. I don't know anyone else around here who would help.' She rung off.

I lifted the lid of my laptop and tapped in the password. I had mail to read. A good excuse for not attempting to make a start on the novel once again. I topped up my wine glass and deleted most of the mail without opening it. They were either junk mail or press releases from sports governing bodies that no longer concerned me.

I must remember to unsubscribe them some time soon.

There was, as predicted by Katie, a missive from her solicitors, the charmingly named Slaughter & Slaughter, outlining her instructions to proceed with a divorce and asking me for postal contact details.

Our daughter Alice had written a short note telling me of her new part in a drama production at school. She said school lunches were getting worse, which was good for her diet, a sentence she finished with a smiling emoji. She attached a 'selfie' showing off a new radically short haircut. She also reminded me that it was parents' evening next week.

Jimmi Valgren was perched on the arm of the sofa holding one end of a banner. He had a pale, thin pleasant face. He looked cold in his green tee-shirt. His dreadlocks ended in little coloured beads.

I looked at the photographs from the *South Coast Gazette* that I had printed off and thought about his parents: what must they be feeling right now? They would never see their young son again. It was every parents' worst nightmare. On Jimmi's right shoulder was the strap of what I assumed was a camera. That camera might hold some answers if I could find it.

I looked at the faces of the others in the sofa gang. There was a middle-aged couple in smart clothes who could well have been man and wife, an elderly lady in a 'ban the bomb' home-knitted sweater, a man aged about thirty with shoulder-length hair who was giving a clenched-fist salute, and, next to Jimmi, two shaven-headed youths with enough piercings to make a colander envious.

Staring blankly out of the cottage window into the interminable darkness of the shoreline, I knew that Jimmi's fate had assumed far more importance than fictional smugglers and ripped bodices. It had set my journalistic juices flowing again. As I cradled the last dregs of red wine in the glass I saw in the blackness outside three small but bright lights moving and flashing in the middle distance.

6

'No more fibs, Tom.'

Jo Etheridge came straight to the point but she said it with a grin rather than a grimace. I liked her style. In fact, it was quite easy to like most things about the Head of Communications for Genor-X, the company that ran the Shoreness Nuclear Power Station.

'Such as?' I smiled back at her.

'Well, for a start, Tom, you said you worked for the *Herald*. That was a small lie wasn't it? You did work for the *Herald*,' she said with the emphasis on 'did'. She wagged a forefinger at me.

'You must have known we would check out your background. We do for everyone who visits the site. It's normal safety procedure these days because we have to be so aware of the threat of terrorism.'

'Yes. Old habits …' I let the sentence trail away.

The security around the plant had been obvious as soon as I had turned into the long straight entrance road that morning for the ten o'clock appointment with Ms Etheridge. Both sides of the road were flanked by stout wire fences topped at regular intervals by closed circuit security cameras and floodlights. About six feet beyond either fence was another slightly higher mesh fence running parallel. The double fencing ran all the way to the small police station totally enclosing the approach to the nuclear plant. Three vehicles in blue, yellow and white police livery stood in a lay-by beside the station. Across the road was a red barrier controlled from a booth, which had a bank of CCTV cameras on its flat roof. A board on the front of the booth said: 'All visitors must report to security'.

My car registration and ID were checked by an unsmiling female officer holding a clipboard. She nodded to a colleague standing on the other side of the Audi.

These were no ordinary police who were giving me and my car the once over. The second officer moved around all four sides of the Audi checking underneath with a mirror on a metal pole. He nodded back at her. These were members of the Civil Nuclear Constabulary, the specialised armed branch of the police that guard power stations.

Waved through the raised barrier, I drove towards the monstrous bulk of the plant. It was only from close up that I realised just how big the place was. I was greeted with a series of signs telling me that I was in a nuclear licensed site and that 'Safety is our priority.' Every sign carried the Genor-X logo of a fluffy white cloud and a flying bird. So eco-friendly.

Jo Etheridge had been waiting in the visitors' centre, a new wooden structure on stilts that overlooked the pebble beach and English Channel, and where the welcoming smell of freshly brewed coffee filled the air. She stood up to shake my hand. No rings, I noted. She was dressed in a smart dark-blue trouser suit, her black hair tied back in a bun. I reckoned she was in her mid-to-late thirties, but I was hopeless at guessing a woman's age. Behind the warm welcome, she also gave off the air of someone not to be messed with.

Her initial gambit of 'No more fibs' confirmed that initial assessment.

I told her the basic facts of Jimmi Valgren's death and said I was looking into it on behalf of a friend rather than as a journalistic investigation. I showed her the picture of Jimmi and his fellow protestors on the sofa outside the nuclear plant.

'You think we're in some way involved, Tom?' She shook her head to answer her own question. 'Look, security is heavy around here, but not that heavy.'

'I appreciate that. I'm just trying to put together a few pieces of the jigsaw, which at the moment is still in a thousand little bits.'

Like most Australians I had met through my work, she appeared genuine and helpful. I hoped appearances were not deceptive.

'Our security is all about two things,' she said, putting her coffee down on the low polished wooden table between us and sitting back in the leather chair.

'The first is ensuring we don't suffer the kind of catastrophe that hit Fukushima in Japan in 2011. That disaster haunts this industry, and all sorts of safety measures are taken to guarantee these plants can withstand the worst earthquake and tsunami that darling Mother Nature can throw at us.

The second threat is a terrorist attack. We're well aware that this sort of place is a potential target for any nutter with a cause. These places are designed to withstand anything up to and including a suicide plane being crashed into them.'

She was in full flow, enthused by her topic. 'To be honest, Tom, a few environment-nutters on a sofa is the least of it. After you mentioned it yesterday, I asked our security chief and he told me that they were no more than a gnat's nuisance to our twice-weekly transportation of nuclear waste from here to the disposal facility at Sellafield.'

She was impressively well across her brief.

'I can see that. But I thought if Jimmi and his little group had been getting in the way, one or two of your over-zealous security guys might have got themselves involved.'

She shook her head. 'They're too professional for that. Anyway, the train deliveries are no big deal. We don't keep them secret – you can go on the Greenpeace website, they even print a timetable of when we take the waste material from here to the north – plus all the stations it travels through.'

'What is it exactly that's being delivered to Sellafield?'

'About ninety per cent of the material in the flasks is low level waste, only three per cent is regarded as high-level waste.' The facts tripped off her tongue as if she had recited them many times for inquiring journalists.

'The flasks are incredibly strong – strong enough to withstand a ground-to-air missile hit.'

She was convincing, but I decided to press my point. If nothing else, I was enjoying being in the company of Jo Etheridge.

'I see all that. But if Jimmi's protest group held up your plans for a second reactor here at Shoreness, wouldn't that make him more than simply a gnat's nuisance, as you say?'

'Not really. The Government need at least two more water-cooled reactors up and running by the mid-2020s to keep the lights on. This site is ideal, we're confident the plans will go through.'

Jo Etheridge paused to let her words sink in. I had heard PR-speak so many times before that I was a committed sceptic, but I had to admit she was good. I decided, however, not to respond. The secret of a good interview was to let the interviewee do most of the talking. A well-timed silence could work wonders: the person across the table felt they had to fill it.

She did.

'Tell you what, email me a copy of the photo of the sofa group and give me any names of those involved that you know. I promise to look into it. And while you're here, let me give you the trip around. What size chest are you?' she asked, eyeing me up and down.

In the locker room, rows of high-visibility jackets were draped on hangers. Below each one on a bench were helmets, ear-mufflers, safety glasses and gloves all wrapped in sealed plastic bags.

She explained that public tours of the site were becoming increasingly popular and, since Fukushima, Genor-X had been keen to promote them as a sign of confidence about the safety of their plants.

'The public are understandably concerned,' she said, zipping herself into a tight-fitting hi-viz jacket. 'We want to show them we've nothing to hide and that we're 100 per cent confident about our safety precautions and contingency plans. Fukushima just couldn't happen in this country. There are so many fail-safe systems in place, we wouldn't have a serious leakage problem whatever happened.'

The sign above the lockers read: 'Long trousers and closed footwear to be worn at all times. Genor-X runs an empty-pocket policy.'

She saw me reading it: 'You have to empty everything from your pockets into the locker except a handkerchief. If you have essential medication you need, that has to be carried by me or one of the guides. Once inside, the handrail must be held for every flight of steps, even if it's only one step. Even the chief exec has to follow this rule. We can't have injuries on site.'

Feeling – and no doubt looking – like a fool in the helmet, ear muffs and safety glasses, I followed her to a security office where I was signed in and given a pass to wear. A bright yellow box the size of a cigarette packet was pushed into the clear plastic top pocket of my hi-viz jacket. On its front was a dial and a series of numbers.

'That's your dose monitor,' said a smirking security officer. 'It measures the radioactivity you're exposed to.'

'Don't worry,' said Jo, anticipating my growing sense of alarm. 'You could stand on top of the reactor here and the dosage of radiation would still be less than if you stood in a field in Cornwall. The radon naturally occurring in the rocks in Cornwall is greater than anything you'll get here – unless there's an accident.'

A dose monitor sounded like something a prostitute might have a use for, but I decided to keep this rather lurid thought to myself.

Through the security turnstiles was a wide concrete walkway flanked on one side by a twelve-foot-high wall and on the other by the mountainous power station that rose up in square blocks like a giant Lego building. The wall was the sea defence but it was also topped with intruder-sensitive wire and security cameras.

Everything appeared neat and well-kept inside the complex. Gravel areas were weed-free. Pipes were painted reds, blues and greens. Walkways were wide and clear, yellow lines denoting their edges. A garden with benches and a lily-covered pool was being used by employees on a break. It could have been a small park in Harrogate or Tunbridge Wells if it had not been for the vast bulk of the generating hall looming behind it. At the back of the park was an outdoor, open-fronted shower unit painted bright green.

She nodded at it: 'You'll see them dotted all around the place as we do the tour. If there's an accident or a spillage, staff might have to use them to douse down. Just don't pop into one to wash off if a seagull poops on you … as soon as a shower is activated it alerts security, our on-site fire brigade and the control room. You'd be surrounded by armed police and firemen within two minutes, and in the control room they'd be thinking about shutting down the reactors.'

We walked past a maze of pipes and valves and then a vast deep pit at the bottom of which swirled muddy green water. This was the sea intake, she explained. Seawater was being drawn in from the English Channel, collected and filtered before being used as a coolant in the turbine room.

Another swipe of our security passes took us into a lift and up six floors to a look-out area that provided spectacular views over the Channel and Shoreness Lighthouse. The place smelled like the London Underground: oil and electricity.

'See that swirling, bubbling area out there?' she said, pointing to a spot about two hundred yards off the shore. 'We call that "the boil". It's where the clean seawater is pumped back into the sea. The water is about two degrees warmer than it was when it came in, and because of that, the fish flock to the area. There's a thriving sea bass nursery there because of the outflow, and that's good news for the local fishermen.'

She took me by the arm and led me across the viewing gallery to another window that looked down on a scene like something from a James Bond movie.

Three men sat in swivel chairs at three horseshoe shaped desks with a mass of dials and knobs on their banked sides. In the middle of each desk was a red mushroom-shaped plunger. Around the walls were more dials and screens. The dials flickered and hovered as the three men lounged back in their padded comfort as if overseeing an ice-cream factory.

'This is the Central Control Room. The whole operation works from here,' she said. 'They continuously monitor the two reactors, the flow of coolants, the power output, everything. If there's a problem they can hit those red buttons. The whole place can be shut down in just ten seconds.'

'Very reassuring,' I said. 'But it still gives me the creeps.'

On the way back to the visitors' centre, I brought the subject back to Jimmi Valgren and asked about his involvement in the fracking protests at Dead Oak Farm.

'The test drilling for shale gas has recently been shut down but I don't know why the anti-fracking mob were bothered in the first place,' said Jo (she had insisted on being on first name terms). 'Octagon Fossil Fuels were never going to get permission to carry on. Fracking can cause earth tremors and no government in its right mind – even this current shower – would give the go ahead to deep drilling near a nuclear plant.'

Safety clothing dumped in a plastic dustbin in the locker room, I was relieved to be told my dose monitor had remained firmly in the green zone, which I assumed to be good news.

I promised Jo Etheridge I would send her the details of Jimmi Valgren and stay in touch. She said she hoped I would. I got the impression she meant it.

There was no sign of Eve in The Lighthouse Inn that Thursday lunch time. I had not intended to drop in at the pub, but as I drove out of the power station, I decided to do what I had often done as a journalist: sit down, make notes and take stock, and where better to do that than in a pub?

Behind the bar was Eve's father William Hathaway, as I had read on the Licensee Notification Board over the front door. He gave me a curt nod, showing no sign of having recognised me from a couple of days ago. That suited me and so did the fact that the bar had no other customers. I ordered a pint and a sandwich and sat in the window seat where the two lady walkers had been when I last visited.

Hathaway did not look the conversational type. He leaned on the bar studying the sports section of his newspaper, sucking on a pen, ceasing only to circle something. Horse racing picks, I guessed.

He was as long and lean as his daughter was short and curvaceous. He had a small mean mouth, and his lips glistened as he sucked on the end of his biro deep in thought. Judging by the powder blue Thomas Pink bespoke shirt he was wearing, Hathaway had done well on the nags. You could not afford shirts like that on a publican's wage. The ginger cat jumped on to the bar beside him. 'Get out of it.' He swiped a hand at it, but the cat was too quick and hopped back on to a bar stool out of reach.

'Here you go, luv.' The cheerful Mrs Hathaway presented me with my sandwich and trotted back to the bar.

'Stop funding the bookie's Caribbean holiday, Will,' she said to her husband, who looked up, grunted and returned to his trifecta. Perhaps he did not do so well on the horses.

I fished a small red cash book out of my inside pocket. I had always used these instead of the traditional spiral topped reporter's notepad. They were more convenient and discreet.

I jotted down what I knew, which was precious little if I was honest: young, pot-smoking, nature-loving artist living half-rough drowns at sea. Naked. Seemingly no close friends locally other than Eve. Friend or Lover?? I was not sure which but I felt it was important to know, so I added two question marks.

Enemies? Power station security possible, but unlikely. Fracking company? Yet to be checked out, but doubtful. Locals? Possible, but what motive? Police? Seemingly not interested.

I took a swig of the pint and considered my notes. It did not amount to much. I glanced up to make sure Hathaway was not watching. He was not. Instead he was talking into his mobile as he ran the pen down the page in the newspaper. I guessed he was pouring some more cash into the bookie's holiday fund.

I returned to my little red book and wrote 'Bats Wing and smuggling??' Two question marks again. What could Eve have meant by that? I must ask her before I did much else.

Then there was Jimmi's Dormobile. Why had it been ransacked?

As I wrote the word 'camera' I became aware of somebody standing over me.

'Another drink? We're about to close,' said Hathaway. I shut the notebook as I looked up and shook my head. 'No thanks. Better not. I'm driving.'

'I shouldn't worry 'bout that round here,' said Hathaway, grasping my empty glass and plate.

'Eve not in today?'

'Na, some design project up in London she has to get finished for college, waste of time if you ask me.'

'Her art course? She told me she was keen.'

He rolled his eye. 'Bloody art college. I keep telling

her she needs to do a course that'll get her a proper job. She's also needed here with the season starting soon. But kids – they don't listen.'

'No, guess not.'

'Anyway, how you settling in at the cottage? I hear you're a writer.'

'Word gets round. Yes, fine thanks.'

'Small place, Shoreness. Not much goes on here without everyone knowing. Nice to see you again.'

The publican nodded and walked back to the bar. Conversation over.

Sitting in the Audi, I dug deep in the glove compartment to find Hunky Dory, David Bowie's best album. As 'Changes' came on, I cranked up the volume and drove out of The Lighthouse Inn car park. I had a vague idea of trying to find my whereabouts among the little roads that snaked inland from the vast pebble promontory. The stony Ness with its unregulated ramshackle properties had become a retreat for all sorts wishing to escape the rat-race or possibly even the long arm of the law. Poets, painters, authors and avant-garde film makers had made the Ness their home, but there was not a blue plaque in sight. The anonymity of the place was one of its attractions.

One sign I had seen earlier, however, was for the nature reserve where Jimmi had apparently holed up. I decided to try to find it again. By the time Bowie had start enquiring about Life on Mars, I felt I was in another world.

Down-at-heel Shoreness had given way to the manicured affluence of Sanctuary Bay. A row of brick-built bungalows looking out to sea backed on to the golf links. Between the two communities, almost like a border post, stood The Lucky Fisherman, a pub that looked a cut above The Lighthouse Inn. Its swinging sign showed a grinning bearded fisherman with his arm around a mermaid. Beneath it, the blackboard announced that Friday Nite was Quiz Nite.

The Lucky Fisherman sat beside a five-way junction centred on a grassy roundabout. I opted for the third exit and was soon surrounded by flat pasture land with a smattering of wind turbines churning lazily above the grazing cows and sheep.

I passed Danish Farm, which offered fresh duck eggs and horse manure; Abbey Farm, which offered Bed and Breakfast, and then Dead Oak Farm, which offered nothing but a muddy drive behind a broken gate that lay at a drunken angle across the entrance.

Fortunately there was nothing behind as I came to a slithering halt. Dead Oak Farm. Both Eve Hathaway and Jo Etheridge had mentioned that name as the site of the exploratory fracking drill by Octagon Fossil Fuels of FUCK OFF OFF fame.

I reversed and poked the nose of the Audi down the rutted track towards the austere farmhouse. The corrugated barn roof had several holes in it. An old tractor surrounded by waist-high weeds had clearly not moved for months. There were no animals in the fields. In fact, there was little sign of agricultural life until out of the barn came a whining quadbike driven at speed in my direction by a wild-haired man.

As the bike drew closer, I noticed two bedraggled

collie dogs were hanging on grimly behind the driver, their tongues trailing saliva in the wind. The quadbike stopped immediately in front of the Audi's bonnet.

'Yes?' said the farmer, his eyes glaring at the front wheels of the car which had just reached the cattle grid inside the entrance.

'Sorry, must have taken a wrong turn back there, just turning around.' I tried to sound nonchalant. 'Perhaps you can help: is there fracking going on around here? I heard there was.'

'It was going on. Not anymore it ain't. What's it got to do with you?' the farmer demanded, his dogs eyeing me suspiciously as I stepped out of the car and stood by the open driver's door.

'Nothing really.' I had always been wary of dogs since an unfortunate incident with a yappy Jack Russell when I was ten and trying to retrieve a football from a neighbour's garden. The farmer's two dogs appeared to sense my cowardice and growled softly. This conversation was going to be brief. 'I'm just a friend of a friend of one of the protestors.'

'Which one?'

'A young lad named Jimmi. With dreadlocks.'

'Him.' The farmer spat out the word. 'Sodding busybody with his fucking camera. Those fucking protestors cost me a fortune. Do you know what it would have been worth if Octagon had decided to go ahead with fracking here?'

Before I could hazard a guess, Farmer Angry gave me the answer.

'About a quarter of a million quid, that's what. Would

have saved my farm. Now I've got to sell up. No point in carrying on. The Government, the supermarkets and the EU are killing small farms like this.'

Farmer Angry was at war with virtually the whole world by the sound of it. Retreat was the best tactic.

'Well thanks. Hope it works out,' I said through the open window as I slipped back into the Audi. I did not think it was worth explaining that the aborted fracking exploration had nothing to do with the protestors and everything to do with concerns about earth tremors and the power station. As I went to reverse, my rear view mirror was filled with another quadbike and a younger version of Farmer Angry sitting astride its seat.

'Who's this, father?' shouted the boy above the drone of the engine.

'Someone asking about the fucking fracking fuckers and that kiddie with dreadlocks and a camera.'

Blocked in, I had no option but to get out of the car again. Using the vocabulary of Farmer Angry, I decided my situation was fucked.

I addressed the boy: 'I'm no supporter of the protest, just asking about Jimmi, who has gone missing. Wondered if your Dad had heard anything,'

'Nothin' to do with us mate, although he was a pain in the arse, all the protestors were,' said the lad with a weariness that suggested he was telling the truth. 'He pissed off a lot of people round 'ere.'

'Really. In what way?'

'You can't come around protesting about everything, telling everyone the only important thing is the wildlife when jobs are scarce. Looking like a poof don't help either, particularly with the TA guys.'

I assumed TA meant Territorial Army. 'How did he meet up with the Terras?'

'They train at Cheyne Camp, don't they? Drink in the Lucky Fisherman. Your mate went there too, I hear. Not the sort of bloke the army guys really get along with.'

I could imagine the scene: ecological warrior meets army warriors with their very different ideas on how to save the planet. I needed to pay the Lucky Fisherman a visit, but first I needed to get out of Dead Oak Farm in one piece.

The young lad got off his quad and walked towards me. I clenched a fist fearing the worst.

But he took me by surprise.

The boy, who was probably about the same age as Jimmi had been, lowered his voice: 'I heard he drowned, is that right?'

I nodded.

'There was no love lost between us, but I'm sorry to hear that. If you're a friend, as you say you are, and you know of Eve, tell her to take care. She's a good girl, but folk round here didn't take kindly to her going off with an outsider like him. Her old man would've gone berserk if he'd known Jimmi was shagging her.'

'Was he?'

'Don't know mate, but they spent a lot of time in his Dormobile. Don't suppose they were studying birdlife all the time.'

I sensed I might have an ally in the farmer's son. 'Thanks for the info. Good luck with the farm.'

'We'll need it,' said the lad over his shoulder as he

mounted the quadbike and reversed to allow me to pull out on to the road.

As the rain started to splatter on the windscreen, I wondered what to do next. I really needed to talk to Eve, and when I was out of sight of the farm, I pulled over to send her a text. Within two minutes, she had rung back.

'Any news?' she asked hopefully.

'No, sorry. Not yet, anyway.'

'I hear you were in the pub this lunchtime. Did Dad say anything?'

'No. Not too keen on your college course, though, is he?'

'Was he going on about that again?' She sighed. 'He doesn't like my college work and he didn't like Jimmi either. In fact, he doesn't like strangers, full stop.'

'I rather got that impression. Look Eve, can you give me some idea of where Jimmi's Dormobile is, and can we meet up soon?'

'The VW was on the approach road to the RSPB nature reserve as it sweeps around behind the lake. You can't miss it if it's still there. There's a nice little café at the reserve. Not many people go there. How about there – tomorrow at eleven?'

I headed back towards the five-way junction at the Lucky Fisherman where a brown tourist sign for the RSPB nature reserve was virtually hidden in the blackthorn hedge.

The road took me inland, down what was little more than a farm track with passing places and potholes that were turning into puddles. After about a mile, the track swung around to the left in almost a complete circle keeping the lake on the left. The speed limit sign indicated ten miles per hour and there was a hand-painted plea for drivers to take care: 'ducks crossing'.

To the right was a steep pebble bank that gave the lake some protection from the sea winds. Around the next corner was a low brown building at the end of the track but before it, perched on a stony ridge off to the right, was a Dormobile, blue and white police tape flapping around it.

I pulled over and reluctantly got out of the warm Audi. The bitterly cold rain stung my face as I walked up to the Dormobile, 'Police Aware' said a sticker across the windscreen. I ducked under the police tape and tried the driver's door but it was locked, as was the passenger door. I then felt rather foolish as I noticed one of the sliding doors on the side had been yanked off and lay in the gorse a few feet away. I stepped inside, relieved to get out of the wind.

Whoever had got here first had done a thorough job. The little cupboards down each side were open as was the storage space under the seat. Cooking utensils, empty cereal boxes, biscuit packets, photographs, and several sketch pads were strewn around. I picked one up and flicked through the pencil drawings of birds in flight. To my amateur eye, if this was Jimmi's work, he had been a talented boy.

The photographs, many of them trampled under muddy boots, were mainly black and white shots of ducks and seabirds, either in flight or floating on the lagoon, feeding or playing hide-and-seek in the reeds.

The back window had been broken too, tiny beads of shattered glass lay everywhere like little jewels. The intruders had not been subtle. It did not appear to be the work of thieves either because they had left behind two cameras strewn in the foot well of the front passenger seat. One was an old-fashioned Olympus OM1 film camera, its back hanging open and nothing inside. The other was a modern Canon digital. The memory card was missing. Whoever did this was interested in what was in the cameras. Not the cameras themselves.

Near the rear doors was an upturned cardboard box, its contents of magazines splayed across the floor. I picked up one and used it to brush the broken glass off a bench seat before sitting down. The pages were full of beautiful illustrations of plants. I looked at the cover: *Curtis's Botanical Magazine*. I had never heard of it. There were copies of *National Geographic* and *Amateur Photographer*, too. I looked through the pages not sure what I was expecting to find.

There was only the whine of the wind through the broken VW window and the mocking of the herring gulls to keep me company. This was an isolated spot. Had Eve seen the state of the Dormobile? If she hadn't, she would tomorrow when she drove here for our meeting, and that would upset her even more.

I drove on to the building by the edge of the lake. As I pulled up, a figure with his back to the car park was locking up.

'You closed?' An elderly white-haired man turned around with keys in his right hand.

'Sorry, we are. Close at dusk – but you're still welcome

to walk around,' said the man, who sounded more like a City banker than a wildlife warden. 'Just stick to the marked paths. All the hides have been locked for the night though and most of the birds are settling down for the evening, so there's not much to see'

'Actually I wanted to ask about the young artist who lived in the van back there,' I said, jerking my head in the direction of the Dormobile that was just about visible in the slate grey gloom.

'Oh him. Frightfully sad what happened,' said the man with a shake of his head. 'I didn't know him, I'm just a volunteer here. I do two days a week. You want to talk to Janice Woodcock. She's head ranger and I think she knew the boy quite well. She'll be in at eight in the morning.'

So, I had a double date tomorrow morning: first with Janice and then with Eve. Katie would, no doubt, be convinced I was up to no good.

Out of the wind back in the warmth of the Audi, I telephoned Lander to ask him about the power station sofa protestors in the photograph with Jimmi Valgren. Of the seven pictured, Lander said only four had been willing to give their real names to the photographer: Valgren, the middle-aged couple and the elderly lady.

The two shaven-headed youths and the other long-haired man had given what Lander referred to as 'eco-names.'

'The photographer said they called themselves Capricorn, Amazon and Santiago or some such bollocks,' said Lander. 'We don't bother to put those names in the caption or the story, it only gives them a buzz. Idiots.'

I wrote down the details and emailed them, together with a copy of the photograph, to Jo Etheridge. I wanted to seem keen and efficient – and I wanted to meet her again.

7

I did not see the punch coming but I certainly felt it. At first, there was no pain, just that sickening feeling when you know what is about to come.

I crumpled like a deflated toy, the air forced out of me by the force of the blow to my kidneys. I fell to ground beside the Audi, my head hitting the driver's door on the way down as the palms of my hands scraped across the rough tarmac of the car park. The car keys I had been holding clattered away into the darkness under the vehicle.

Then came the cry of agony as my brain registered the shaft of sickening pain from deep inside. I curled up into the foetal position, my face a few inches from the front tyre, gasping for breath. I lay there looking at the tread waiting for the next blow, helpless to defend myself. It came. A kick in the small of the back that lifted me off the ground. I think I tried to plead with my assailant but no words would come out. I was close to passing out when two crunching blows came as my ankles were stamped on.

'Enough.' I just remember that word.

Someone spat on my head before I heard two, possibly three, pairs of feet hurry away. There was laughter. A door banged shut, at least I think it did. I was about to lose consciousness.

I am not a big man and had never been one for physical violence. I was even a coward on the football field in my youth, volunteering to referee rather than get scythed down by a right back with malicious intent. My hands were made for writing, not punching. They say the pen is mightier than the sword, but lying in the dirt of the pub car park with rain seeping through my jeans, feeling sick with the pain in my gut and reaching for my keys with a bleeding hand, I did not take much solace in the thought that I knew the difference between an oxymoron and a poxy moron.

My fingers found the keys and I hauled myself to my knees. Looking up, I could swear the Lucky Fisherman's grin on the swinging sign had grown wider. I do not know how long I had been lying there. There was no-one else in the car park, or at least no-one I could see among the row of four-wheel drives and the battered khaki green minibus with Cheyne Camp painted on its side.

I fell into the Audi and locked the doors internally, driving off without bothering to put on a seat belt. It was little more than a five-minute drive along the pitch-black deserted beach road to the cottage but every gear change was agony.

I had not intended to go out that Thursday night, but sitting in the kitchen of the cottage contemplating another microwave curry and wrestling with the crossword – 10 across: *The Communist Party's net gains could be misleading (3,8)* – I had decided to treat myself to dinner at the Lucky Fisherman, the more salubrious-looking of Shoreness's two drinking holes. How deceptive appearances can be.

The visit to the nature reserve and Jimmi Valgren's ransacked Dormobile that afternoon was troubling. Perhaps there was some substance to Eve's suspicions about her boyfriend's watery end. If so, why had the police seemingly closed the case convinced that the Dover Coroner would record a verdict of accidental death when the inquest hearing came up next week?

Jimmi had not been Mr Popularity around these parts and he frequented the Lucky Fisherman. It was time to pay the place a visit.

Showered and in my smartest denim shirt, I set off after checking that the Dictafone battery had plenty of life in it. The recording device was the size of a matchbox but had a good range for picking up conversation. As a journalist I very rarely recorded conversations surreptitiously, but when taking out a notebook and making notes might cause alarm, it was worth having the recorder as back up if there was too much information to remember. It slipped easily into the top pocket of the shirt.

Before I left, I checked out the pub's website. The classy home page suggested it was the South Coast's 'premier bistro for locally caught fish with a wide range of English wine and beer'. Clicking on the tab marked history, I discovered there had been a pub on the site for about four hundred years. It derived its name from a local legend of a poor fisherman who worked all hours in a futile attempt to keep his nagging wife happy. It was a miserable, childless, marriage until one day at sea he hauled in his nets to find he had caught the most beautiful mermaid. When he took the mermaid back to his fisherman's cottage, his wife, who was already eating the supper she had prepared, was so contorted with fury at the sight of the mermaid's bare breasts that she choked to death on a fishbone. After that the fisherman and his mermaid lived a long and happy life together. There was no mention as to whether the happy couple had any little tiddlers but it was the sort of tale American tourists lapped up. The website also told me that the landlord was Romeo Turk.

When I arrived at the Lucky Fisherman, with its red velveteen bench seats and polished wooden tables, I could see why Romeo might live up to his name. The buttons on the white shirt of the man behind the bar were straining to contain what appeared to be a muscular frame. His swarthy complexion and wavy well-groomed hair suggested he had some Mediterranean blood in his family tree. The eyes were as deep and dark as Loch Ness water, the teeth were a set of white tombstones. If Romeo was his given name, his parents had chosen well.

To add to the effect, a neat scar ran down the left hand side of his face from just below his eye to the middle of the cheek, and a small diamond stud sparkled in his left ear.

'What can I get you, sir?' He flashed the tombstones. 'Miserable night again.'

Pleasantries over and pint in front of me, Turk turned his attention to other customers. A stool at one end of the bar gave me a good view of the clientele at the Lucky Fisherman.

Through a large arched opening was a games room with dartboard, pool table and flashing gaming machines.

Around the pool table were four laughing young men in army fatigues with the cross-sword badge of the Territorial Army on their sleeves.

I had had quite a lot of dealings with the military in my previous life as a journalist, particularly at the 2012 London Olympics where the servicemen and women had fronted the security operation. I had the utmost respect for regular soldiers, the majority of whom were utterly lacking in desire to throw their muscle around.

The Terras, on the other hand, enjoyed the swagger. I had met quite a few of these too: the bank clerks, the shop workers, the school teachers, the self-employed builders who loved dressing up and playing soldier games in their spare time. They tended to wear their machismo, like their shaven haircuts, as part of the uniform. The group in the games room fitted my jaundiced view of the TA boys.

As well as the four at the pool table, two others were banging the buttons of the quiz machine and cursing loudly because they did not know that Canberra was the capital of Australia.

They were exactly the sort who would not find themselves warming to a skinny artistic type with dreadlocks who was into his flora and fauna but who was still able to pull one of the local birds.

There was a seventh person in the room with the squaddies, who was not wearing fatigues. Someone I recognised. Idly throwing darts at the board was the farmer's son from Dead Oak Farm.

Two of the pool players came out clutching four empty pint glasses which were deposited on the bar in front of Turk. 'Four Stellas, packet of dry roasted, packet of scratchings and two packets of those hedgehog flavoured crisps.' There was not a 'please' at the end of the sentence but Turk did not seem to mind as one of them dropped a £20 note on the counter.

As Turk pulled the pints of lager, a woman appeared in front me holding a notepad. She was the perfect match for Turk. I guessed that her pneumatic figure came courtesy of a cosmetic surgeon, her smooth face courtesy of a botox syringe, her pearly even teeth the efforts of her dentist and her glowing golden skin the result of many visits to a local tanning studio.

'Have you decided, sir?' she asked. The accent came from somewhere between Southend and Crouch End. I ordered the fisherman's pie and a large glass of English sauvignon blanc.

As she walked back behind the bar, Turk gave her well-padded backside a lusty pinch. She giggled and gave the back of his hand a slap.

Turk, having served the TA boys and two other men, who had settled into a window seat, made his way to where I was sitting and nodded towards the games room. 'Bit noisy but they don't mean no harm. And their money's as good as anyone's, that's what I always say.'

'Of course.' I felt obliged to agree. 'Are they from the local MoD place? Cheyne Camp?' I knew the answer but wanted to engage Turk in conversation.

'Yes. Terras. They come down here for courses on the shooting ranges and tank driving routes. They were here last week too so they must be on a two-week exercise. Mind you, if they ever got called up to join in the real thing, they'd be shitting themselves.' Turk laughed and I decided to join in.

'How about the lad in there not in uniform? I'm sure I was talking to him earlier today.'

'Danny Lawton, farmer's son,' said Turk moving away to serve two customers who had just walked in.

Danny Lawton had struck me as being straightforward. He had suggested that Jimmi Valgren had rubbed the Terras up the wrong way – but he had not said anything about being friendly with the Territorial Army bunch himself. Now he was racking up the balls on the pool table.

I reached inside my top pocket and pressed the record button before Turk returned.

'I hear there was a local tragedy last weekend,' I sipped the icy white wine. 'Young artist swept out to sea and found some miles down the coast.'

'So I heard. Not one of my regulars, though,' said Turk, as if that lessened the tragedy. 'Daft to go swimming this time of year.'

Turk turned away as more customers arrived hurrying in and shaking the rain off their golfing umbrellas. 'Four pints of Pedigree, please Romeo,' called one of the group as he hauled off his coat.

It was a busy pub, much more so than its Shoreness competitor, the Lighthouse Inn. The newly arrived foursome were laughing loudly about a golfing story. Two couples were eating, the games annexe was noisy and in the far corner sat two men who had been there since I had arrived. One of them was the surly looking soul from my first lunchtime visit to the Lighthouse Inn. The boy racer without the driving licence as Eve had informed me. Gary Wilde. The man with Wilde looked equally powerful. Even his eyebrows had muscles.

The ambience, like the fisherman's pie that had been placed in front of me by Romeo's Juliet, was very good.

'Enjoying that, sir?' Turk wandered back up the bar. 'Another glass of sav-blanc?'

I nodded and said that the pie was delicious.

'Should be. Only the freshest ingredients in here. Landed this morning by the Wilde brothers,' said Turk, tipping his head towards the two quiet men sitting in the corner nursing pints of lager.

'Local fishermen?'

'A dying breed,' said Turk, re-filling my wine glass. 'The Wildes are the last two of the Shoreness fleet still making a living out of commercial fishing. The others rely on tourist fishing and diving trips to keep them afloat. Quite literally.'

Turk paused and pointed at my chest.

'Hope you don't mind me mentioning, sir, but there appears to be something switched on in your top pocket. There's a red light showing through the material. Wouldn't want you to run the batteries down.'

My blood turned to ice as I glanced down and saw the tiny red recording indicator light blinking away, clearly visibly through the blue denim.

'Oh, sod it. Thanks.' I scrambled my mind for a plausible explanation as I fumbled in my pocket to turn off the recorder. 'It's a little recorder that I use to make notes.' I held it up to show Turk. 'I'm a freelance journalist for the *South Coast Gazette*, I do restaurant and pub reviews … and the Lucky Fisherman will certainly be getting a top write up. I must have knocked it on by accident.'

Turk grinned but I had no idea what he was thinking.

'I look forward to reading it. When's it coming out?'

'Oh, in a couple of weeks I guess. That's really up to the editor, a Mr Lander.'

'I know him,' said Turk. 'Often pops in for a pint. I'll have to stop charging him if we get a rave review.' The landlord laughed and moved away. The Terras were back for refills.

I went to the toilets to gather my thoughts only to be confronted by two of the TA boys smoking roll-ups beside a sign on the wall with a red line through a cigarette.

They thought they looked hard in their ill-fitting uniforms but the acne spreading across their pale chins gave them away.

'Too wet to go outside for a fag, ain't it?' stated one looking at me as I desperately tried to act normally and pee in the urinal. Amazing how you can barely wring out a drop when you are being watched. I nodded, washed my hands and left.

The most natural thing for a food reviewer to do would be to linger over a dessert. I ordered cheesecake and a coffee. As I ate, I took out my phone and made as if to check for messages, but instead sent a text to Lander:

'If anyone asks, I'm doing food reviews for the SCG. Explain later.'

A few moments later, my phone bleeped. Lander had replied by text.

'OK – but we don't pay much! Cops tell me another

body has been found in the sea near Shoreness. Talk tomorrow.'

Another body. I decided it would have to be a police matter now. I drained the coffee, mouthed a 'thank you' to Turk, who was serving another customer, and left my money including a generous tip in the saucer containing the bill.

Out in the car park, as I fumbled for my keys, I failed to hear the footsteps behind me.

Back in the holiday cottage, I slid the bolt on the top of the front door as well as ensuring the Yale lock had clicked shut. I drew the curtains and sat at the small dining table feeling nauseous. A quick check on all moving parts left me content that no bones were broken but the blow to the kidneys was sending wave after wave of pain through my being. My raw hands hurt like hell, too. A brandy was not a good idea but I poured one anyway.

I felt for my top pocket. Shit. No recorder. It must have fallen out during the attack. I certainly was not going back to look for it tonight.

I was glad that tomorrow evening I would be heading far away from this place on the Caledonian Sleeper to Edinburgh, but before I left I had a couple of appointments in the morning at the nature reserve.

I looked down at the newspaper on the table and the crossword clues: *The Communist Party's net gains could be misleading* (3,8). I sipped the brandy, the fiery liquid numbing the pain a little, and filled in the answer.

Red Herrings.

How many of those was I chasing?

8

It was just after seven in the morning. I had forgotten to set the alarm but the pain in my side and back ruled out the possibility of enjoying a lie-in.

I had not wanted to look at the damage done by the car park beating when I had undressed the previous night but this morning the bathroom mirror revealed a dark reddish-purple circle the size of a saucer on my right side. I prodded it and winced. I gingerly felt my ribs but could not identify any serious damage.

'You'll live,' I said, mimicking a phrase my mother had regularly used when I had come home from school with a grazed knee or cut finger. She had never been one for making a fuss. My father was quite the opposite. He was ready to race to the nearest Accident & Emergency Department at the first sight of blood.

Perhaps their different make-up was the chemistry to my parents' long-lived marriage, unlike my relatively brief one with Katie. The first five years with Katie had been good, or so I thought. The second five years slipped into a routine, but since then, I now realised, it had been a case of existing together. The only good thing throughout had been our daughter Alice. She had been the cement that had held the marriage together for so long. Not any longer.

Alice was now approaching womanhood, and Katie was approaching other men. Me? I was approaching what the Sunday magazines loved to call 'the male mid-life crisis.'

When I peed I was relieved to see there was no sign of blood. My assailants had done a swift, simple job. It was enough to warn me off rather than seriously hurt me. Whether I heeded that warning or not was another matter.

Yesterday's rain had given way to sunshine – the sort of March sun that misleadingly looked warm. Getting into the Audi was a painful exercise but it was a good morning for a drive to the Shoreness Nature Reserve, where I hoped to meet the manageress Janice Woodcock and find out more about the boy Valgren. On the way, though, was the less enticing thought of passing the Lucky Fisherman.

The pub car park was empty apart from a highly polished black Toyota Rav4 complete with smoked windows and the number plate ROM 3O. I assumed it was meant to be read as Romeo, as in Romeo Turk, the landlord.

I stopped the Audi near enough to where I remembered parking the previous night and got out without shutting the door. No need to announce my presence by slamming it. I wanted to see if there was any sign of my missing recorder although I did not hold out much hope. If it had not been found and picked up, it would almost certainly have been crushed under the tyres of cars leaving.

The Lucky Fisherman looked bigger and more imposing than I remembered. It was one of the very few two-storey buildings in Shoreness and was fronted by red brick instead of the painted weatherboarding used for most of the buildings. On top of what appeared to be a newish extension was a small tower topped by a glass dome making it look like a miniature lighthouse. To one side of the car park was a beer garden with a giant red-painted anchor. In another corner was a small rowing boat sunk in the ground and made into a children's sandpit. There was a dinosaur slide and swings. It all appeared so innocent in the morning sunshine.

There was no sign of the recorder or last night's fracas. Not even a drop of blood. The pub door opened and Turk emerged.

'Morning Squire. I heard what happened last night,' he said, holding eye contact. 'I'm very sorry about it. Are you OK?'

'Yes, fine I think,' I lied, putting one hand inside my jacket and feeling my ribs.

'That's not the sort of behaviour I expect in my establishment and I won't tolerate it. I intend to find out who did it. I suspect it might've been one of the TA boys, I heard you caught them smoking in the bog.'

'Yes, I did – but why would they react with violence? I didn't even tell them to stop smoking.'

'Who can say? Perhaps they were smoking weed and you spooked them,' said Turk, who seemed oblivious to the cold sea wind despite being dressed in only a tee shirt with Antigua Haven written across the chest, Bermuda shorts and flip-flops. 'When young lads get a bit pissed, they can do odd things. Whoever it was, they'll be banned from here. I assure you of that. And the next time you're in, dinner's on the house – if there is a next time, that is.'

'Oh, OK thanks.' I doubted I would ever return to take up the offer. 'By the way, you haven't come across my little recorder I suppose? I seem to have lost it.'

Turk scanned the tarmac. 'No, but I'll keep my eyes peeled. Got to get on, expecting a brewery delivery at ten.' He turned on his heels and walked back inside the pub leaving me shivering in the wind and wondering whether the landlord had been expecting me.

It was too early to visit the nature reserve, so I took a circular route past the Cheyne Ministry of Defence Camp. I put Dire Straits' Alchemy in the CD player and selected my favourite live track: Romeo and Juliet. Somehow it seemed appropriate.

The MoD training range looked just as inhospitable in the sunshine as it did when I first drove around its perimeter fence on my first day in Shoreness. Beyond the cluster of red-brick army homes with their regimented gardens outside the camp's guarded gates, acres of stony ground inside the fence stretched as far as the eye could see to the coast. The land was criss-crossed with tracks, tank ramps and craters. The occasional sorrowful tree struggled for survival, no doubt wondering what it had done wrong to take root in such a hostile environment. There were watchtowers dotted around. There was also what remained of a battered village centre with houses pock-marked by bullets and gaping holes where windows had once been.

Had Much-Bombing-in-the-Marsh once been a vibrant local community that was forcibly cleared when the training camp was set up, or had it been purpose-built solely for the war games? It was impossible to tell. Further around the boundary fence, were some four-storey concrete tower blocks, windows missing, masonry battered and blasted. It looked like a scene on the news from Beirut, which is perhaps what it was meant to be.

I pulled up on the verge beside a sign that read: 'Strictly No Parking. MoD Ranges'. A fraying red flag flapped from a pole inside the fence which carried more signs – these were black and yellow triangles warning 'Unexploded Ordnance'.

Three figures in khaki with guns slung over their shoulders abseiled down the side of the Beirut tower block and swung in through the open window feet first. Tenderly feeling my side again, I wondered if they were my assailants. I drove on as Mark Knopfler growled his way through 'Private Investigations'.

It was not yet nine when I pulled up outside the visitors' centre at the RSPB nature reserve but it was already open. The early bird and all that, I thought.

In the warm entrance hall was a whiteboard with writing in blue marker pen scrawled in three columns down its length. Each column had a title: Seen this month, Seen this week, Seen today. Lists of birds were written with dates, times and initials recorded in brackets by each one. Most of the initials were JW but there were others including JV.

Marsh harrier sightings dominated but there were several goldeneyes, smew, a black-necked grebe, goosander (two females), a chiffchaff, a short-eared owl, ten oystercatchers, an avocet. The lists went on. I had no idea there were so many different species on the lake. As far as I could make out, there were just a lot of ducks and reeds.

Next to the 'sightings board' was a large childlike map showing a blue lake with a green path meandering around it linking brown boxes at the water's edge. The boxes were marked: Newman's Hide, Rupert's Hide, Robin's Hide, Danish Hide, *South Coast Gazette* Hide, Lighthouse Hide, Genor-X Hide, Todd's Hide.

The smell of fresh coffee dragged me away. A case of hide and seek, I thought. The main building had a vast floor to ceiling window overlooking the water, which gently lapped against the stony shore just a few feet away. In front of the window on the inside was a long bench and in front of the bench, monoculars were set up on tripods pointed towards the lake.

At a small desk sat a woman, her head tilted back as she looked through half-moon glasses at a computer screen. She looked about fifty, her grey hair cut stylishly short. She wore a dark blue RSPB sweatshirt. Around her neck hung powerful Zeiss binoculars and she had a name badge on her left breast with Janice written on it in the same hand that had listed the birds on the board in the entrance hall. She peered over her glasses and seemed surprised to see me standing there.

'Oh, the early bird,' she said. Wise minds, I thought. 'I didn't hear you come in. Are you a member?'

'No.'

'No matter. It's free to walk around the reserve. We just ask you keep to the designated footpaths and make a donation in the little box over there if you feel you can. Lovely morning for it – and we have binoculars for hire if you wish.'

'Actually,' I said. 'If you are Janice Woodcock, it's you I want to see rather than the ducks.'

'Really! What have I done wrong now? Not another library fine?' she said with mock horror.

'Not this time. You can keep the *Bird Watcher's Guide* for another week. My name's Tom Kidd, and I'm making some inquiries on behalf of a friend.'

The triangular nameplate on the front of the desk told me that she was: Dr J R Woodcock. She looked like everyone's favourite auntie.

'If it's OK, I wanted to ask you about Jimmi Valgren, the young lad who lived in the Dormobile back along the track and who drowned last weekend.'

Her smile disappeared. 'So, so sad,' she said shaking her head. 'He was a lovely human being – and so talented. We still have some of his photographs and sketches for sale in the gift shop. He donated them to us.'

'Can you spare a minute Dr Woodcock – over a coffee?' I looked towards the drinks machine in the corner of the shop. 'I've not had breakfast yet.'

'Of course, we're not busy as you can see. And please – it's Janice.'

I fetched two coffees and explained how I had been the one who had spotted Jimmi Valgren's body in the sea at Samphire Hoe. I told her about my chance meeting with Eve Hathaway and her fears about Jimmi.

'I'm puzzled, Janice. Jimmi's van along the track has been ransacked yet the police have written off the case as an accidental drowning.'

She snorted. 'The police? They're hopeless around

here. We're continually reporting the theft of eggs from nests – protected rare species too – but they don't give a flying fig. There's a small police unit based at the nuclear plant and their over-riding concern is security there. All we have is one community bobby covering Sanctuary Bay and Shoreness, and he's a lazy so-and-so. Anything for the quiet life, for him. Says he is too busy with house burglary and car crime to worry about a few duck eggs, but I don't believe it.'

'Why?'

'He spends most of his time in the Lucky Fisherman. If you ask me, he gets backhanders for turning a blind eye to the late night drinking sessions that go on, and he never bothers with drink driving, unless they happen to be tourists. No-one round here has much faith in PC Trotter.'

'So, Janice.' I paused to choose my words carefully. 'Do you think anything untoward could have happened to Jimmi?'

She looked taken aback, as if the idea had never crossed her mind. 'I shouldn't think so. Why? I thought his death was simply an accidental drowning.'

'It probably was – but a few things don't make much sense. For a start, I hear he had a bit of a phobia about the sea and wasn't exactly the sort to go swimming in the freezing Channel in March. I'm just trying to piece a few things together. Can you tell me a bit more about him?'

He had arrived at the bird sanctuary about three months ago, she said. He spent most days and evenings watching, photographing and sketching from the hides dotted around the shore of the lake.

'It was a two-way arrangement because we thought his presence in the van at night would deter anyone looking to get up to no good. In return for letting him stay, he also donated several of his works to the RSPB, which we sell to help raise funds.'

'Was he in trouble with any of the locals? And why would his Dormobile be ransacked?'

'That I don't know. He never said if he was. He seemed such an inoffensive young man. I can't imagine anyone disliking him,' said Janice. Her eyes moved to the wall over my right shoulder and she nodded. 'That's one of his.'

There was a striking photograph of a cormorant in familiar pose with its vast black wings hung out as if to dry. With its long sad face it looked like the undertaker of the bird world.

'He took that from the Danish Hide, which was his favourite spot. It's sponsored by the local Danish family who are farmers here. I think it was just a coincidence that Jimmi was half-Danish himself. That particular hide does have lovely views of the reed beds and the beach beyond.'

Janice suddenly lifted her binoculars to her eyes and gave an excited giggle. 'How lovely,' she muttered. '*Anas acuta*'.

'What's that?' I could not seeing anything different in the flock of ducks floating happily on the water outside the windows.

She pointed. 'A pair of *Anas acuta* – pintails. They winter here but this pair look as if they might be a breeding pair, which is very rare in the UK. I must put it on the board.'

I followed her to the entrance hall where she put the details of her sighting in the empty 'Today' column on the white board, scribbling her initials beside it.

'The sightings with JV beside them – were they by Jimmi Valgren?' I asked.

'Yes. He contributed almost as many as I did.'

I looked down the 'Last Month' entries and JV appeared almost every day. Under 'Last week' he had initials besides sightings on Monday, Tuesday and Wednesday and then they stopped.

The officer who had given me a lift back to my cottage on Monday evening, said he had been told that the body at Samphire Hoe appeared to have been in the water for at least four days. That would fit with Jimmi disappearing at the end of last week.

'Can I ask you a few other questions, Janice?' I said as we moved back into the café area after she had insisted it was her turn to get the coffee. 'Do you know the Lawtons who run Dead Oak Farm?'

'Poor Ian.' She sounded sad again. 'His place has been going to rack and ruin since his wife died a couple of years back. Such a tragedy, and he seemed to lose interest in the land once she'd gone, although it was always a losing battle for them trying to make a profit. His farm's on the driest, stoniest soil in these parts – hence the farm's name.'

I sipped the coffee she had handed me and waited for her to carry on.

'His daughter's at university, in Reading I believe. His son Danny went to agricultural college and helps out on the farm but I'm not sure he wants to stay around here, not since he and Eve split up.'

I almost dropped the cardboard cup. 'The same Eve who was with Jimmi?'

'Yes,' she said, pausing as if anticipating my thought processes. 'But I can't imagine Danny would've done anything nasty, even if he was feeling jilted. He doesn't seem the sort.'

A spurned lover's rage knows no bounds. I thought it but did not say it.

'Funny we should be talking about Eve,' I said instead. 'I'm meeting her here shortly. What's her Dad like?'

'No idea,' she shook her head. 'He runs the Lighthouse public house I believe and I rarely go there. I tend to go to the Lucky Fisherman if I do use a local.'

'But I notice you have a Lighthouse Hide. Did the pub sponsor that?'

'No, it's called that because it has the best views of the old disused lighthouse that had to be replaced by a new one when the power station was built and obscured its light. Now it's just a tourist attraction. We're still looking for sponsors for that hide. Interested?'

I laughed. 'I don't think my redundancy money would stretch to that but I'll tell you what: if my first novel is a blockbuster, I'll happily sponsor the hide.'

'It's a deal. I'm afraid I'd better get on with my chores, but if there's anything else, here's my card if you want to chat again,' she said, taking a business card from her top pocket. 'Feel free to look around. Our feathered friends might surprise you.'

I stepped outside. Before any twitching, I wanted to talk to Larry Lander about the news that a second death by drowning had been discovered, but as I was dialling the number, a small white van with 'The Lighthouse Inn' emblazoned on the side pulled up. Eve looked out as the driver's window rolled down.

'Hello Mr Kidd. I haven't got long. Dad thinks I've just popped to the cash-and-carry in Normanden to get some more crisps. Hop in.'

I sat in the passenger seat. Eve was wearing a different but equally cheeky tee shirt: 'Anglers do it dangling over the side,' said the legend across her breasts. I wondered if she had bought a job lot of saucy shirts. Her mood, though, was anything but cheerful. She looked anxious and upset. She also looked very young and vulnerable.

'Eve, I need some honest answers if I am to make any progress.'

She nodded.

'Were you and Jimmi lovers?'

She nodded again, reddening slightly.

'How did Danny Lawton take that?'

'Badly at first. He threatened to knock Jimmi's block off, and kept sending me texts telling me how much he loved me. Then he started stalking us at the Dormobile, driving around outside on his quadbike, revving the engine. But, Mr Kidd, I don't believe Danny could've done anything nasty.'

Another female giving Danny Lawton a good character reference.

'Do you know that a second body has been found at sea?'

She looked alarmed and shook her head.

'Who do you think ransacked Jimmi's VW? Whoever it was appeared to be looking for something rather than just nicking stuff.'

'I've honestly no idea, Mr Kidd.'

'What about Romeo Turk?' It was a stab in the dark.

'Hate him. He gives me the creeps. He's always staring at me.' Eve folded her arms self-consciously across her bosom and looked embarrassed. 'Jimmi went to his pub a bit, though. That's where he scored his pot when he wanted it. The Lucky Fisherman is known as being the place to do deals. Dad's pally with Turk but I just get the feeling he's a bit of a perv, if you know what I mean.'

I did. Alice my daughter was about six years younger than Eve, but still attracted the sort of looks from men that made me want to neuter them.

'What did you mean the other day when you said bats wings and smuggling?'

She hesitated. 'I've no idea what bats wings are or what Jimmi meant. He said it one night last week when he was high and babbling on. He seemed very agitated and kept going on about people vandalising nature. Said he was going to get photographic proof.'

'And smuggling?'

'I'm not sure exactly what Jimmi was talking about, but smuggling goes on, everyone knows it does on quiet stretches of the coast like this. The customs people can't stop it, the police don't seem bothered. We're that close to the French coast, it's easy, I guess. Drugs, fags and booze are smuggled. There's even rumours of people smuggling now. The European quotas have made sure there's not much profit from fishing these days, so the fishermen have to do something to earn a living. I don't approve of it but I also can't say I blame them. Do you?' She looked at me.

'Are the Wilde brothers involved in that?'

'I don't know but I wouldn't be surprised. They never seem short of cash judging by the cars they drive.'

'Why aren't the police on to this?'

Eve rolled her big blue eyes skywards as if I had just asked the most naïve question imaginable.

'We have one local bobby – Peter the Pig, we call him – PC Trotter, who has his snout in any trough going,' she said. 'Just ask my Dad. He's always after a free meal or a drink. As long as no-one's murdered, the heavy mob in Normanden nick are not bothered about little old sleepy Shoreness.'

'And you think Jimmi might have been murdered?' For the first time I contemplated the ultimate crime.

'Yes …' she started to sob and put her hands to her face. A muffled whisper came out. 'I'm scared, Mr Kidd.'

I wanted to give her a reassuring hug but was concerned it might be taken the wrong way. She clearly already had a certain view of middle-aged males and their motives. Instead I put a hand on her shoulder. 'Don't be scared, Eve. Nothing's going to happen to you. And I promise I'll do all I can to find out what happened to Jimmi.'

She dabbed her smudged eyes with a tissue and tried to smile. 'I'd better go or Dad will get suspicious.'

I waved a hand as I watched her speed away bumping along the rough track back past Jimmi's ransacked Dormobile, a symbol of the sadness in her young life.

I dialled Lander's number.

'Where's that bloody restaurant review?' Lander didn't even say hello, but then burst into laughter. 'What's that all about, you doing reviews for the *SCG*?'

'I used it as a cover story last night in the Lucky Fisherman. The landlord – Turk – got suspicious of my questions and then spotted my recorder was on. And he said he knew you.'

'Hardly. Been there a couple of times for a pint, though. It's got a dodgy reputation although the food's meant to be good. Kids and Army types use it for scoring dope, I hear. And there's often the odd scuffle on a Saturday night.'

'There was one there last night, too.' I felt my side but did not offer Lander any more details. 'Anyway, if Turk asks, back me up, Larry. I want him to believe my cover and not think I was just snooping around. And what's this about a second body being found?'

'False alarm.' Lander, sounded disappointed. 'At first the police thought it was linked because the deceased was another male, similar age to Valgren and found naked in the sea. The body came ashore about three miles from Shoreness, but this time to the west, not the east.'

'So?'

'Don't you remember anything from geography? The predominant currents are west to east up the Channel, so he couldn't have been dumped in the sea at Shoreness and floated westwards. Anyway, the deceased has now been identified as an unfortunate bridegroom-to-be who went skinny-dipping with his mates on a stag night in Brighton. Silly bugger.'

Lander's compassion knew no bounds – but my crossword had come up trumps. A red herring indeed.

'We've carried the Valgren story in this week's paper. Seen it?'

'No not yet. You were sold out at the local newsagents.'

'Yeah, sure,' said Lander.

I told him I would be in contact again after my weekend in Edinburgh, and hung up. It was time to get back to the holiday cottage, pack and head for London and the sleeper north.

Back at the holiday cottage, a police car was parked outside. Standing beside it on the verge was a uniformed officer smoking. As I pulled up, he hurriedly dropped his cigarette and squashed it underfoot.

'Afternoon officer, anything wrong?' I said getting out of the Audi.

'Mr Kidd, is it? Police Constable Trotter.'

He was short for a policeman and carried too much weight. In a chase on foot, he would not have caught many villains. He had the bolshie air of someone who liked getting their own way.

'I heard about your spot of bother at the Lucky Fisherman last night, sir. Did you get a look at your assailants?'

'No'

'Pity. We'll look into it of course, sir, but if I were you, I'd give the place a wide berth while you're here. Two weeks, isn't it?'

I nodded. PC Trotter was well informed.

'Any serious damage, sir?'

'I don't think so, officer. Just a few bruises. The landlord thought it might have been the Territorial Army lads, for some reason.'

'Yes, well. We can't go on supposition, can we? But I'll make some inquiries and keep you informed. In the meantime, I wouldn't go around asking too many questions in a place like this, if you get my drift.'

I said I did. I felt I was being warned off.

'One other thing, officer: any developments on the drowning of Jimmi Valgren? And I see his VW at the bird sanctuary has been ransacked.'

'Dover police are dealing with the drowning, sir. Nothing to do with me,' he sounded irritated by the fact that I was still asking questions specifically having been warned not to. 'As for the Dormobile – looters, I suspect. Leave a place empty with valuables inside and you're asking for trouble. I'd bear that in mind, sir, if I were you.'

I parked in a quiet residential cul-de-sac near Normanden Station where I thought the car would be safe for the weekend, bought a coffee and a copy of the *South Coast Gazette* from the kiosk and caught the train to London in plenty of time for the eleven o'clock evening departure to Edinburgh.

One glance at the paper's front page took me back to my early days in journalism in Nottinghamshire. Not much seemed to have changed. There was a splash headline about a ring road protest, a story of a local TV weatherman standing as a UKIP candidate in the upcoming General Election, and one on school governors starting a fund to repair a leaky gymnasium roof. Also on the front page tucked in the bottom right hand corner was the headline: ARTIST'S TRAGIC DROWNING.

> *Local wildlife artist Jimmi Valgren was found dead in the sea at Samphire Hoe last weekend.*
> *Valgren, 23, a former Brighton student, had lived in the Shoreness area for three months, working on his art at the RSPB Nature Reserve.*
> *His naked body was spotted by a walker at the Hoe. It is believed he had been in the water for at least three days.*
> *A Normanden Police spokesperson said the death was being treated as a 'tragic accident.' The coroner has been informed.*
> *Head Ranger at the Nature Reserve, Dr Janice Woodcock said: 'It's a tragedy. Jimmi was a truly talented artist who cared deeply about the centre, the birds here and our conservation work. Our thoughts are with his family.'*
> *Valgren's family live in the Bristol area.*

Short and to the point. It was not quite the big news story Lander had envisaged when he first became suspicious about the drowning. But there was still time.

The journey to London was a slow one. The Normanden 'Express' appeared intent on stopping at every isolated station on its way to Charing Cross although no-one got on or off at most of the halts. Meanwhile, several trains packed full of commuters leaving London after another week's graft rattled past in the opposite direction.

Time to attack the SCG crossword. 1 across. *All women do (3,5).* Too easy, I thought, filling in the first clue: *hen party.* The crossword was completed long before my train trundled over the Thames and into the cavernous mouth of Charing Cross.

The Caledonian Sleeper was waiting for its passengers on Platform One at Euston. I found a mini-supermarket to stock up for the journey north before heading down the platform to find Carriage F, berth three.

If I was lucky, I would be alone in the tiny two-berth cabin. Unlucky and I would be sharing with a stranger. I was lucky. When the old rolling stock groaned and complained as the two-gang locomotives at the head of the vast train eased out of Euston, I was still alone in my cabin. I pushed the upper bunk, which had been made into a bed in case of a late arrival, back into its recess and settled on the lower bunk by the small window table that hid a sink underneath.

I plugged my laptop into the power supply and logged on to the train's complimentary wi-fi in the hope that the signal would stay strong enough for me to check my emails before it faltered. I unscrewed the Chilean merlot I had bought and poured a healthy measure into one of the plastic cups provided.

By the time Watford Junction was flashing past the window, I had read the emails I had been waiting for, plus a couple I had not, one offering a complimentary supply of Viagra, another asking for my bank details to pay in a prize I had won from a lottery I had not entered.

Following the assault in the pub cark park the previous

night, I had emailed two trusted former colleagues who worked as crime reporters on national newspapers.

I wanted to know more about my new neighbours in Shoreness. If there was anything juicy to be found out about the two landlords – the monosyllabic mine host of The Lighthouse Inn, William Hathaway, and the unctuous Romeo Turk at the Lucky Fisherman – they would do it through their network of police contacts.

Both journalists had come back with roughly the same findings.

Hathaway was as unremarkable as his public house. He had received a police warning in his youth after being involved in an altercation at a football match at Chelsea, but since then he appeared to have led a blameless life, certainly as far as the police were concerned, apart from two speeding offences and a non-payment of TV licence. He had been in the army for eight years after leaving school, serving in Germany and the Middle East, reaching the rank of sergeant. He had also dabbled in the private security business in Saudi Arabia before returning to England and the pub trade, first in Gillingham and then Shoreness. His file showed he had been marked down as once belonging to the National Front but had been non-active for at least twenty years.

Turk's CV was far more entertaining. Officially he had kept his nose clean apart from two civil fines for non-payment of council tax on a property in East London. The police press officers, however, clearly had been happy to give my colleagues a more thorough off the record briefing.

Turk's father, Donald, had run two London pubs in the

Bethnal Green area. Both establishments were suspected as being 'holding houses' – used for storing and passing on stolen goods. An uncle had done time for an assault and extortion. Romeo Turk's elder brother, also named Donald, known as Donny, had died fifteen years ago in suspicious circumstances in a car fire in Rotherhithe. It was believed that Romeo and Donny had started to become involved in drug dealing around this time. After Donny's death, Romeo left London. The police believe he made himself scarce before he suffered a similar fate to his brother at the hands of rival dealers.

After six years in Spain, Romeo resurfaced in Shoreness with seemingly plenty of legitimate money to purchase and refurbish the Lucky Fisherman. To all intents and purposes, Turk was an honest citizen running an honest business. His wife Charmaine, the daughter of a Dartford haulier with a fleet of vehicles, likewise had a record that was as blemish-free as her complexion. I wondered whether both had needed some diligent cosmetic work.

So Turk had connections with a haulage firm, very handy for moving goods – or people – around on the QT. He also knew men with boats who drunk in his pub. He had links with the continent and a reputation for dabbling in the drug world.

Tread carefully, Tom boy, I thought to myself before drifting off to sleep somewhere near Crewe.

9

Any romanticism about travelling by sleeper to Scotland is dispelled by the dawn shunt at Carstairs Junction, where the snaking Caledonian Sleeper is divided. Half heads for Glasgow, Loch Lomond and Fort William on the west coast; half trundles to Edinburgh, Perth and Inverness on the east.

The grinding and jerking of the carriages added to the shouts of the railwaymen on the platform at Carstairs is enough to wake the heaviest drunken traveller. I lifted the blind on my little compartment window, wiped away the condensation and peered out on to a bleak Lanarkshire day breaking over a row of grimy pebble-dashed houses. For all its natural beauty, Scotland was also home to some of the grimmest, most uninspiring architecture in the United Kingdom.

There was little point in trying to get back to sleep. Edinburgh was only an hour away. The empty wine bottle rolled across the floor and under the bunk as the train lurched forwards. The little sink served as a handy urinal.

Edinburgh's Waverley Station was a mess. Refurbishment work had closed half the eating places, while passengers were directed on long detours around bollards and red and white tape. The sound of hammering and pneumatic drills was incessant, even at this early hour.

Time to escape the station bedlam in search of breakfast.

The magnificent façade of the Royal Scottish Academy with its imposing columns glowed in the low early morning sunshine as the commuters hurried down the steps into the bowels of the station. I bought a copy of The *Scotsman* from a pavement newspaper seller and headed up the hill along busy pavements to George Street and an Italian café I remembered from my last visit.

The place was still very popular. The staff with their hybrid Italian-Scottish accents were calling out orders, buttering toast, filling plates and pouring coffee in perfect synchronisation. I ordered porridge, toast and coffee, and found a stool at the front window counter so I could look out on the world. Edinburgh, like London, never seemed to sleep. There were those passing who were hurrying to work, those on their way home after a very late night out. Shoppers and beggars, tourists and joggers. They moved around barely noticing one another.

One of the new bull-nosed silver and black trams rumbled by. It was virtually empty despite the hustle and bustle on the pavements. The new Tramway was still as unloved in Edinburgh as the Millennium Dome had once been in London.

I turned to the back page of the newspaper first, an old habit. Hearts, one of the two Edinburgh football clubs, were riding high in the Championship. Hibernian, their city rivals, were hot on their heels. Today the two met in a sectarian derby and the back five pages of the sports section were taken up with match previews.

As well as a sporting rivalry, these two teams represented an ingrained divide in the capital city. Hearts were the team of the Protestants, Hibs was the Catholic club. The rivalry had become a hatred and ran deep through most families in the city. The police would be busy this afternoon.

I scan-read the features before thumbing through the pages to find what I was really looking for: the crossword. I ordered another coffee and took out my pen. 24 across. *One in church moving to transept (10).* Before I could fill in the answer, the mobile rang. It was Larry Lander.

'If you want your restaurant review, you're wasting your time. I'm on a weekend off in Edinburgh.'

'That can wait.' Lander chuckled. 'Look, just a quickie. Got a pen handy?'

'Always.'

'I've had an email from a Commander Gerald Marler, who was the driving force behind the anti-fracking mob that campaigned against the exploratory drilling at Dead Oak Farm. He saw the story about Jimmi Valgren on the front page yesterday and wants to talk to me about it. I've done one or two pieces with Marler before. He is an old naval type. Bit pompous but he's no one's fool. Lives in Sanctuary Bay. I thought it might be best for you to talk to him, just say you're doing something for the paper. He could shed some light on things, you never know.'

'OK, what's his number?'

Lander passed on the number. 'It might be something, might be nothing. Enjoy your weekend eating haggis.' Lander hung up.

I filled in the crossword answer: *Protestant.*

It was still early, barely nine o'clock, but on the assumption that old military men did not slum around in bed, even on a Saturday morning, I dialled the number.

'Marler speaking.' It was not so much a reply as a proclamation.

'Mr Marler, Tom Kidd here. Larry Lander at the *South Coast Gazette* asked me to give you a ring.'

I could almost sense the hackles rise at the other end of the line. The commander was probably not used to being referred to as plain Mr Marler.

'I really wanted to talk to Lander. It's about the deceased artist chap.'

'Yes Mr Marler. I'm dealing with that for the *Gazette*.'

'Well look, I think there's something fishy going on. Don't know what. Just a feeling in the old bones. The hippie-lad was a bit of an idealist but a decent chap all the same. What did you say your name was? Tomkins?'

'Tom Kidd.' I shouted over the hubbub of the café, making heads turn.

"Ah. Kidd. Right Mr Kidd, I'd like to meet up. Can't discuss this on the telephone, don't you know?'

'That's perfectly understandable, Mr Marler. I am in Scotland at present but I will be back down south on Monday. I'll call you then.'

'Scotland? What the devil are you doing there? Thought this business was going on in Shoreness, not Loch Ness. I was based there you know. Scotland. At Faslane. Damn cold place.'

'I'm sure Mr Marler. Look, I have to go. I will ring on Monday.'

I could almost feel my teeth rattle as Marler barked his farewell down the phone. I was happy to end the conversation although my interest had perked up with the mention of Faslane, the naval base on Gare Loch where Britain's nuclear submarine fleet was based. Was there a link between there and the Shoreness nuclear plant? If Commander Marler had served as a submariner, he might know something worth knowing after all.

The red double-decker bus was heading to Inverleith Row and the Royal Botanic Garden. From the crest of Queen Street, the view across the city from the top deck never ceased to impress. The proud sandstone houses stood in well-heeled crescents behind pointed railings. Church spires, still blackened from the days of coal fires, spiked the horizon like dark needles. Cobbled streets ran off to either side, their character unaffected by the redevelopment of the city centre. Edinburgh had style and just knew it.

The bus bumped along Great King Street, passed the Edinburgh Academy, swung over the Water of Leith Bridge and up the steady climb of Inverleith Row, where the Royal Botanic Garden was identified by the rank of flags outside: the Scottish Saltire, the Union Jack, the EU flag and, no doubt to please today's special visitors who were being shown around by my sister, the flag of Japan.

This was the unimposing administrative and educational block of the Garden that the public barely even noticed as they passed by. The main entrance used by the thousands of visitors each year was on the other side of the Garden on Arboretum Place.

The overweight man sitting behind the reception desk still had some of his breakfast on his official RBG tie. He slid a glossy magazine out of sight and eyed me suspiciously. He probably knew all the staff and students entitled to use this entrance – and I was not one of them.

He seemed disappointed when I told him I should have already been signed in by Dr Fleur Kidd. The man ran a chubby finger down a list of names and grunted when he found mine. Reluctantly he handed over a visitor's lanyard and pressed a button that unlocked a glass door into an internal hall.

The corridors that led to offices and classrooms could have been those of almost any educational establishment. I had met Fleur there many times. What gave the place away as somewhere special were the display cabinets along the corridors. One of them contained seed pods, dried fronds and a ship's log from Charles Darwin's five-year voyage on HMS *Beagle* in the nineteenth century. Another cabinet contained exhibits and photographs from a more recent expedition into the Chilean mountains to conserve rare conifers that were found nowhere else in the world. Another cabinet showed the work of a student team from Edinburgh in Tasmania's unspoilt northern forests.

Up a flight of polished wooden stairs on the mezzanine floor was an area that appeared to have been laid out to welcome the Japanese delegation for breakfast, the remains of which were being cleared away by two women in black and white aprons. Had the guests from the Far East been offered deep fried sushi as a local delicacy?

The walls of the mezzanine were lined with portraits of the men who had been charged with running the Edinburgh Garden, the Regius Keepers, stretching from 1699 to the present day. One of them, Sir Isaac Bayley

Balfour, had had a lecture theatre named after him and that was where Fleur had said I was likely to find her.

The sign on the plinth outside the two large oak doors said 'Lecture in Progress, please enter quietly.' I looked through the glass panel beside the doors and could see Fleur addressing the Japanese delegation. Two rows of grey-suited solemn men looked down intently from behind desks on the banked crescent of seats. I slipped into the darkened room and took a seat in the shadows of the back row.

She was only a slight figure in her white lab coat, but Fleur exuded confidence and conviction. Working the laptop projector, she spoke fluently about her favourite subjects: preserving plants and saving the world. Her words simultaneously appeared in Japanese sub-titles at the top of the screen behind her. She had the solely male audience in the palm of her delicate hand.

They had, she told them, a wonderful opportunity to make a difference: to make the world a better place for their children and their grandchildren by supporting the conservation work done by Edinburgh's Royal Botanic Garden.

'If a modern-day Noah had to take two groups of people on his Ark to save mankind, the two he would choose would be the medics and the horticulturalists,' she said. 'We all need medics to keep us healthy but it's the horticulturalists who help provide the food we eat and the drugs we need. All the medicines we use today came originally from the plant world before being refined by the chemists and developed synthetically.

Take the humble yew tree. The bark of that provides

us with Taxol, the basic element in the treatment of most cancers including breast cancer, ovarian cancer, lung cancer and pancreatic cancer. It was the work of botanists that led to this breakthrough with a drug we now consider essential.'

Images of plants flicked across the screen behind her as she spoke. 'Take the Elephant Foot Yam. Ugly to look at, delicious to eat and widely used as a treatment for all sorts of ailments throughout South-East Asia. It was this plant that gave us the basis of something that has changed the world – the contraceptive pill.

Or take the great Scottish explorer and botanist John Kirk. During work in Africa he saw the natives using a plant extract to tip their arrows when they went hunting for monkeys. That extract came from the plant *Strophanthus petersianus* – or Sand Forest Poison Rope to give it its more common name. The poison caused the monkeys to slow down, lose their grip in the trees and they could be easily captured for food. Kirk actually tried the poison on himself and discovered it slowed his heart rate. He brought samples back here to Edinburgh and it formed the basis of synthetic drugs now used to treat heart conditions.

In this establishment alone we have two hundred to three hundred new species of plant waiting to be categorised and listed. Worldwide, I estimate that at least three hundred unknown species of plants, from mosses to vast trees, are discovered every week. Yes. Every week. Yet, gentlemen, there is so much more.

The spread of man, the demands for more food and space to build homes and factories means we are wiping out species today before we even know about them and the possible properties they possess.

When a plant series disappears it reduces the variety of genetic material available, that, in turn, reduces the potential for medical research. Its compounds are lost forever.

The cure for dementia, an answer to malaria: they will be out there somewhere in the botanical world but only if we have time to find them. That's why our work here is so vital – and why your support is so important to us.'

Fleur paused for dramatic effect as images of suffering babies and distraught old people passed across the screen behind her.

'Yes, we do seek your financial support for our work which you saw on the tour this morning, but we also need you, as highly influential businessmen, to put pressure on your government in Japan to stop the industrialisation of unspoilt areas of your beautiful country and the clearance of the forests in the east of the mainland and on your islands, many of which have yet to be fully explored.'

I admired my sister. As well as outstripping me academically, Fleur's work had always seemed so much more valid than scribbling sports reports for something that would soon be tomorrow's chip paper – and which involved the felling of vast quantities of the trees that she was trying to save.

'What's with the white coat, Sis?'

Fleur glanced down as if she had just realised what she was wearing. She shrugged off the coat quickly and let it slide down her back onto the chair in the cafeteria.

'Forgot I had it on, Tommy. It's worn for effect. Our oriental visitors expect to see scientists in white coats, so a white coat it is for their visit. They're important to us and it's a small price to pay if it impresses them.'

Fleur was the only person who still called me Tommy. It was a name she had used when she had first learned to speak and it had stuck.

She looked radiant, and I guessed it was not just because of the successful presentation she had given an hour earlier and the series of bows she had received from the Japanese delegation as they filed out of the entrance hall for a coach tour of the city and Edinburgh Castle. Her boss, resplendent in kilt, had touched her on the arm as the guests left and whispered in her ear: 'Wonderful job, my dear.'

'You look very happy Fleur,' I said. 'Work going well, or is it because of this Chris you told me about?'

'Bit of both, Tommy. Yes, a bit of both. Life's good right now. I'm sure you'll like Chris.' She giggled just as she used to do as a child when she played a trick on me.

We finished the pot of green tea that Fleur had ordered, telling me it was good for the digestion.

'Do you think the Japanese business delegation will come across with the readies?'

'I certainly hope so. They're increasingly keen to show their green credentials, partly to get one up on the Chinese, who are one of the world's great polluters.'

'Was that right what you told them: that there are still thousands of unknown species of plants in the world and we're destroying them before we know about them?'

'That's right,' she said. 'And mankind is the species

that will pay the highest price in the long run. In layman's terms, the scientists are in a desperate rush to find out what's growing in this world before it disappears.'

'You amaze me. I thought we'd explored just about every corner of this planet and discovered just about everything there was to discover.'

'If only. As I said in the lecture hall, we have at least two hundred species waiting to be classified here in Edinburgh alone. Come with me. This might interest even you.'

We walked past the Fossil Garden, the giant Victorian greenhouses, the Palm House and the Chilean Terrace Garden, where Saturday visitors mooched with pushchairs and ice creams. Fleur led me around an administration block to a muddy track beside a yard full of wheelbarrows, ride-on mowers, bags of compost and gardening tools. We arrived at a locked head-high wooden gate marked 'No public admittance'.

Fleur unlocked the gate and we went through. It was not quite the same level of security I had encountered at the power station, but then cacti did not pose quite the same threat to the world as nuclear fallout. Here the greenhouses were not so grand, and there were no benches for visitors to sit on and pretty borders to admire. This was the working area of the Garden.

'The public don't get to see around here, partly because it probably wouldn't interest them, but principally because of security,' she said.

Fleur unlocked a greenhouse door with another key on the chain she wore around her waist. As we stepped inside, the heat hit me like a slap in the face with a warm soggy flannel.

'Hot isn't it? And humid. We keep a lot of the rarer orchids in here,' she said, locking the door behind us to keep the heat in as well as intruders out.

There was barely space to walk along the aisles between the waist-high slatted wooden work benches where potted exotic plants flourished, their large leaves spilling over into the walkways. Even more foliage hung down from wires above, roots grasping at thin air.

'A quick lesson in orchids,' she said, seeing me look up at the airborne plants. 'Orchids are highly evolved and by far the largest family of flowering plants in the world. There are more than 22,000 known species and thousands we still don't know about.' She paused to let me absorb the facts.

'Most orchids are epiphytic – that is they grow on trees, their root system hanging down, and they have no soil contact.' She pointed to the plants above us. 'You probably know that vanilla is the most harvested product from the orchid, but the rare exotic ones are highly collectable and worth a great deal of money. That's why we guard this lot so carefully. If we didn't, we'd have wee collectors in here digging up specimens, taking cuttings and stealing seeds.'

'No?' I said, the sweat dripping off my nose and running down my neck as I craned my head up to look at a curious maroon growth that looked like a giant phallus.

'Ha – if you think that's impressive, you should visit the orchid house at Kew in London. Your landlord – Gideon Squires – is the curator and one of the world's leading authorities on orchids.'

'He dropped in to see me at the cottage earlier this

week. Told me he'd been trying to convince you to move to Kew.'

'He has been, but, while I like Gideon, I couldn't work with him.'

'Why's that?'

'We've been on a few projects together and he certainly knows his stuff, but he's from the razzmatazz commercial side of botany: wants to get it out there to the public on TV programmes, and launch big projects like a garden bridge over the Thames. I'm not sure conservation is top of his list of priorities. I think he's getting disillusioned with what he sees as a lack of ambition by his bosses. He feels his career is being stymied.'

Fleur beckoned me through another set of double doors that she locked behind her, and led the way through into the cooler Mustard House and then the Ginger House.

'I never realised there were so many types of ginger, Sis'.

'Oh yes. The *Zingiberaceae* family is one of our major research programmes. There are about 1500 species. Come on, before we leave, I'll show you my pride and joy.'

She locked another door behind her and we were out in the fresh air again. It suddenly felt bitterly cold. I was wet through with sweat. It was a relief when we reached the last greenhouse in the row tucked into a corner underneath a high external brick wall. Taped on the inside of the glass door was a hand-written sign that read 'Socotra'.

Fleur punched a code into a keypad. As we entered, a

young oriental women looked up from the tray of pots she was planting on a bench.

'Hi Nia, how's it going? Just showing my brother some of our little secrets.'

Nia nodded and continued with her work.

'One of our very brightest students,' said Fleur, when we were out of earshot of Nia. 'She's from Singapore on a scholarship, but she's so valuable, I hope she doesn't go back.'

The temperature here was far more comfortable. It felt like a balmy evening in a Mediterranean resort. A large industrial fan hung from the roof struts and turned lazily, a warm breeze floated around the mounds of stony ground where the plants were housed.

'This is the Socotra House,' said Fleur proudly, as if introducing a newborn baby. She looked around and beamed.

Socotra, she explained, was a small island in the Indian Ocean that was governed by the Yemen. It was half the size of Wales but so unique was its flora and fauna that it was designated a UNESCO World Heritage Site.

'Never heard of it.'

'You won't have done. It's very isolated and barely touched by the Western world. It doesn't have a tourist industry and that's what keeps it so special. On our last survey, there were 825 plant species there of which more than 300 are unique to the island. That is, they are found nowhere else on earth other than Socotra.

Imagine that, Tommy. More than a third of the plants there are unique to that one little island. Three of those species are on the red endangered list. Forty-five are on the amber list.'

I had not heard of the red and amber lists but it did not take a genius to guess how they worked.

'That means that if we don't protect them, they will be lost forever, and we are only now beginning to find out what properties they have.'

'We?'

'Yes, us here at Edinburgh and Gideon's team at Kew. The Yemen Government have granted Edinburgh with the sole licence to conduct field studies on Socotra and bring back samples to propagate here and at Kew. In return, if we find anything of value, they hold fifty per cent of the commercial rights.'

'What does that mean?'

'We think some of these rare plants could hold very special pharmaceutical properties,' she said, holding up what looked like a potted daisy.

'The population of Socotra is just over 40,000 and the only medicines they have really come into contact with are the traditional ones garnered from plant sources. They're relatively long-lived people, which says much about their life style, but here's the exciting thing: none – and I mean none – of the older islanders over sixty suffer from any sort of dementia. They may have, unwittingly, discovered the answer to the curse of the modern world – dementia among the elderly … Alzheimer's disease.'

'Wow,' I said, looking more closely at the little plant in Fleur's hand with new-found interest.

'The people of Socotra use root extracts and crushed seeds for all sorts of ailments and we're narrowing down what we think may be the plant that is helping them stave off dementia. Meanwhile, the pharmaceutical companies are ploughing huge amounts of time and money into research into this problem because whoever comes up with the answer first will be on to the biggest thing since Viagra – bigger.'

I thought of making a smutty joke but decided against it. Instead, I stayed silent as Fleur carried on, enthused by her subject.

'Those companies would do anything to be in on the research we're doing here but we have to do it in a totally ethical way – not for gain but for humanity's sake. That's why security has to be high, because word is seeping out that we might be on to something. There's been speculation, some of it pretty accurate, in horticultural and scientific magazines about our work.

The thing is, Socotra's principal language is unwritten. The native people have no way of writing down what they know. That means there's no written record of anything. Everything is passed down by word of mouth from one generation to the next. Once outside influences move in, as they surely will, the past knowledge could be lost forever. We need to be very sensitive in our work in Socotra, and to keep it as discreet as possible. Follow me.'

Fleur walked between the aisles, past a dehumidifier humming softly, to the far section of the glass house where small delicate plants were dotted around a pile of stony, chalky soil.

'You've probably heard that saffron, the spice we get from the crocus, is the most expensive flower product in the world,' she said. 'It's always said it's worth more per gram than gold.'

She pointed to a little bundle of green among the pebbles in front of her with flat, limp leaves and a tiny white flower. 'Well, this little beauty will make saffron look cheap if we're right about what we've found in its roots.'

'What's it called?'

'Orchis vespertilio'

'You know Latin was never my strong suit, Sis. What does that mean in English?'

'The Bat's Wing Orchid.'

10

'Your driving's not improved, Sis.'

I hung on grimly to the door handle as Fleur slipped her bright red Mini Cooper into the smallest of gaps seemingly oblivious to the football traffic pouring out of Easter Road after the derby match between Hibernian and their detested rivals Hearts. She was cutting across the flow to head for her flat in Pilton in the fashionable north of the city where terraced piles had been converted into desirable apartments for young professionals.

I had a thousand questions to ask about orchids, but for now I was just interested in survival.

'Och, these Scottish drivers are useless,' she muttered. 'Who does he think he is giving the finger to?'

Fleur lowered her window and blew a kiss to a burly driver festooned in green and white shirt, scarf and hat who was fulminating behind the wheel of his Skoda while the Mini cut across his path. I sunk lower and lower into my seat.

As we left the maelstrom of football traffic behind, our way was clear at last. Fleur swung left into leafy residential roads and then Pilton Gardens, where her flat occupied the ground floor of a once grand Georgian family home.

She pulled into the parking spot reserved for her flat in front of a neat walled front garden where a few exotic shrubs that Fleur had planted struggled to impress, huddled, fighting a losing battle with the Edinburgh climate.

'Come on,' she said. 'Tell me all about it while I make us some tea.'

By 'it' Fleur meant my loss of a job with the *Herald* and the pending loss of a wife. Sitting in her kitchen, I filled in the details without trying to sound sorry for myself, but it was matters botanical that really filled my mind right now.

Fleur had explained that the Bat's Wing Orchid, a different species to the colourful and popular Batwing Orchid, took its common name from its wide ribbed translucent leaves that, when held up to the light, looked very much like a delicate bat's wing with its scalloped edges and veins of cartilage. It was the roots of the plant, though, with their potential for providing the answer to the onset of dementia that enthralled my sister.

'Can they grow in this country outside of your greenhouse?'

'They can. Just about,' she said. 'That's my big project at the moment. We have set up controlled experimental sites around the country to see if the orchid can be cultivated here, although we are not having much luck as yet. We are trialling the plant at sites on the west coast of Scotland where the Gulf Stream comes in and keeps the weather mild. There are sites in West Wales too, and near the Eden Project in Cornwall. Also in Guernsey. But the most exciting development is at a site near Dover in Kent, although that is slightly different.'

'Go on,' I said, topping up our tea mugs from the large brown pot.

'Well, we thought the Bat's Wing was unique to Socotra and to all intents and purposes, it is. But six months ago, an orchid with an almost identical genetic make-up was identified on a site in Kent that has a unique microclimate.'

'That place wouldn't be Samphire Hoe, by any chance?'

Fleur's eyes widened. 'How did you know that? It's meant to be very hush-hush.'

I told her about my discovery of a body in the sea at the Hoe, how Larry Lander had asked me to make a few inquiries and of my conversations with the distraught Eve.

'Well, apparently one of the last things Jimmi Valgren said to Eve was something about 'bat's wings.' It didn't make sense to her at the time nor to me when she told me, but it might now. He had a keen interest in nature and he was found dead at Samphire Hoe. I don't know if it means anything or not.'

Fleur looked unconvinced.

'It's possible he had read something about our work with the *Orchis vespertilio,'* she said. 'A few features have appeared in science journals. They were a bit speculative but the basics of our work with the Bat's Wing Orchid were accurate.'

'Was the *National Geographic* one of those publications?' I remembered the magazines I had found scattered around Valgren's vandalised Dormobile.

She nodded. 'That one among others. They reported that the plant was of high scientific interest and that it was being grown at various protected sites. The details, though, were pretty sketchy although there has been plenty of speculation on social media sites, some of it accurate. Your dead young man may have read about it.'

'You said the site near Dover was slightly different to the others?'

'Because we didn't plant it up. The orchid was found growing there naturally. That's the most exciting thing. But there's been a problem: I normally visit the site about once a month but I've been summoned down there, there's something of a crisis. I don't exactly know what, but I've got to be on the first flight to Gatwick at 6.25 on Monday morning. It made me wonder if you'd like to travel south with me instead of catching the train. I'd like that.'

I readily agreed to catching the flight with her. I wanted to find out as much as I could about Samphire Hoe. I could use the rail ticket I had purchased for my return trip another time. I left Fleur to do the flight booking online while I went to the spare room to unpack.

I laid on the bed watching a spider scale the dusty lampshade as I worked my way through the crossword clues in the Scottish newspaper I had bought that morning: 10 down. *A suitable sucker (7, 5).* I certainly felt like one at times. I filled in the squares: *tailors dummy.*

I must have drifted off to sleep, because the next thing I knew, my mobile was warbling frantically, its volume increasing with every second I failed to answer it. I did not recognise the number flashing on the screen.

'Tom Kidd.'

'Hello Tom, it's Jo. Jo Etheridge from Genor-X.'

I sat up and, for some reason, checked my appearance

in the wardrobe mirror opposite the foot of the bed. She said she had spoken to the power-station police and security staff and found nothing to suggest they had been overly concerned with Jimmi Valgren nor his protesting pals.

'The sofa blockade on the railway track has never ended in violence, and I think they were genuinely surprised to hear about his death,' she said. I sensed there was more she wanted to tell me.

'OK, thanks. Don't suppose I'll be bothering you again then,' I said, putting the ball in her court. She volleyed it back.

'Actually, there is something else. You've had a good career in journalism, you know your way around, and I wondered if a new challenge might appeal now you are out of work.'

She paused.

'Go on,' I said.

'We are launching a new in-house monthly magazine called *Power Post* – and are looking for an editor. Fancy talking about the job?'

Working for an on-message company publication was an easy number, but such a job had never appealed to me. On the other hand, Jo Etheridge did.

'Why not? I'm back down south on Monday morning.'

'Can you do Monday evening? Over dinner near our head office on the South Bank just by London Bridge?'

I said I could. She gave me a time and address and hung up. I might have to get a shirt washed while I was in Edinburgh. For now, I needed to get shaved and showered. I wanted to make the right impression on

Chris, Fleur's new love.

'We're meeting there,' said Fleur as I strapped myself into the Mini Cooper for another episode of Top Gear Edinburgh style. Heading into the gentrified district around Leith Docklands, Fleur flung her red rocket down cobbled streets originally made for horse-drawn carts.

We came to rest beside the quayside. The place was bustling with well-heeled diners and drinkers out for a Saturday night. Where once five pints and a fish and chip supper with curry gravy would have been considered fine dining, now the clientele were cooing over their medallions of monkfish in a caper and saffron sauce with hand-cut potato wedges and pea purée as they sipped a chilled pinot from Italy.

It was not really my scene but I did not say so. Fleur was clearly part of this chic world these days. She looked every inch the elegant professional in a tight cotton navy blue dress that revealed more than it covered, and was topped off with a tiny silver jacket.

'Come on, we have a window table booked at The Chandlers. You must have heard of it.'

I shook my head.

'Oh Tommy, you are so out of touch. You know the Scottish guy who won the recent MasterChef series, it's his place. The food is wonderful, and all sourced locally.'

The quay was full of boats and barges that once used to transport coal, grain and whisky but which were now permanently moored and converted into bars and restaurants. A girls' night out was in full swing in one called the *Saucy Sailor* judging by the screeches of delight drifting down the gangplank.

The Chandlers was an old solid square warehouse on the water's edge. Built to sell provisions and equipment for the boats, it now provided 'an elegant dining experience'. The décor was all polished wood and red-brick with a few mementos of the building's history dotted here and there. Beside me hanging on the wall was a faux coil of rope. Tacked to the wall beside Fleur was an oar.

'So you think Alice is coping OK with the separation?' asked Fleur, who had always been very fond of her niece.

'She seems fine with it,' I said, sampling the blush wine Fleur had ordered. 'You know what thirteen-year-olds are like these days, much more mature than we were at that age.'

'Don't be so sure, Tommy. They may appear more grown up but underneath they are still vulnerable children. These will be difficult times for her. Might you contest custody?'

The question shocked me. I had never considered that option. But then, two weeks ago, I had never considered divorce.

'I don't think so. I don't know. It's a real mess as I guess these things are. For a few days after Katie kicked me out, I think I hoped that we'd get back together but I now realise that won't happen. Oddly, I feel relieved about it. Is that wrong?'

Fleur shook her head.

'I'll do what Ali wants I guess. If I get settled somewhere near her school, she might want to live with me, but I sort of assumed a daughter would want to be with her mother.'

'Not necessarily,' said Fleur. 'Particularly if she feels it's Katie who's caused the split. Poor girl. I'll ring her next week to see if she wants to talk about things.'

Fleur was upset. For the first time, I realised a divorce affected more than just the two people involved and their children.

'I'm seeing Ali on Tuesday at a school open day. I'll chat to her then if I get the chance. It'll all work out, I'm sure.' I tried to sound upbeat and Fleur was beaming again.

'Here's Chris.'

I scanned the well-populated restaurant. The only person I could see weaving between the tables towards Fleur's waving hand was a handsome, tall black woman in a flowing red dress over matching leggings.

11

Dressed in a man's denim shirt several sizes too large for her – and very little else as far as I could tell – Chris poured the thick dark coffee from the French percolator into mugs.

'You take it black don't you? Like me,' she said.

As she leant across the breakfast table in Fleur's kitchen to pass the coffee, the shirt gaped open. She seemed happily oblivious. I made a point of looking down to butter my toast and thanked her, relieved when she finally sat down and cradled her steaming mug in both hands in front of her chin like a survivor rescued from the mountains in winter.

'It was a lovely meal last night.' She had a soft sing-song accent that I placed as being from South Wales.

'It was. I don't usually go in for that sort of dining myself but I have to say I was impressed. For that money, I ought to be too.'

'Oh, we don't do it very often, but Fleur wanted somewhere special for us to meet.'

The previous evening had gone well once I had picked up my jaw from the floor after the initial meeting with Chris. Or Christina Coverdale to give her her full name.

The two girls had both giggled when the introductions had been made as if they were in on a private joke at my expense. Later in the evening, when Chris slipped off to the loo before the desserts arrived, Fleur put her hand on mine and apologised.

'You should've seen your face,' she said, shaking her head. 'Sorry I led you up the garden path a bit but I wondered if you'd twigged that my Chris was a female Chris.'

'No, I didn't, but it makes no difference. She's lovely.'

'I'm glad you think so. Did you honestly not know I was gay, Tommy?'

'No … well, I suppose I never thought about it. I just assumed your lack of a male partner was because you were so wrapped up in your work.'

'That was part of it, I guess, I wasn't that bothered about hooking up with anyone of either sex really – until Chris came along a year ago.'

'And now?'

'We're an item. Chris is selling her flat and moving into my place, and we're going to get hitched. I wanted to tell you first. Next it's Mum and Dad. I don't know how they'll react.'

Before I had had time to consider our parents' reaction to being told their only daughter was a lesbian, Chris returned to the table. The pair were radiant in each other's company. They also had much in common including their love of horticulture.

Chris had studied at Cardiff University before working on forestry projects in Wales and the Lake District. Her speciality was conifers and she had moved to the Royal Botanic Garden in Edinburgh to join their team that ran conservation projects.

I liked to consider myself as broad-minded. So why

did I feel slightly shocked to discover that Fleur was gay? I came to the conclusion that the only shock I felt was with myself for not realising – or even contemplating the idea.

Still, when the two lovers had retired for the night at Fleur's flat after the meal, I turned the volume up a little on the late night football show on television just to ensure I did not hear any noises off.

The next morning, Chris greeted me in the kitchen as if we had been friends for months. She had a warm, easy-going personality to go with her striking looks.

The toaster popped up and Chris got up from the table again as the front door slammed shut. Fleur came in with a collection of Sunday newspapers that she spread across the end of the breakfast table.

The morning was the perfect family Sunday morning: lazing around reading and chatting. I attempted the Sunday crossword but did not get beyond the first clue: *Girlfriend's three-wheeler is an aerial hazard (4,6).* As I filled in the answer – *bird strike* – I started thinking again about Jimmi Valgren, the wildlife artist who for some reason had ruffled too many feathers.

I was convinced there was more to his death than a simple sad drowning accident. Had he seen something he should not have at the secretive Samphire Hoe?

We went out to lunch in one of the fashionable pubs that lined the waterfront in South Queensferry, a popular weekend destination for Edinburgh's smart set. Scotland looked magnificent in its Sunday best. Well wrapped up, we ate on the outside terrace in the shadow of the cantilevered Forth Rail Bridge, the March sun threatening to provide some warmth as it glinted off the icy estuary with the Cleish Hills and the Kingdom of Fife reaching to the horizon.

We talked about Fleur and Chris' plans, Scotland's future as an independent country if that ever happened, the etiquette of using smart phones at the dining table and the latest James Bond movie. Everything but the Bat's Wing Orchid, the small delicate plant that had grown to be the elephant in the room.

My chance came when Chris excused herself. She had work to do at the Garden and had to get away.

'Is there a lot of security around the site at Samphire Hoe?'

'Not a lot, I think,' said Fleur. 'Where the plants grow is pretty inaccessible, it's half way up a cliff. There's not much need for security.'

'Your team working there, I wonder if they might know something about Valgren? After all, it's where the body was found. They might have heard something.'

Fleur shrugged. 'Did he die there or did his body end up there brought in by currents?'

'That, I'm not sure about. Where I saw the body, there was a lot of debris floating around. It seemed to be trapped in a corner against the sea wall. He could have been there for days and not been seen.'

The mobile warbled. A text had arrived. It was from Eve Hathaway: 'Someone has broken into your holiday cottage. Don't ring back, father in a stinking mood.'

'Important?' asked Fleur.

'I'm not sure,' I said. 'It seems as if some people have taken exception to me being in Shoreness.'

12

I picked up the circulars lying on the mat inside the front door of Lighthouse View Cottage and hesitantly walked into the lounge, not sure that I wanted to see what awaited me.

The front door had been ajar. Not broken, just left gently swinging on its hinges in the breeze coming off the Channel. Whoever had got in had had access to a key because there was no sign of a broken window or forced entry.

The place was a mess.

Drawers were open and empty, their former contents scattered across the floor. The cushions had been pulled off the small sofa, a storage chest was open, the box games of Monopoly, Cluedo, chess and draughts that had been inside had been thrown out, their contents scattered across the floor. The television was switched on and the presenter was burbling on about house improvements. Scribbled across the screen over his face in thick black marker pen was a message in capital letters: 'FUCK OFF KIDD'.

In the kitchen it was the same message only in not so many words. The fridge door had been left open leaving the beer and wine to get warm. The remains of a carton of orange juice had been poured on the linoleum floor.

The two eggs that had been on the little rack in the fridge door had been thrown at the wall. The bedroom had been given similar treatment, although in here the intruders had considerately left a calling card. They had pissed on the clothes they had thrown out of the wardrobe and drawers.

Rather than stealing anything, these intruders had done the opposite. They had returned something. The pocket tape recorder I had lost when I was punched to the tarmac of the Lucky Fisherman car park was on the bedside table. It still worked but its files had all been wiped clean although one message had been recorded on it: *'Just fuck off if you know what's good for you.'*

I played the message three times. I could not be sure but I thought I recognised the rasping voice.

Chris had given us a lift to Edinburgh Airport at an ungodly hour that morning to catch the 6.25 to Gatwick, but at least we had beaten the crowds and avoided delays at check-in and security, where the staff had been too sleepy to care.

Over coffee and croissants in the depressing airport café, Fleur told me, as she had promised to do, more about the Bat's Wing Orchid and why it was such a secret project at Edinburgh's Royal Botanic Garden.

'We don't want to delay any research that might benefit mankind – and we have genuine reason to believe there's something in the root system of the plant which could help prevent dementia – but if our research goes public too soon it could be disastrous.'

'In what way?'

'For a start, Socotra would be invaded by pharmaceutical companies as well as trophy hunters from the plant world. The limited number of plants that grow on the limestone plateau there could be destroyed and lost forever in no time. We need to find out the properties of the plant and how to grow it commercially – and by sheer serendipity, we may have stumbled across something at Samphire Hoe.'

Fleur explained that the chalky soil on the south coast of England was similar to that found on the Socotra plateau where the Bat's Wing flourished in the semi-desert climate.

'But Kent is hardly semi-desert.'

'No, but Samphire Hoe is unique. For one thing, it has not had hundreds of years of interference and influence from man as it was created only a couple of decades ago when they dug out the Channel Tunnel and dumped all the soil at the foot of the cliff. But it's more than that,' she said, lowering her voice and looking around suspiciously as if to make sure that the other customers, who had their noses buried in newspapers, were not eavesdropping.

'At Samphire Hoe there are giant air-conditioning units for the Channel Tunnel. The electric trains that use the tunnels generate a lot of heat, and the tunnels have to be air-conditioned otherwise they would be unbearable to travel through.

The air-con sends cool fresh air down into the tunnels and sucks out the warm air with giant fans. This warm, dry air is pumped out of big funnels at the foot of the cliff at Samphire Hoe – and half-way up the cliff we have our own unique microclimate that stays relatively steady for twelve months a year – and it's almost exactly the same as in Socotra.'

'Wow.'

'Wow, indeed,' agreed Fleur.

'But you didn't plant the Bat's Wing there?'

'No, that's the incredible thing. We have other projects at Samphire Hoe because it is so unusual, but a team of our horticulturalists found it growing there naturally.'

'How did it get there?'

'That we don't know: at least, we have a few theories, but we don't really know. Yet. The best guess is, and it's my opinion this is right, is that some seeds from the same orchid group as the Bat's Wing had lain dormant for thousands of years in the ground and were brought up by the Channel Tunnel excavations.'

'Is that possible. Can seeds lie dormant for so long and suddenly start growing into plants again?'

'In theory, yes. Seeds are remarkably resilient things. Once exposed to light and rain, given the right conditions, there's no reason why they can't germinate.'

I sat back and tried to take in what Fleur was telling me. My journalist's training taught me to be sceptical because history had shown 'experts' to have been wrong so often in the past.

'What about birds or animals bringing the seeds here from Socotra. Or the wind, come to that?'

Fleur dismissed both suggestions. No animal from Socotra migrated to northern Europe, she said. The orchid seeds were not air-borne even if the winds from the Indian Ocean made it all the way to Dover, which they did not, she informed me.

'What really matters, however they got there,' said Fleur sounding exasperated, 'is that these rare plants with their potential properties are growing in the United Kingdom, and they could provide a medical breakthrough to rival penicillin.'

Fleur was met at Gatwick Airport by the Samphire Hoe project manager. I mentally chastised myself for being surprised to see he was a young black man. Why had I assumed all Edinburgh scientists were white? He had the look of someone worn down by life: worried and harassed, yet he was clearly pleased to see Fleur. He greeted her with a handshake and took her case from her before ushering her hurriedly towards the lifts for the short-stay car park.

She turned and held her thumb and little finger to the side of her face mouthing silently 'I will ring, later.' I nodded and she was gone. I was quite sure that Fleur's colleague was in such an agitated state that he did not even notice me standing there.

I had about an hour to kill while I waited for my chauffeur – Larry Lander – to turn up, so I adjourned to a coffee shop with a newspaper and harbouring dark thoughts about what might have happened at my holiday cottage. I had not bothered to tell Fleur about the break in. She had enough on her mind, and anyway, as I had no facts to go on, only Eve's bare text message the previous night, there was not much to tell. The only thing for it was the *Guardian* crossword. 2 across: *Disdainful prisoner is sent down (13).*

Two large Americanos later, an unshaven, dishevelled

Lander shuffled into the arrivals hall looking troubled. Having been warned about the break-in, I had asked him to look in at the holiday cottage before picking me up.

On the drive south, he gave me a few details, omitting to mention the urine-christened clothes: 'It's a bit of a mess but not too bad. I didn't touch a thing, just in case you intend to call the police. What were they looking for Tom? It clearly wasn't a simple robbery because nothing seemed to be missing.'

'I honestly don't know, Larry. Possibly the same thing they thought they might find in Valgren's Dormobile. But if I had to guess, I suspect they were simply trying to put the frighteners on me. And they are beginning to succeed.'

I felt the bruise that remained from last Thursday night's assault in the Lucky Fisherman car park.

We both slipped into silence as the traffic heading south on the M23 towards Brighton was reduced to a crawl.

I tried to jam a few pieces of the jigsaw together: Jimmi Valgren's dalliance with Eve Hathaway had upset her former boyfriend Danny Lawton, but, by all accounts, not to the extent that he would resort to violence, let alone murder. If anything, Lawton appeared keen to find out what had happened – yet I had seen him hanging out in the Lucky Fisherman with the Territorial Army recruits. It was the Terras, I suspected, who had jumped me from behind in the car park that night. The brief beating was probably a warning shot after I stumbled across them smoking pot in the pub loo.

I closed my eyes and tried without success to doze

as Lander came off the motorway and headed east, the Sussex hedgerows rushing by as we made for Normanden, where my car had been left for the weekend.

By the time we had reached our destination, I had finished the crossword including 2 across: *condescending.*

'Too early for a pint, I s'pose?' asked Lander.

The hour hand on the retro-style clock on the dashboard had not quite reached eleven. 'Yes, it is. Definitely.'

'You're right, it's just that I've been up so long it feels like lunch time.'

'Me too. I feel I need something to line my stomach before I see what a mess the cottage is in. Come on, I'll buy you a full English in the Station Café and you can tell me the latest about Mrs Lander and the lovely Jasmine. How's her shorthand coming on, Larry?'

13

I put my bag with my worldly possessions in the boot of the Audi. It was considerably lighter than when I had arrived in Shoreness a week ago. I had dumped the clothes that had been urinated on by my weekend callers in the wheelie bin marked for 'non-recyclables'. I cleaned the floor and the walls of the kitchen as best I could with a disinfectant spray I had found under the sink, checked the windows were all shut, and locked the front and back doors before returning the keys to the upturned flower pot at the rear.

I had intended texting Eve later to tell her of my decision but as I drove past the Lighthouse Inn she was outside watering the flower tubs that were full of thrusting daffodils. I swung the car to the far side of the car park and she looked up, alarmed when she saw it was me. There were no other vehicles there but that did not mean there were no prying eyes looking out of the darkened windows of the pub. She was wearing one of her range of uncomfortably tight tee-shirts, this one explaining that gardeners just love getting mucky.

I nodded at the blooms. 'Lovely aren't they? I always think daffs are the real sign that spring is just around the corner.'

I hoped to relax her with small talk and to make the conversation appear as innocent as possible. She managed a half-hearted smile but her red-rimmed eyes suggested she had been crying or not getting much sleep. Or possibly both.

'Thanks for the tip off about the break-in, Eve.'

'I heard some of the locals talking about it in the bar yesterday, did they take much?' She sounded frightened as she glanced over my shoulder towards the pub.

'No. It's more what they left behind. Who exactly was talking about it?'

'A couple of the old boys and Constable Trotter. He seemed to think it was quite funny from what I could gather.'

'Do you think they had anything to do with it?'

'What? The old fishermen? No – and while I wouldn't trust Trotter, that's not his style. But I expect he knows who did it.'

'I bet he does. Look, Eve, I'm sorry, but I'm leaving.'

Her chubby face started to crease as she fought back the tears. 'Why? Please, not yet.'

'I'm no private eye, Eve, and I'm no hero. If you really think something nasty happened to Jimmi, go back to the police, but not the local copper. I was attacked at the Lucky Fisherman the other night, it was nothing serious but it was nasty. Now I'm receiving threats and having my belongings trashed. I'm sorry. This isn't for me.'

I turned away from Eve and headed back to the Audi, convinced I had glimpsed a face at the pub window. As I turned to reverse, Eve looked a picture of despair – like a child, bewildered and hurt. I did not like myself very much for leaving her with her misery, but I had to do this.

As I drove away from the wind-blown bleakness of Shoreness, I slipped Van Morrison's 'Blowin' Your Mind' into the CD player and 'Brown Eyed Girl' reverberated around the car. I had a date that night with an attractive woman, and possibly the offer of a new job and a new start.

The rutted track to the Shoreness Nature Reserve seemed to have got worse. Where puddles had been on my last visit, there were now crater-like potholes. I drove at a crawl, fearing the worst for the Audi's suspension. As I turned the last corner, I saw that Jimmi Valgren's ransacked Dormobile had been removed.

There were six cars parked in a neat row outside the visitors' centre. It was a cool, crisp day, presumably good for bird watching.

Dr Woodcock was wobbling precariously standing on a low stool just inside the entrance, a felt-tip marker in her right hand as she reached up to add another addition to that day's sightings:

Bittern – one at Cowslip Marsh, one at Christmas Dell
Great White Egrets – both at New Diggings
Buzzards – over Quarry Pit and Shoreness Water
Curlews – on Salt Island and Cowslip Marsh

'Good day for it?'

She almost toppled backwards as she looked round. 'Oh, it's you. Yes, lovely. Perfect, in fact. Nice to see you again Tom. Have you made any progress on the Jimmi front?'

'None. In fact, I'm heading back to London for the time being. The novel was going nowhere and Jimmi's death is really nothing to do with me, so I've moved out of the cottage, but before I go I wouldn't mind looking around the nature reserve.'

'Feel free,' she said, peering over the top of her glasses at the list of sightings to check her handiwork. 'Did you notice the Dormobile has gone? Jimmi's parents had it picked up by a tow-truck. It must be awful for them.'

'It must be. Did you say Danish Hide was one of Jimmi's favourite viewing spots?'

'It was.' She sounded sad. 'He spent hours in there with his cameras and sketchbook. If you follow the signs for the Moss Trail around the north of the lake, it is the third hide you come to, just after Todd's Hide.'

Fortified by a coffee from the visitors' centre, I stepped out into a biting cold westerly that was ripping up small white-crested waves across the lake. I pulled up the zip on my jacket as far as it would go and buried my chin into the fleece liner.

I followed the Moss Trail. I was struck by how little there was to see. To the left were fields with sheep and their lambs, blissfully unaware that they were destined for the Easter Sunday roast. To the right were stony dunes dotted with gorse and ferns. There was plenty of quacking to be heard but no ducks to be seen. The lake was out of view, which, I realised, was the whole point: if I could not see the wildfowl, then they could not see me. The local inhabitants of the nature reserve remained totally unconcerned by the visitors. Only once inside the hides could the humans peer out and admire them.

Danish Hide had two doors at the rear, one marked

in, and other marked out. I was disappointed to see it was already occupied. A couple around retirement age glanced up and nodded their acknowledgement without saying a word. It was as hushed as a library.

They sat in the front row, elbows on a ledge, binoculars trained through the narrow slit of a window on a nearby reed bed. The woman took her binoculars from her eyes and nudged the man, excitedly whispered something and pointed. As she made a note on a pad in front of her, the man trained his binoculars on the swaying mass of reeds.

Along the back wall of the hide were colourful posters behind Perspex showing pictures of the birds that might be seen at the sanctuary. They depicted the birds both in the water and in flight to make recognition easier. Other posters, clearly intended for school parties, had maps showing migration patterns of the birds, their life cycle and where they made their nests. One was devoted to the other inhabitants of the sanctuary: foxes, otters, mice, water voles, and, if you were lucky enough to spot them, brown hares. Another schools poster referred to the history of the area, the fishermen, the smugglers and then the arrival of the power station and its impact on the community.

I sat in the front row feeling underdressed without a pair of binoculars. I tried to look interested in the watery landscape hoping the couple would soon leave. After five minutes, I got my wish. They stood up and, to my surprise, spoke in a normal voice and not a whisper.

'The cormorants are particularly active today,' said the woman, pointing to a stony spit jutting out into the water covered by large birds hanging out their black wings.

The hide to myself, I started to look around, not sure what I was expecting to find in what was a large bare shed with seats and desks in two rows, the back row higher than the front. Judging by some of the lurid graffiti on the window frame, it was a popular spot for courting couples despite the fact that splinters from the wooden benches might be a problem.

The view from the window across the lake was perfect on a day like this. Beyond the lake and the stony dunes, was the road into Shoreness, and beyond that the pebble beach and the sea. It was almost the same view I had had from the holiday cottage window.

I looked around again at the posters mounted on the back wall. If Jimmi was being harassed by the locals, he was very vulnerable in his Dormobile. The hide, on the other hand, was more obscure.

I scanned the posters more carefully and my gaze stopped on the one about smuggling. It depicted two bearded pirates at night on a beach, one holding a lantern, the other dragging a chest. I moved along the back row to the poster and studied it intently. Jimmi had said something to Eve about smuggling – and Eve had said it still went on today.

The posters were in frames attached to the back wall by batons. Between the batons and the wooden walls there was a small gap. Small enough to slide photographs into. Something was there. It looked like a large envelope but it was wedged in tight and was impossible to reach with fingers. I dug into the jacket pocket and took out the Swiss Army knife that I always carried. You never knew when a corkscrew or bottle opener would come in handy.

Using the blunt side of the longest blade, I levered the brown envelope out of its musty hiding place. It was sealed with tape. I was keen to open it but did not want to do that in the hide in case I was disturbed, so I hurried back to the car park.

As a journalist there had been moments when one document or one phone call had confirmed a big story. That sense of excited anticipation was flowing through me again as I sat in the driver's seat with the doors locked. I slid the penknife into the envelope and opened it carefully. Inside was a small plastic bag meticulously taped up. Inside that was a camera memory card.

I reached over to my backpack on the rear seat, fished out the laptop and slid the card into its slot. A few clicks later a series of beautifully framed pictures of birds either taking off or splash-landing on the water came up on the screen, with a low sun on the horizon adding to the dramatic shading. Shards of light bounced off the luxuriant colours of the birds as the sun's rays stabbed through the gaps in the reeds. Moments in time of life on the lake were caught perfectly by Jimmi's lens.

The shots were taken from the Danish Hide judging by the vista beyond the lake which was softly out of focus. I hurried through at least one hundred pictures before I started to get more interested. The last group of ten pictures were very different. In these, the distant beach was in focus and viewed through a longer lens. Night had fallen but the soft silver light of the moon illuminated two large vehicles on the stones. There was also a tractor with a winch that appeared to be attached to a small fishing boat that had been hauled clear of the water. I could make out about six figures walking away from the boat. They were punctuated by two ferociously bright pin points of white, which I guessed were torch beams. At the bottom right hand corner, the camera had recorded the time as 22.30. The date was two weeks ago. About three days before Jimmi's death.

I snapped the lid of the lap top shut. My heart was pounding. I was not sure what I had discovered, but I had a fair idea. Whatever it was, Jimmi Valgren thought it was important – and thought it was worth hiding. Whoever had ransacked his Dormobile had presumably been hoping to find it too.

'Marler speaking.'

'Commander Marler, Tom Kidd of the *South Coast Gazette*. About Jimmi Valgren ....'

I had decided not to antagonise Marler by calling him plain mister. It went against the grain, but if using his services rank pleased the old boy, then why not play along?

'Good. Been waiting for your call. How was Jockland? Catch the monster?'

This was, presumably, the commander's stab at humour.

'About Jimmi?' I wanted to move on from small talk.

'Yes. Well, I don't like it, you know. Something makes me feel very uncomfortable about his drowning. Are you free today to meet and have a chat?'

'I'm pretty busy today, commander. I've got to get up to London later for a business meeting. Will it take long?'

'No more than twenty minutes. Do you know the

Sanctuary Bay Golf Course? How about there in an hour? At the club house. I'll sign you in.' It was more an order than a request.

'No jeans, of course. Dress code.' The commander hung up.

I was wearing jeans, but fortunately had a pair of crumpled cords in the bag in the car boot. These would have to do, I thought, as I changed self-consciously in the car park, hoping no twitchers were getting twitchy.

I was there early. It was an old journalistic habit that had been drilled into me as a cub reporter. It gave you a slight advantage over whoever you were meeting. Golf had never been a game I enjoyed covering as a journalist. Not even The Open. Its class-ridden structure grated. It was evident even at small clubs like Sanctuary Bay where the sign beside the parking spot closest to the clubhouse warned that it was reserved for 'The President'. Next to it was the chairman's spot, then the captain's and the secretary's. A little further away was the space for the 'Ladies captain'. Non-members were signposted to the far pot-holed reaches of the car park.

The walls of the clubhouse were decorated with photographs of grinning golfers in lurid sweaters holding trophies aloft. A huge honours board in green and gold hung behind the bar while in one corner a discreet television showed the *Sky Sports News* channel regurgitating its diet of football rumours with the volume switched off.

I ordered a sparkling mineral water and sat at a window table with the crossword open aware that curious eyes were upon me. 3 down: *Seaside hairdresser is looking for crabs (11).*

'Mr Kidd?'

I rose to shake the outstretched hand, and, to my surprise, the commander added: 'Pleased to meet you. It's Gerald.'

'Nice to meet you too Gerald, I'm Tom.'

The barman arrived with a gin and tonic on a tray for the commander, who offered me a refill, which I declined.

'Sad business,' he said after his first sip.

The commander looked to be in his mid-seventies. He was lean and had clearly been a handsome man in his youth. His greying hair showed no sign of thinning and his eyes shone. The link between a ramrod straight pillar of society and a young artist living semi-rough was not an obvious one.

'How well did you know Jimmi?'

'Fairly well, although we'd only known each other for a couple of months. He came to the first residents' meeting in the village hall after we heard about the shale gas exploration at Dead Oak Farm and was all for helping set up a protest group. He was pretty well informed – more than most of us – about the possibility of the area being turned into an industrial zone if they found the stuff.'

The commander said the F.OFF OFF movement was born with a unanimous show of hands. They launched a poster campaign, lobbied local councillors and the constituency MP, and planned a road blockade if and when it was necessary.

'And do you think the protest had anything to do with

Jimmi's drowning, Gerald?'

The commander signalled to the barman for a refill and lowered his voice. 'Oh no, nothing like that.'

'So why the suspicion that his death was anything more than an accident?'

'I used to take Jimmi to Shakespeare Cliff at Samphire Hoe about once a week. He said it was a special place for photographing wild life, especially birds. I'd drop him off late afternoon and pick him up the next morning. You see, he had no transport of his own except that camper-thing and that was rather too conspicuous.'

'Conspicuous?'

'He didn't want to park it at the Hoe overnight. He'd have been seen – and the public aren't meant to stay there overnight. I suppose I shouldn't have done it but I didn't see the harm, so I gave him lifts there and back. He wanted to get the birds at feeding time in the dawn light, said it was a special light for photography.'

'Where did he sleep, then?'

'I think he bunked down in an old rail-workers' hut beside the line. He took a sleeping bag with him. The last time I took him there was almost two weeks ago. When I went back on the Thursday morning as arranged, there was no sign of him. I went back again the next day and he still wasn't there at our usual pick-up time, so I assumed he'd moved on. He was that sort of restless lad. Then last week, I heard he'd drowned – found at the Hoe.'

Marler took a sip of his gin and tonic and added grimly: 'Thing is, I can't imagine he went into the sea voluntarily.'

'Could he have slipped and fallen trying to get a better

vantage point for his photographs?'

'No. The cliff is set well back from the sea these days behind the new land at Samphire Hoe. Fall off the cliff and you land on bushes or the railway line. Is all this going to be in the paper?'

The last question caught me off guard. I had almost forgotten I was there under the guise of being a freelance journalist for the *South Coast Gazette*.

'Not sure yet, Gerald. We need some facts first, not just suspicion or speculation. One thing I don't quite understand is that you seem to have put yourself out a lot for Jimmi. Why?'

'I'm not sure I know what you mean.' The commander idly turned over the beer mats on the table between us. Then turned them over again. 'Just doing a favour for someone who seemed a good sort. Nothing wrong with that. Let me know how you get on.' And with that, he drained his glass and left.

I filled in the crossword answer. *Beachcomber*.

It was time to head for London and my dinner date with a long-legged Australian.

14

Fleur's flat in Loughborough Junction. It was six in the evening and the packed commuter trains were taking their sardines back to the suburbs.

Although Fleur was in the south of England on field work at the Samphire Hoe site, her employers at the Royal Botanic Garden in Edinburgh wanted her close to the coast and had booked her into one of Dover's less seedy hotels for the week. So the flat was all mine again.

I looked again at Jimmi Valgren's photographs on my laptop. The pictures of the beach at night were indistinct. It was impossible to identify the figures on the stony dunes or the vehicles parked there. If something illegal was going on, these pictures were too inconclusive to convict anyone. They were hardly worth killing for.

I had felt guilty about lying to Eve Hathaway by telling her I had given up trying to find out what had happened to her dead boyfriend, but I wanted to throw those who had trashed the cottage, ruined my clothes and left me with sore ribs off the scent. I was pretty sure word would soon get around the close-knit Shoreness community that I had done a runner. I could work much more safely, at least for a few days, if they thought I was not on the scene.

The role of Danny Lawton, Eve's ex, was not clear either. He certainly had reason to dislike Jimmi. And why had the old commander gone coy when questioned about his friendship with Jimmi? I pondered both as I shaved. I was keen to create the right impression on Ms Jo Etheridge, my first 'date' since Katie had declared our marriage was over.

'Date might be wishful thinking,' I told the reflection in the mirror as I tried to stop a shaving nick bleeding with a piece of torn off loo paper. 'More like business opportunity.'

Still, you never knew. Jo was a handsome woman and, I'd guessed, only a few years younger than me.

I pulled a new white cotton shirt out of its cellophane. It fitted well. I rejected a dark blue knitted tie deciding the casual look was best: suit jacket, plain shirt, and jeans, which always looked good on top of well-polished leather shoes.

'You'll do,' I said, taking one last glance in the mirror and peeling off the bloodstained loo paper.

Jo Etheridge had booked a table at Ted's Place, a popular bistro just off More London, one of the coming places in the capital on the booming South Bank. The London mayoral office was a few paces away in the council headquarters over-looking Potters Field and Tower Bridge.

I was early as usual, but Jo was already there, sitting at a window table. Her long dark hair, confined to a bun when we had first met at Shoreness Power Station, had been let loose to fall on her shoulders. Gone was the sensible work suit, in its place she wore designer jeans and a loose pink linen blouse.

'My, Mr Frost, you do scrub up well,' she said with

a smile, taking the words out of my mouth. Good start.

'Thank you, kind lady. It's important to make the right impression at a job interview.'

'Business and pleasure, I hope,' she said. 'What do you fancy?'

We opted for sharing a tapas board accompanied by chilled Spanish beers drunk straight from the bottle. The evening was going well.

'I've made a few inquiries about the photo you sent of the dead artist and his sofa protestors,' she said after the food had arrived. 'Our men at the nuclear constabulary base have not heard anything. But I did pass on the photo to our head of security, who has good contacts, and he did come up with something interesting.'

She took a piece of typed paper from her clutch bag and unfolded it. 'The four sofa protestors named in the newspaper caption all checked out: Jimmi, Jack and Elizabeth Brenkley, the middle-aged couple, who are retired teachers from Normanden Primary School, and Brenda Llewellyn, a Shoreness pensioner who runs a pottery business with her son.'

'What about the other three who refused to give their real names?'

'The two kids with the piercings – Capricorn and Amazon as they called themselves – are students from Brighton who knew Jimmi and went along for the laugh. They're harmless as far as we can tell. But it's the other man in the photo who's intriguing.'

'Go on,' I said as two more beers arrived.

'He gave his name as Santiago. Nothing too sinister in that, lots of eco-protestors use pseudonyms, particularly when they talk to the media. But there's something about this guy. When our security starting making some progress with their enquiries, the shutters came down high up the food chain. They were, in fact, told to forget about asking any more questions.'

'What do you make of that?'

'Our security boss is not sure but he has a pretty good idea. He thinks Santiago was an undercover police officer – the sort that infiltrate protest groups working under a false ID. Once their cover is blown, they're useless. It's a hugely sensitive and secretive area. Santiago appears to have gone to ground. If your Jimmi got on the wrong side of him, it may not have been very pleasant. These guys can be a law unto themselves apparently.'

I took a long pull from the bottle letting the information and liquor sink in, not sure where it left me.

'Our security people won't take it any further,' she said. 'It's none of their business really. Their antennae only prick up when they sense there might be a threat to the security of the site.' She reached for the sharing platter, which had still not been touched.

'And Jimmi wasn't that?'

She shook her head, her mouth full of stuffed vine leaves.

I got the feeling she was waiting for me to ask the questions: 'What do they do most of the time, your security guys? Shoreness is the back of beyond.'

'I think it's a routine job ninety-nine per cent of the time but they have to remain alert to anything out of the ordinary. For instance, they watch shipping activity within five miles of the plant, particularly at night, and lately they've been aware of more comings and goings. I don't think it's anything to worry us regarding security, but French and Spanish trawlers come for the sea bass around "the boil" as do local craft from Shoreness and Dover. Whether their catch includes anything more than fish though, it doesn't really bother us.'

I caught her drift. 'Smuggling?'

She nodded: 'Smuggling is the jurisdiction of the coast guards and customs. They can call up the navy if they need help, but it's no threat to our security, so we don't get involved.'

She asked about my career in journalism. I told her about the travelling and the occasional big stories; the hairy trips up the Khyber Pass and into downtown Sochi; drunken adventures in Cape Town and Miami. I also mentioned the harm the job had done to my marriage – just so she knew my situation.

I also thought it would help to mention that Australia had always been one of my favourite destinations, which smoothly brought the conversation back to her. A much more interesting topic.

She said she had been through a messy relationship in her home city of Adelaide, which had prompted her to seek a move abroad. Like so many Australians, she wanted to visit 'The Old Dart' as England was often known as Down Under, and here she had stayed, working her way up the pecking order at Genor-X. Now she was so far up the management ladder that she was the one offering the jobs.

'It's part of the corporate thing, Tom. We feel we need an in-house magazine: glossy, good quality. It would be distributed among our 2000 employees in the UK as well as our suppliers and trade journalists. We would also use it to make our views known on certain political issues, or to answer public concerns if and when they arise. It wouldn't be propaganda but it would be the news slanted our way – not much difference from any of the national newspapers really. What we need is a wise journalistic head to edit it and give the publication credibility.'

'There are plenty of those around looking for work.'

She sighed. 'There may be, but I've already interviewed seven for the job and they were either too greedy or useless or lazy – or all three. I probably shouldn't say this, but I'm now under pressure from the board to make this appointment. Does it interest you, Tom? Seriously?'

'It does.'

The proposal was to launch a monthly publication for a six-month trial period. The salary on offer was not much less than the one I had been on at The *Herald*. It all seemed just about perfect for an out of work, unattached journalist.

How could I say no?

How could she say no?

15

When I woke up on Tuesday morning I thought I was having a heart attack. Something was pushing down on my chest, making breathing difficult. I had pins and needles in both arms.

The weight shifted and smiled. It was Jo's face.

'G'day cobber,' she said in a mock Aussie accent. She playfully licked my chest, then kissed me on the mouth and sat up, totally unabashed by her nakedness. I had never intended nor expected to spend the night with Jo Etheridge but I was not complaining. And, if memory served me right, neither was she.

'I take it that you'll take the job then?' she said. 'There are plenty of fringe benefits.' She waggled her shoulders to make her small pointed breasts bobble and then leant over me so that they brushed my face as she switched on the radio on the bedside cabinet. She kissed me lightly on the nose and got out of bed.

I watched appreciatively as her backside disappeared into the en-suite bathroom of her Thames-side tenth-storey flat. Divorce might not be so bad after all. It was the first time I had slept with any woman other than my wife for more than twenty years. I had let Jo take the lead and my trepidation had melted away in her warm and generous embrace.

The radio clock said it was 8.30. It really was time

to stir but the soft snug duvet smelled deliciously of her body and I closed my eyes again to dream of Anglo-Australian relations.

'C'mon, your turn in the shower – although I know you Poms don't like washing too much.' She stood beside the bed with a white bath towel wrapped around her, her damp hair hanging down on her naked shoulders and her toes still glistening with water.

She turned and padded across the polished wood floor towards the kitchen leaving little damp prints in her wake. 'I'll put the kettle on. You've got five minutes'.

She made tea and toast, offered me some granola and fruit, which I declined, and a lift to the Tube, which I accepted. Before I got out of her sporty Volvo V40 on Vauxhall Bridge, she said she had enjoyed the night before and would be in touch about the job.

'I know you're busy tonight with the parents' evening but perhaps we can do it again sometime soon, Tom.'

I felt myself blush. Australian candour was lovely but discomforting. 'Yes, I'd like that. And I'd like the job too.'

By comparison to Jo's Volvo, which still had that showroom smell, my old Audi A4 had that lived-in feel. Over the past week it had collected the smells of takeaway food and dirty laundry. I made a mental note to get it valeted before I offered her a lift.

I was heading back down the M2 towards Dover and Samphire Hoe, where I had arranged to meet Fleur. She had telephoned the previous afternoon. She had some information about Jimmi Valgren, which puzzled me, but she was clearly upset about something else. When I pushed her for an explanation, she said she was busy and would explain when we met.

I slipped Bob Dylan's best album, Blood on the Tracks, onto the CD player and thought about my divorce-seeking wife Katie as the American balladeer raged his way through 'Idiot Wind'.

The mobile rang over the car's hands-free connection.

'Tom Kidd speaking.'

'Billy, it's Larry. Where's that restaurant review for the Lucky Fisherman?'

'Piss off, Larry.'

A laugh crackled over the car speaker. 'Ha, almost had you there. But seriously, I've heard something that might interest you.'

'Go on.'

'At police calls today I was told that three Afghans had been picked up in the Shoreness area sleeping rough in one of the old boat huts. They don't speak any English but it seems they're genuine asylum-seekers. The police won't know until they get an interpreter in, but they think the Afghans are telling them that they arrived at night by boat a few weeks ago and were landed at Shoreness. It smacks of people smuggling.'

Another piece of the jigsaw slipped into place.

'Thanks Larry, that is interesting and may tie up. Valgren had taken pictures on a long lens of something suspicious happening on the beach there. I wouldn't mind betting the two are linked. I will pass the pics on to the police – but not just yet.'

'OK Billy. And take care.'

Lander hung up. As the motorway gave way to an A

road, I mentally sifted through what I knew and what I thought I knew: on that first night at the Shoreness holiday cottage I saw lights in the distance on the beach. Could they have come from the same source as the lights in Jimmi's blurry photographs taken the week before? Were the Afghans the figures in the dark?

Fleur had been right. Finding the road entrance to Samphire Hoe was not easy. Coming from the west on the A20 dual carriageway, I had to double back via a roundabout to search for the poorly signposted slip road. Once on it, I was almost instantly halted by traffic lights that controlled the road into the single-track tunnel that burrowed steeply down through the towering mound of Shakespeare Cliff.

Having waited an eternity for the lights to turn green while nothing came in the opposite direction, I drove past a raised barrier and into the eerie narrow ill-lit tunnel. The footpath I had walked along a week earlier was on a higher level to my left. It was not a place to meet anything coming the other way. I was relieved to emerge into daylight again on the seaward side of the hills to be greeted by the sheer white cliffs to my right and the grassy seventy-acre Hoe sticking out into English Channel. On my left was the high concrete wall of what I now knew was the air-conditioning plant for the Channel Tunnel. It followed the road for a short while before curving away. It was broken only for two tall gates. Beside them was an intercom and a sign that said 'Groupe Euro Tunnel SE Property. All visitors must report to security.'

There were three other vehicles in the car park. In one

that was looking directly out over the rolling grey water, a couple were reading newspapers, cups of hot liquid on top of the dashboard steaming up the windscreen. At the rear of another, a man was letting two excited black Labradors out of the tailgate. The animals barked furiously at the wind, which showed no inclination to ease off, as their owner wrestled with their leads.

To the left of the car park was a blue wooden lookout tower near the water's edge. To the right a large concrete obelisk carved with the names of the eleven men who had died during the construction of the Channel Tunnel. Behind me, a train clattered along the line at the foot of the cliffs and above it on the precipitous chalky slope was an area marked off with red and white tape that was flapping in the wind, desperately trying to break free from its moorings. Inside the tape was a group of figures looking down intently at the crumbly, stony ground.

Fleur was waiting, as promised, in the otherwise deserted visitors' centre sitting at a table beside a woodburner that gave off welcome heat. Around the walls were murals telling the history of Shakespeare Cliff.

The first attempts to dig a channel tunnel were started here in the 1880s but, having got little more than a mile underground, the project was abandoned. There were fears that if the tunnel was completed, the French might invade, although the lack of finance for the project was another factor in the hole being boarded up. The existing excavations then persuaded a mining company to start digging for coal under the sea but continual flooding and explosions ended that enterprise soon after the Great War. That left the fishermen and gatherers of the rock samphire to work the area for a few more years until even they gave up trying to scratch a living from this inhospitable stretch of coastline.

'How's it going, Sis?'

Fleur hugged me as if we had not seen each other for a year. 'Not well,' she said. She sounded defeated. 'You know I told you about the Bat's Wing Orchid growing here on the cliff? Well, word has clearly got out because the site has been raided. Half the samples have been dug up or trampled on.'

'So it's widely known how potentially valuable the plant could be to the pharmaceutical industry?'

'Possibly that, or possibly it's just plain thieving for plant collectors who have heard about the rarity of the Bat's Wing. There are private collectors in America, India and the Far East who will go to almost any lengths to get rare species. The horticultural world is a close-knit one, news of projects gets around no matter how much you try to keep things under wraps. There's been gossip about this plant on social media sites for a month now.'

'When did this happen?'

She shook her head. 'We're not sure. In fact, the people here think it's happened more than once. Most of the damage looks pretty recent though, so probably towards the end of last week – when I got the call to fly down.'

Fleur suggested a conducted tour of the cliff site. I was not keen but I wanted to play the supportive brother. I had some trainers in the boot of the car and, to my disappointment, Fleur told me they would be fine for what was a relatively easy climb.

'I'm not very good with heights, Fleur. You'll have to hold my hand.'

'There's an old path that makes its way up the cliff, you'll be fine,' she said. 'It used to be used by the samphire collectors and keen walkers until about twenty years ago. It's now closed to the public and has become slightly hazardous in places because it's crumbling away, but it's OK if you take care – and there are some of the old metal posts that used to carry a wire fence still dotted around here and there to hang on to.'

I looked up at the brooding cliff face far from convinced.

To get to the path we had to enter the air-conditioning plant at the foot of the cliff. Inside the security gate was what looked like a large corrugated metal warehouse with vented sides. It rumbled gently. I was sure I could feel the ground tremble under my feet. In two smaller corrugated units linked by umbilical-like power lines to the main building were generators, and beside them was a Portakabin marked 'Security. All visitors must report inside.'

We were checked in by an unsmiling uniformed guard who, judging by the rank smog inside the hut, had ignored the 'No Smoking' sign behind his desk. He wrote our names on a clipboard, handed over passes to attach to our jackets and nodded. Clearly a man of few words.

Behind the main building in the concrete perimeter wall next to the cliff was a small iron gate that clicked open when we ran our passes over a sensor. We walked through onto the rough ground that immediately started to rear up the cliff.

'The rest of the team are already up there,' said Fleur. 'Follow me and tread carefully. I suggest you keep your right hand on the cliff as we go up, and hold on to the metal posts as we pass them.'

Within two minutes we were looking down on Samphire Hoe. The handful of cars in the parking area seemed like toys below. The heaving sea stretched away to the west, inhospitably cold and dangerous. Immediately below a London-bound train emerged from the tunnel, its four carriages in cream, green and yellow livery rattling along the short stretch of line beside the countryside park before disappearing into another cliff tunnel.

It had started to spit with rain, the drops stinging my face as the wind whipped along the cliff to the annoyance of the screeching gulls that glided overhead. And yet, it felt surprisingly warm. Almost hot.

Down to our left was the Eurotunnel air-conditioning plant. In the roof of the large warehouse were four wide shallow funnels angled sideways and pointing to where we were perched on the cliff. Each was big enough to swallow up a car. They were covered in wire mesh and below that, giant blades rotated steadily. This was the outlet of the air conditioning, and warm dry air was being churned out and up the cliff. It reminded me of the rush of wind you got standing on a Tube station as a train approached.

The warm air bathed these few acres of cliff and made the temperature feel like a pleasant summer's evening on a Caribbean Island. No wonder I was sweating in my North Face walking jacket complete with thermal liner.

Fleur was pulling ahead as I paused for breath. I

was clearly not as fit as I thought. This, though, was no place to hurry in an effort to catch her up. With every other step, I could feel my left foot slip slightly on the unpredictable limestone path, forcing me to lean to the right into the rock face, where there were clumps of coarse grass to hold on to.

Fleur was far more sure-footed in her walking boots, and even when she disturbed a small rock, that rolled and bounced down the hillside and thudded into the mesh fence beside the rail lines, she did not slow down.

I caught her up by the red and white tape pegged around the scientific site. Above us, two people in green overalls and safety harnesses that were attached to stakes were on their hands and knees. A third person was talking to Fleur. It was the man who had met her at Gatwick the previous morning.

'David, this is my brother Tom. Tom, this is Dr David Ntini, our project manager here at the Hoe.'

'Good morning'. He sounded irritated. 'Please take care up here.' With that he turned back to Fleur and pointed to where the two workers were going about their precarious business.

'We're still assessing the damage. It's awful,' he said to Fleur, blinking at her intently through thick black-framed glasses. 'We're trying to save what we can. Hopefully they'll recover but you know how fragile they are in this environment.'

Dr Ntini had a cultured Scottish accent – not at all what I had expected. I chided myself again for having preconceptions about people.

'I'm so sorry about this, Fleur. This is my first big

project for Edinburgh, and now this happens ….'

She put a hand on his arm. 'Don't blame yourself. That would be silly. We'll get the site back to what it was, David. Just give it a little time. In the meantime, we have to beef up our security and talk to the police about this. You concentrate on the horticulture, I'll see to the logistics.'

'If I could get my hands on who did this ….' His hands were clenched tightly into fists.

'I know, David, I know. But thinking like that doesn't help. We'll get through this.' Fleur turned to me. 'Now David, can you tell Tom what you know about Jimmi Valgren, the lad who was found dead in the sea down there.' She pointed towards the far end of Samphire Hoe, where the waves were sending spray over the concrete barrage.

Several of the horticulturalists on the site had got to know Jimmi from his visits to Samphire Hoe on photographic expeditions, said Ntini. They also knew he stayed overnight sleeping rough in an old rail hut.

'We discouraged him not because we feared he'd damage the plants, but because of the dangers of climbing on the cliff as well as crossing the electrified railway line. We didn't, however, inform the countryside project management.'

'Why not?'

'Our team members said he seemed a genuine laddie, keen on his birds and his snaps and not up to no good. He didn't come into our site so we let him be,' said Ntini. 'Aye, it was a great shame what happened to him.'

'Do you think the trouble you've had here with the

plant thieves had anything to do with Jimmi's drowning?'

Ntini seemed taken aback. 'Och no. Never considered it. Why should it?'

'Well, I'm not sure – but two unexpected events happen at roughly the same time in the same place. They might be linked.'

Another train, this time heading towards Dover, rushed into the tunnel some two hundred feet below us, the clatter of its bogies drowning out Ntini's reply, but I guessed that, by the shrug of the shoulders, the doctor did not have much more to offer on the subject.

'We must get on,' he said turning to Fleur.

She nodded and told him she would be back shortly, after escorting me down the cliff path.

Going down was no easier than climbing up. If anything, it was more hazardous, my weight encouraging me to rush downwards along the old, eroded path. I watched the stones I disturbed roll and bounce down the cliff, a few hitting the rail tracks below.

'Was it much help?' asked Fleur after we had reached the gate back into the air-conditioning plant. 'I thought you'd like to see for yourself what we're doing here, as well'

'I don't know how much help it was but I'm glad you brought me.' I looked back up the cliff, thankful to be on flat solid ground again. 'It's fascinating stuff, Sis. But your Dr Ntini, he seems a bit on edge about it all. Have you known him long?'

'No, he's newish. Joined us in Edinburgh about six months ago. He's well qualified, hails from Glasgow where he went to university. He seems a nice guy who is just wrapped up in his work like so many scientists are. I've never worked with him directly before this trip, though. Why?'

'No real reason, just wondered.'

'He specialises in orchids, that's why he's here. He was working in the Orchid House in Edinburgh. Don't know where he was before that.'

'Well, I'm no expert at body language but I get the distinct impression he would like to get to know you a lot better, if you know what I mean.'

Fleur blushed. 'Oh, don't be silly, Tom.'

I sat by the woodburner stove in the visitors' centre cradling a coffee from the machine that tasted like ditch water. That day's crossword was proving equally dense. Solving the cryptic clues usually required some lateral thinking, and that, I concluded, was also what I needed to do to find the answer to who killed Jimmi Valgren.

1 Across*: Such a quiet room is required by the jury to make a decision (10).*

I chewed the end of the pen. It was almost as good as the coffee. The link between Jimmi and Samphire Hoe was Marler, who brought him here in the evenings and picked him up again the following morning. The retired naval commander was certainly putting himself out for someone he did not know that well. I needed to speak to him again.

The other more immediate poser was where I was to sleep that night, having given up the holiday cottage. I could stay in the Dover hotel with Fleur if they had a spare room but I did not particularly want to bump into

Dr Ntini again. I would return to London and Fleur's flat.

London. Something pleasant inside stirred. I realised I was thinking of Jo Etheridge and the unexpected delight of the previous night spent in her bed. It was by far the best job interview I had ever had. I then remembered Jo's reminder that morning about my parental duties: I had promised my daughter, Alice, I would be at the parents' evening at her school tonight. The smile on my face disappeared.

I had always found schools forbidding places, both as a parent and as a pupil. I had tended to do the bare minimum at school except in games. Teachers made me feel uncomfortable. Even now, as an adult, they had the same effect on me. Playing at happy families with Katie was not an enticing prospect either.

I looked up at the speckled cliff where the rare orchid had decided to make its home. There were two routes there: one up, the other down. If the old walkers' path was out of bounds, could the raiders have abseiled from the cliff top to the site? It was Fleur's favoured theory. A little light bulb flicked on in my memory bank. I had witnessed abseiling only a few days ago at Cheyne Army Camp, where the Territorial Army recruits were on exercise.

I filled in the crossword answer. *Soundproof.*

'And that's exactly what I don't have,' I said quietly to myself, dumping the half-finished coffee in the litter bin. 'Sound proof'.

The top sign on the gate said 'Beware of the Dog'. Below

it was a hand-painted warning that read 'no cold-callers.'

I was certainly one of those: both cold and a caller. I looked around for any sign of a Rottweiler, although an irate poodle might have been enough to keep me the other side of the gate. The only dogs I really warmed to were on a racetrack.

It seemed quiet enough. There was no car in the gravel drive alongside the garden with its trimmed borders and orderly line of daffodils underneath a front window shrouded by a net curtain. There was a short concrete ramp instead of a step up to the varnished wood front door that had one of those small spyholes that allowed those inside to see out but not the other way around. I pushed the bell and heard a muffled chime that sounded like the tune 'Colonel Bogey'. There was no barking. That was a relief. Perhaps the sign on the gate was just a bluff.

The person who opened the door was sitting in a wheelchair. She was, I guessed, in her mid-sixties, well-groomed and clearly once very attractive but now looking a little worn down by life.

'Yes?' she said.

'Sorry to bother you, my name's Tom Kidd. I'm an acquaintance of Commander Marler. Is he in?'

She said he was and, to my surprise, expertly spun the wheelchair around, and headed back down the hall. 'Gerry's in the garden, Come in. Shut the door behind you Mr Kidd. I'll call him.'

I followed her electric powered chariot through a long hall and into a wide uncluttered living room with a vast picture window that looked across another manicured lawn fringed by weed-free flower beds. There was a sweet smell about the room that I recognised but could not quite place.

In the fence at the bottom the garden was a small picket gate that led directly onto the Sanctuary Bay Golf Course. Beyond the clipped dunes and raked sand traps of the course, was the Channel that was dotted with the sails of yachts braving the blustery afternoon. It was a stunning view.

The commander was on his haunches at the picket gate, back to the window, paint brush in hand, white paint pot on a sheet of newspaper beside him. He stopped painting to take his mobile phone out of his pocket. His wife had sent him a text message. He looked around rather alarmed and marched back towards the bungalow.

'Tea?' I'm Penny Marler, by the way,' she said, offering her hand.

'Yes please. That would be lovely. No sugar. Thanks.'

She had left the living room by the time Marler, paint brush still in hand, pushed back the sliding glass door and stepped inside.

'What are you doing here?' he said in hushed tones.

'I wanted to ask a few more questions. Is it inconvenient?'

'Why didn't you ring? I don't want my wife bothered. You can see how it is.'

'Yes, sorry.'

I could, of course, have rung in advance. But I had found, as a journalist, that it was usually better to ask awkward questions without giving the interviewee advance warning and time to work out their answers.

Cold calling could work.

Penny came back into the room, a tray carrying a tea pot and cups on a flap attached to her wheelchair. 'Gerry, would you get the biscuits please?' Marler huffed and marched out of the room.

'Are you a golfer, Mr Kidd?'

'No.'

'I only ask because most of Gerry's friends seem to be members of that golf club,' she said tilting her head towards the window. 'Most of them are frightful bores, and a lot older than you,' she added conspiratorially.

Marler, now minus the paint brush but plus a plate of chocolate digestives, walked back in on the conversation: 'Tom is on the anti-fracking campaign committee, aren't you Tom?' he said looking intently at me as if daring me to contradict him.

'Yes, that's right. Eff Off Octagon Fossil Fuels, that's what I say.'

For the next five minutes, we discussed the perils of fracking, earth tremors and house prices on the sought-after Kent coastline before Marler suggested we take a stroll around the garden while Penny washed up the cups and saucers.

When he was happy his wife was out of earshot, the commander appeared to relax: 'So for what do we have the pleasure, Tom?'

'If you want me to help find out what happened to Jimmi, I need to know all the facts, Gerald. Something tells me you're keeping something back.'

'Like what?'

'Well, like why were you so helpful giving him lifts

backwards and forwards to Samphire Hoe?'

'Jimmi was very helpful to me. One good turn and all that.'

'Go on.' I let the silence hang between us. The Commander shuffled his feet and then spoke.

'Oh well, no harm in telling you, I suppose. As long as it doesn't go any further.'

I nodded.

'Pot. Cannabis. Jimmi got it for me.'

Marler hardly looked like a junkie, I thought. Then the Penny dropped. 'Your wife, Penny?'

'Yes,' said Marler, his voice wavering from the normal businesslike military bark. 'She suffers from Multiple Sclerosis, has done since she was fifty. It's a bloody horrible business but she's very stoical. She's tried all sorts to alleviate the pain: pilates, aromatherapy, yoga, even bee sting therapy, but nothing brings her the relief that cannabis does. It helps with the muscle spasms.'

'Can't the doctors help?'

'There are now legal cannabis oral sprays on the market but they're not as effective as smoking the stuff,' said Marler. 'I don't understand why the Government cannot make the weed legal for MS sufferers but they won't, of course. Too much of a political hot potato.'

'So you have to get it whichever way you can?'

'Yes,' said Marler, looking back towards the lounge, where Penny was sitting, giving us a cheerful wave from behind the picture window.

'A few old navy pals with young sons who had contacts helped me out for a while getting it for me, but it was dodgy and they weren't keen, then Jimmi stumbled into my life when he joined the fracking protest. He seemed the type to know where to get it, and he was. Apparently it's readily available at the Lucky Fisherman from the army chaps believe it or not. He was a good egg. He would get the stuff for me knowing it was for Penny, and he insisted on only charging me what he'd paid for it himself.

He even showed Penny how best to prepare it and roll it into what he called "a spliff". Penny and he got on really well, in fact. In return, I was more than happy to help him out with lifts to the Hoe. It's a damned, damned shame. He was such a good lad.'

Marler made a fist with his right hand and thumped it into the palm of his left. 'If I knew *who* did *what* to him … God, I'd like to get hold of them.'

Even in his retirement years, the old commander looked as if he could handle himself but, even so, I did not fancy his chances against whoever had used my ribs for football practice the previous week. They did not stick to Queensbury Rules.

It was starting to rain. Marler beckoned me to walk back to the bungalow: 'Please, not a word to Penny. She just thinks Jimmi moved on somewhere else. She didn't see the story in the local rag. I don't want her upset. As it is, I've got to try to find another source of the stuff. Might have to go in the Lucky Fisherman myself, although I'm dreading that.'

I could understand why but could offer no solution to the old man's dilemma.

'I'll keep in touch, Gerald. I'm still trying to find out what happened to Jimmi but the fewer people who know that, the better. I may ask you to show me exactly where you dropped him off at the Hoe and where you think he kipped down for the night. I believe it was an old rail hut, wasn't it?'

Marler nodded. 'Anything to help.'

When we walked back into the lounge from the garden I realised now why I had recognised the sweet herbal smell in the room that I had noticed earlier. It took me back to the parties and rock concerts of my youth.

I had never liked the private all-girls school in Sidcup that Alice attended. It was Katie's idea. Surrounded by suburbia and trees, its pupils were self-obsessed little madams as far as I could tell. Apart from Ali, of course.

It was not so much the cost I objected to – although at £9000 a term it did make the eyes water and the bank manager fret – more the fact that I had grown up in the state system. What was good enough for me, and all that. I also believed it would have been far healthier for Ali to mix with boys in the classroom everyday instead of regarding them as some alien race to be giggled about.

The car park at St Jeavons School 'for young women' was full of Mercedes, Jaguars and BMWs. I decided to leave the unwashed ageing Audi under an oak tree in the far corner so it did not spend the evening feeling inferior. The other parents would probably think it belonged to the groundsman in charge of the lacrosse pitches.

In the entrance hall, some of the sixth-form girls welcomed arriving parents with trays of white wine, sparkling water and fruit juice, providing directions to the various meeting rooms for each year.

'Year Eight? That's up the stairs, across the atrium and to the right, sir. If you get to the library, you've gone too far,' said one of them, who looked glamorous enough to be a footballer's wife.

Fortified by a glass of white wine, I headed for my first meeting with Katie since she had told me she no longer wanted to be Mrs Kidd.

I was early for the 7.15 appointment with Ali's tutor, Ms Berry. Both parents accompanied by their child were expected to discuss with the tutor how the academic year was progressing, it being a 'democratic and open society' at St Jeavons. After that, the girls left the room and the parents could discuss specific topics with the heads of departments.

I shuffled into the large Year Eight Common Room, hoping not to be recognised by any of the handful of other parents I had met before. Groups of adults talking in low voices and nodding were studying the art-work on the walls and photographs from a recent 'Ghana Orphanage Project'.

Ali was collecting empty wine glasses from parents on a tray. For all her apparent worldliness at home, she looked young in her uniform of blue and yellow school sweater and pleated skirt. Her face lit up when she spotted me. She put the tray down on a table and rushed into a bear hug.

'Hi Dad, how's my best-selling author?'

'He's got writer's block at the moment I think, but I'm working on something. A whodunit mystery, you might say'

She pulled away. Her eyes were rimmed in red but

there were no tears. 'Dad, I miss you. Please sort this out with Mum. I don't like the way she is. I want it to be like it was.'

'Look Ali, I'm not sure that's going to happen – but we can't talk about it here. Tonight. I think your mother wants us to behave as though everything's OK at home, is that alright with you, Ali?'

'It's too late for that. I've already told Goose about you splitting.'

'Goose?

'Goose – as in gooseberry, it's what we call Ms Berry, although I don't think she knows. She's also a bit of one. Goose, that is.' Ali giggled and looked like a little girl again.

'What did you mean when you said you didn't like Mum the way she is?'

Before Alice could answer, Katie entered the room – although I hardly recognised her at first. Her normally long dark curly hair had given way to a severe short cut tinted with henna. Gone were the sensible slacks and blouse and in their place was a tight red crepe dress she might have worn to a cocktail party. She even had a discreet diamond stud in her nose and strappy high heels. If she was not careful, she would be done for soliciting outside the headmaster's office.

She gave me two air kisses and muttered, 'Hello, Tom' in my ear.

'Hello, darling. How are you? Off to audition for X-Factor?' I said it louder than necessary.

She glared. If looks could kill.

'There's no need to keep up the happy families

pretence. Ali has already told her tutor about us going our separate ways, and probably the whole school knows by now.'

Katie looked mortified and then glared at me: 'And I s'pose you encouraged her.'

The bell rang for the 7.15 appointments. The next quarter of an hour made uncomfortable listening to Ms Berry. Alice's work, she said, had dropped off. So had her behaviour. She had had two detentions in the past week, had quit the book club and the debating society. On top of that, she had been caught texting in class and had had her mobile phone confiscated for the rest of the term. It felt like we were being scolded for our daughter's transgressions. Sitting between us, Ali did not seem perturbed by this litany of misdemeanours.

'We've put this lapse down to the upset caused by your separation. It's quite normal in teenage children when their home life is fractured and is to be understood,' said Ms Berry, looking at us from over her glasses.

'We're quietly confident Alice's normal high standard of work and commitment to school life will resume in the near future. Have you anything to say? Alice first.'

Alice said she was sorry and would pull up her socks, although she did not use that exact phrase. Her sheepish parents both said much the same, and the bell rang for the next set of parents in Ms Berry's diary.

'Sorry, Mum, sorry Dad,' said Alice when we were back in the atrium.

'That's all right, darling,' said Katie. 'But if you knew we were going to hear all that, why were you so keen to have us here?'

'Isn't that obvious?' I said.

Katie glared at me again.

'Ali wanted to get us together again – or have you been too wrapped up in yourself to notice?' I threw back the same accusation that Katie had aimed at me when she had told me that our marriage was over.

'Oh shut up, Tom. You know nothing about my life.'

'I've got a good idea.' I made a point of looking her up and down. I sensed other conversations in the room dying down and eyes turning our way.

'Just what d'you mean by that?'

'STOP IT'. Alice shouted, her eyes brimming with tears before she turned and ran out of the room. The conversations around us started again.

'Well, that went well, Katie.' I turned and left.

16

Perhaps it was an inferiority complex caused by last night in the St Jeavons School car park alongside the Mercs, Beamers and Jags. Possibly it was because I had forgotten to check when the annual service was due. Whatever the cause, the Audi refused to start on a wet Wednesday morning in south London.

To make matters worse, the resident's parking permit for the space outside Fleur's flat expired at nine. It was now 8.55 a.m., and a traffic warden was hovering across the road ready to pounce. Perfect.

The yellow flashing lights of a pick-up truck appeared through the tunnel below Loughborough Junction Station just in time like the arrival of the cavalry. An hour later, wet and cold, I was sitting in a foul-smelling Ford Fiesta with a grubby steering wheel and sticky carpets. It was what the south London garage that had taken in the Audi called a courtesy car. The young female mechanic who had signed in the job had shown as much optimism about getting the Audi back on the road as I felt about finding the truth behind the drowning of Jimmi Valgren.

'Once these old boys start goin' wrong you're in for a pile of trouble, mister,' she informed me with the tone of an undertaker. 'I'll see what I can do and we'll give you a call about the estimated cost before we do anything.'

I called the man I could most rely upon in this world.

'Larry, can you put me up for a night or two?'

Larry Lander did not let me down, insisting I was welcome to stay at least until the weekend.

Perhaps Lander was secretly pleased to have someone else in the marital home to help thaw what was apparently quite a frosty atmosphere since his wife Sue had discovered that the accommodating receptionist at the *South Coast Gazette* gave her husband more than a helping hand with the daily mail.

Sue was a smart lady. A tough one too. I had always thought she and Lander were unlikely bedfellows, yet their marriage had survived longer than mine. She was into aromatherapy, he was into ale; she liked dinner parties, he liked a takeaway; she went on group walking holidays in the Himalayas while he lay on a beach in Barbados.

Even their careers had gone in different directions since they first met as young journalists. She was now the highly popular anchor of the regional evening news programme on the television, he struggled to keep the local newspaper with its dwindling circulation afloat.

I was late. That was the Audi's fault but it did not stop me being annoyed with myself as I pulled the Fiesta into the car park at Samphire Hoe and saw that Gerald Marler's old but immaculate Rover was already there.

A fine rain, almost as thick as fog, swirled in off the Channel. The grey sky and sea merged into one obscuring the French coastline. The waves crunched into the seawall, the spray mingling with the rain. I did not envy anyone out there in the world's busiest shipping lane today. The cliff I had scrambled up with my sister the day before was there somewhere, also shrouded in the mist. Even the gulls had fallen silent. Surely no-one was working up there today?

Marler was in the visitors' centre stamping his feet beside the woodburner stove. There was no-one else there although there were other cars in the car park. Dog walkers, no doubt. Hardy souls used to this sort of weather.

Now that Marler's secret about buying cannabis for his ailing wife with Jimmi Valgren's help was out in the open between us, the old commander appeared more at ease.

He nodded at the window. 'Takes me back to my year in Scotland, Tom. Why they call that place bonny, I'll never know. We had weather like this six days a week – and on the seventh it was worse.'

I fed two pound coins into the coffee machine. 'What were you doing in Scotland, Gerald?'

'My Royal Navy days. It was all very hush hush at the time but I don't suppose I'll be breaking the Official Secrets Act now if I tell you.'

'Tell me what?' I handed him a coffee.

'I was a submariner in the early days of nuclear powered subs, the Polaris class. It was the early Sixties and it was the time of the Cold War with the Ruskies.'

I was a child of the Seventies but I knew enough about history to know that the fear of attack from the Russians – 'The Ruskies' – was very real for a couple of decades. That was why America and her ally, the United Kingdom, had armed themselves to the teeth with nuclear warheads that were carried silently around the globe under the waves by the Polaris fleet and now the Trident class of submarines.

'The all-important thing was stealth,' continued Marler, gazing out to sea. 'The old diesel subs were noisy, you see. They could be heard coming from literally miles away by ships, even in weather like this – and they had to keep coming up for air and fuel.

'The nuclear subs – now, they were silent and could stay under undetected for months on end. We once did a trial run from Singapore to Faslane totally under the waves. It took thirty-two days and the authorities, who were trying to track us as part of the exercise, had no idea where we were.'

'Why Scotland?'

'The boats were built in Barrow-in-Furness and stationed at Faslane, just off the Clyde. It gave us good access to the North Atlantic to keep an eye on the Soviet fleet. It was also a good spot for the trials. We spent weeks and weeks in Loch Fyne running what were called Static Noise Trials. The sub was suspended under buoys in a quiet part of the loch and we would run each part of the machinery on board independently. It was to check whether we could be heard by listening sensors placed around the loch.

Then we ran Under Way Noise Trials. These would be done at various depths and speeds, again to find out if the sub made a noise that could be picked up. It seemed incredibly important at the time. Perhaps it was. We've kept the peace more or less for seventy years, haven't we?'

'Just about.'

The old man looked sad. 'I wish I'd had this discussion

with Jimmi, you know. He was against nuclear weapons, made that pretty clear on the few journeys we had together, but I thought it best to bite my tongue. His generation don't understand the half of it.'

'No. Perhaps not. Fancy showing me where Jimmi stayed when you left him here?'

We turned up our collars and went outside, Marler leading the way to a gravel footpath marked 'West Shore'.

The path led down to the sloping concrete barrier that held back the sea. It was as wide as a three-lane motorway. The spray slapped over the barrage onto the concrete and rolled back through large metal grilles into the sea. There were warning signs telling visitors to beware of the slippery surface.

We kept to the top of the slope to avoid being drenched although it was a lost cause. The wind raged against us as we headed west, making us lean into it as if we were attempting to push open a jammed door. We walked for fifteen minutes passing one man and his soggy but happy dog before the concrete barrier turned right and headed back towards the cliff and the railway embankment.

The incessant wind rattling in our ears made conversation impossible. Marler tugged my sleeve and indicated we should go towards the railings. When we got there, he pointed down into the churning water which rose and fell with each wave, at its highest point reaching six feet from the top of the sea wall.

'That's where the body was found, I believe,' shouted Marler, trying to make himself heard above the roar of the wind.

'Yes,' I shouted back. 'It was. Exactly there.'

I shuddered inside my coat but not through cold. The image of Jimmi's grey misshapen cadaver floated back into my consciousness. The water was sinister and murky as it churned and heaved a few feet below. Bits of wood and plastic bottles clattered against the wall. There was a dead gull among the seaweed and scummy foam.

What an awful place to die.

Marler turned away from the sea and headed inland towards the cliff with the railway directly in front of us as a train appeared out of the tunnel and trundled towards Dover. The path became more sheltered as it dipped between the rolling hillocks of the countryside park where the cattle and sheep grazed.

He indicated a seat overlooking a pond that was fed by a stream from the hillside, the outlet running down a man-made gulley and into the sea. Ducks and a pair of swans had made their home here alongside the skylarks, pipits and herring gulls.

Sitting with our backs to the sea and wind, Marler pointed again, this time towards the railway line that was on an embankment at head height.

'The rhododendron bush there is where I think Jimmi set up his hide. He could get good views of both the cliff and the pond without worrying the birds. He was also sheltered against the worst of the elements.'

'But he didn't sleep there?'

'No. It's too public. The park rangers, who check the site in the evening, would've spotted him and told him to leave. I'll show you where he bedded down.'

We set off along the path that ran parallel to the railway line heading back towards the visitors' centre as two female joggers passed in the opposite direction, glaring at us as if we were intruders on their personal route.

'Here,' he said after a few minutes, nodding towards a rusty three-strand fence that ran alongside the railway. 'That old stone platform is all that remains of Shakespeare Halt. That's where Jimmi stayed.'

The three-strand fence had been pushed down in one place, low enough for a man to clamber over. Just beyond the old platform on the other side of the tracks was a wooden hut by a modern mesh fence that protected the railway line from rock falls from the cliff that rose steeply above. The door hung off the hut and part of the corrugated roof was holed but it was just about habitable.

'I'm going to have a look.' I set off for the gap in the fence.

'All right, old man. I'll be lookout. Two sharp whistles for danger. Like this.' Marler put two fingers in his mouth and gave two shrill blasts.

I almost laughed but thought better of it. Marler was clearly back in his element as a serviceman. 'And don't step on the lines, particularly the live one running down the side,' he added.

No-one appeared to be watching. I stepped over the fence, checked for trains and crossed the double track, taking an exaggerated step over the live line. I crouched on the far side at the end of the old platform to look back. My heart was pounding like it did when I used to retrieve my football from the dog-owning neighbour's garden.

Marler gave the thumbs up. The door of the hut was held at a drunken angle by one bent hinge. As I pushed, it scraped on the ground. I looked down to see the telltale marks of it having been opened recently. Inside it was dank and bare.

I felt disappointed. But what had I expected to find? Jimmi's diary meticulously noting all the events up until his death? A suicide love letter written to Eve? There were, though, some signs of life: a bird's nest inside the broken piece of roof and next to it on a rafter a startled starling eyeing me. It was too early for her to be brooding eggs, perhaps she was just sheltering from the rain. She glared but refused to move.

There was also a small blackened gas camping stove pushed into a shadowy corner that I had not noticed at first. It appeared to have been used recently judging by the absence of cobwebs and dust on it. Along one side of the hut away from the gaping hole in the roof, the earth was flattened and dry, and there were the stubs of a few home-rolled cigarettes.

I picked up one of the stubs and sniffed it. I could not tell if the remains were simply tobacco or something more narcotic, but there were dark brown flecks on the paper. They looked like dried blood. I checked the floor for any signs of a scuffle but found nothing.

Two sharp whistles.

I turned and stood, alarmed at the commander's warning signal, and a metallic roar filled my ears, making me fall backwards into the corner of the hut, sending the roosting bird fleeing in alarm.

It was the 12.35 from Dover to Charing Cross. As it clattered away, I popped my head out of the hut door and I received another thumbs up sign from the commander who mouthed 'coast clear.'

The search seemed pointless. I was no forensic detective, I really had no idea what to look for except the obvious. And there was nothing obvious except that Jimmi had been here, and there were a few cigarette butts on the floor with what might or might not be traces of blood on them.

Outside, however, was different.

Behind the hut was a small gap between it and the mesh fence. There, under the edge of the hut that was raised off the ground about six inches, was some dark blue material that had been partially covered with chalky rubble. I got down on my knees and reached behind the hut, grasped a corner of the material and yanked. It came away surprisingly easily and I dragged it back into the hut so I could see what I had found without fear of being spotted. It was a sleeping bag. It was zipped up. There was nothing inside but the outside was dotted with more flecks of dark brown.

Back inside the boundary of the countryside park, I showed the commander what I had found. 'Recognise it? Is it Jimmi's sleeping bag?'

'Can't be certain. He had one that colour, yes, but there must be thousands like that. God, you're a mess Tom. Have you seen the state of your trousers?'

I looked down. As well as being wet, my black jeans were a mixture of mud and grimy chalk.

'That can wait. Right now we should take this to the police. There are some spots of what could be dried blood on it.'

'What for?' DNA checking? How will they know what

Jimmi's DNA was? The body was cremated in Bristol last Friday. Even if it is his blood, it's proof of nothing.' The commander was probably right.

Back in the visitors' centre, I hovered beside the stove trying to dry out. Marler had got coffees from the vending machine. The murky contents of the waxed cardboard cups still tasted of ditch water, but at least it was hot ditch water.

'Where do we go from here?'

Marler asked the question. I did not have an answer.

The door opened and a group of excited chattering people rushed inside to escape the weather. One I recognised instantly. It was Dr David Ntini, the project manager of the scientific site at Samphire Hoe. When he spotted me, his demeanour changed.

'You back?' he said as he walked over. 'Fleur's not here today and the site is non-operational anyway due to the weather conditions.' His eyes blinked behind his thick spectacles and then he realised I was not alone.

'Dr Ntini, this is Gerald Marler, a friend who knew the deceased, Jimmi Valgren, I'm not here to see Fleur or the site.' I decided to leave it at that, not offering Ntini an explanation as to why I was there, but the doctor did not bite as I had hoped he would.

Ntini moved as if to rejoin his group and then hesitated and turned back to us: 'Look, we're busy doing important sensitive work here. The cliff site is not a place for family visits and sightseers. I made an exception for Fleur yesterday but I won't again. Understood?'

I nodded. Ntini left. Marler raised an eyebrow.

As Marler had opened up about his friendship with Valgren, it was only fair now to tell him most of what I knew. I explained what was going on at Shakespeare Cliff with the discovery of the Bat's Wing Orchid and its potential to medical science. As the husband of an ailing wife, the commander would understand the importance of discretion.

'Raided, you say?'

'Yes. Probably from above, by abseilers.'

'If Jimmi saw them – and, more to the point, if they saw Jimmi – that could be the motive for killing him.'

'That's what I thought, Gerald. But, and it's a bloody big but, we don't even know for sure he was murdered. There were no obvious marks on the body, the police were not interested. He might have simply suffered a horrible accident. We shouldn't jump to conclusions … but, yes, I accept, it's fishy.'

'Damned fishy, if you ask me,' snorted Marler.

Despite the widespread dismal opinion of the local constabulary, I decided to call into Normanden Police Station with the sleeping bag on my way to the Landers' home that was just a few miles out of town.

Behind the desk, a harassed-looking sergeant glanced up from behind the strengthened glass screen, her eyes settling on my mud-smeared jeans.

'Can I help, sir?' Her voice came over the second-rate intercom system making her sound dalek-like.

I told her of my concerns about the death of Jimmi Valgren, the discovery of the sleeping bag at Samphire Hoe and the camera memory card hidden in the hide at the nature reserve.

Duty Sergeant Hopps took down a few details, saying she could remember reports of the drowning but little else. As she wrote, raised voices from another room distracted her.

'Bit busy in here today sir, not your normal quiet Normanden day. Now, where were we ... Shakespeare Cliff taking photographs. Yes. Look, I'll get someone in CID to give you a ring, I've got your cell phone number haven't I?'

She wrote it down as I dictated it a second time and then accepted the sleeping bag through a hatch, putting on surgical gloves before she handled it, stuffing it into a clear plastic bag.

I also offered her a computer memory stick. 'I've copied Valgren's photographs on to this. You might want to take a look.'

'I am sure we will,' she said, putting the memory stick in a brown envelope. 'I'll pass it on to CID and inform them about the photographs you say show lights at night on Shoreness beach. In fact, they could be of great interest to us.'

When I told her I was staying with the Landers for a few days, her interest perked. 'With Larry? Well that's good. We know him well in here. Don't go putting your story in his paper, though, not before you've spoken to us.'

There were more raised angry voices from somewhere at the back of the station and a door slammed. It was time to go.

As Lander had promised, the key to the back door was

under a stone heron that was peering longingly at the gold carp in the small pond in the back garden of their converted barn. I let myself in and took off my muddy shoes, grateful to feel the warmth through my socks of the central heating system underneath the granite floor of the kitchen diner.

Lander was busy putting that week's edition of the *South Coast Gazette* to bed and said he would be home in time to see wife Sue fronting the local evening news programme on television. He had said to make myself at home, which was not difficult in such stylish surroundings.

Leading off the kitchen was a cavernous lounge that went the height of the barn, showing off the exposed eighteenth century beams. The floor was polished oak. The high windows gave spectacular views across farmland. Upstairs, the three bedrooms all had name signs on the doors: Skye, Mull, Arran. They were the Scottish islands where the Landers had spent their honeymoon. They still regularly visited the Hebrides for fishing trips – one of the few interests they had in common – and that is where they were heading on Sunday, by which time I hoped to have sorted out my life.

I was in Mull. Sue had laid out towels and organic toiletries on the white duvet covering the futon. In the en-suite wet room I stood under the monsoon shower and drenched myself with deliciously hot water instead of cold rain.

By the time Lander arrived home, I was showered, shaved and dressed in clean clothes, the dirty ones turning over in the washing machine in the utility room. I had made a pot of tea and settled down to the crossword from a copy of yesterday's *Times*. 5 Down: *Go in after fish and chips (9).*

'Had to rip out the first three pages and make big changes at the last minute today, big news,' said Lander as he flopped into the brown leather sofa at right angles to the matching one I was sitting on. He took a long swig from a can of lager. 'And I hear you've been in the cop shop.'

'Word gets round.'

'Ah, the lovely Sergeant Hilary Hopps – known to the local force as Bunny. She's my eyes and ears at the police station.'

'Is she any more than that?'

'Shit no. Wouldn't dare even trying. Anyway, I think she bats for the other side.' He tapped the side of his nose and winked.

The big breaking story for the *South Coast Gazette*, Lander explained, was the discovery and subsequent identification of three Afghan asylum-seekers found in Shoreness. More than that, two local fishermen were being questioned about their arrival in the UK.

'Gary and Bronx Wilde,' said Lander. 'Currently helping the police with their inquiries at Normanden nick, rather reluctantly too, I understand.'

That may have explained the raised voices I had heard that afternoon at the police station.

'People smuggling has long been suspected along this coast but this is the first time anyone's been nicked for it,' said Lander. 'The theory is the local fishermen go out at night innocently to catch sea bass but meet up with a

French trawler in the middle of the Channel and land a bigger prize. It's the refugees I feel sorry for.'

'What will happen to them?'

Lander shrugged. 'Not sure. I'm told that one of them claims to have been working for the British Army in Afghanistan as a local guide on the promise that when our troops withdrew, he would be looked after.'

'But he wasn't?'

'No. He apparently has his mother and younger brother with him. Says the rest of his family have been killed by the Taliban. The three did a runner and got here via Turkey and Greece and are now claiming the protection he says our Government promised him. I think he might be lucky, too,' added Lander as he headed to the kitchen to collect a second lager from the tall red Smeg fridge.

'There's quite a groundswell of opinion in support of these people, and the Home Office is under pressure to be seen to do the right thing.' Lander returned with two cold cans and put one down on the table in front of me.

'News time,' he said, picking up the television remote control and pointing it at a vast flat screen on the wall above the fireplace. On the screen appeared Sue Lander, elegant and authoritative as she welcomed viewers to *South-East Today* from behind the news desk.

Behind her, images of a fishing boat and Shoreness beach appeared.

'Our top story this evening is … two fishermen brothers are questioned about the arrival of three Afghan asylum-seekers discovered at Shoreness. We now go to our crime correspondent Simon Abraham outside

Normanden Police Station. There may be some flash photography.'

The reporter repeated much of what Lander had already told me and then cut to some film taken earlier of the Wilde brothers arriving at the police station. As they were bundled inside, heads bowed, the waiting press, who had clearly been tipped off about their arrival by the police, called out questions.

One of the angry voices shouting an obscenity back at the media scrum was very familiar. It was the same rasping voice I had heard at the Lighthouse Inn on my first day in Shoreness, and then again on my stolen and then returned Dictafone telling me to 'Fuck off if you know what's good for you.' It belonged to Gary Wilde.

We watched the rest of the local news in comparative silence except for Larry lewdly suggesting that he knew what he would like to do with the weathergirl's warm front when she appeared in an inappropriately tight dress at the end of the bulletin.

'You have to admit, she's very good,' I said.

'It would be better if she was bad,' snorted Lander.

'Not the weathergirl. I mean your missus, Sue. She's a class act on TV.'

'Alright, no need to go on about it. I know it already. I'm always being referred to as the husband of Sue Lander rather than the esteemed editor of the local campaigning newspaper. She's the main breadwinner now. How d'you think we can afford the mortgage on this?' Lander spread his arms and looked up to the beams in the ceiling.

'She's looking good too, Larry. You don't know how lucky you are. You're a fool to mess around with secretaries at your age – and I speak as someone whose marriage has just gone down the pan.'

Lander harrumphed. He could just about take this sort of advice from a close friend. He also knew I was right.

'She's delighted you're staying, you know? She's hurrying home from the studio to make an evening of it. She's picking up an Indian takeaway on the way home if that's OK with you. We've got a cracking one in Normanden. Run by Afghans, coincidentally.'

'Perfect.' I filled in the crossword answer: *Carpenter*.

The foil containers of spicy vegetables, chicken and fish tikka, dals and rice did not disappoint and neither did the two bottles of chilled Prosecco. As we reminisced about our early days in journalism, there was no hint of a simmering atmosphere between Larry and Sue. Perhaps I had got it wrong.

She looked as good as she did on television. Just turned forty, she had kept her trim figure. Her naturally blonde hair was cut in a stylish bob. The blue-rimmed Gant spectacles added to her air of authority. In comparison, Lander was a couch potato gone to seed, but as a couple of opposites they worked despite everything.

When Lander excused himself to go to the loo, burping with each step up the open tread stairs, Sue's manicured fingers touched the back of my hand.

'It's so good to see you again, Tom, and, before you ask, yes I do know about that over-waxed little trollop Jasmine, and yes, I have forgiven him. The poor sap. He can't help himself when it comes to a nubile ninny who thinks she can shag her way to a promotion. I've made him pay in my own subtle way and he's out of the dog house but still on a leash.' She smiled and theatrically fluttered her eyelashes. She was not a lady to cross.

'And how about you and Katie? Any chance of a reconciliation? I always liked her even though I never thought the two of you were well suited.'

'Didn't you? You never told me that.'

'No, well I wouldn't would I? It's not the sort of thing you say to a couple while they're still together … unless you're trying to split them up. And I've never fancied you that way, Tom. You know that.'

I had always liked her frankness. 'No, I don't think there's any chance of us getting back together although Ali wishes it were so. In fact, I've already been out with someone else. Only one date, but it went rather well if I do say so myself.'

'Tell me more,' said Sue, curling her slim legs underneath her on the sofa next to me as Larry announced his return to the room with another belch.

I told them about Jo Etheridge and the job offer to run an in-house magazine for Genor-X without going into too much graphic detail about how the deal had been sealed in her bed.

'Sounds ideal,' said Sue. 'When do you start?'

'I'm not sure yet. I still have misgivings about moving into the world of what is basically PR, and for a nuclear power company at that. But Jo may be right about nuclear energy being the way forward, and it is very tempting. I've become disillusioned with the newspaper business. But before I sign on the dotted line, I've still got a few loose ends to tie up around here.'

'And a restaurant review of the Lucky Fisherman to write,' said Lander, opening a third bottle of Prosecco.

Katie was hysterical. It took me a moment to realise where I was when I answered the mobile phone.

'She's not come home, Oh my god, what's happened to her Tom. What have we done?'

'Katie, Katie ....'

'I'm going to call the police. I just know something awful has happened.'

'Katie, slow down a minute. Is Alice missing, is that what you're saying?'

'Of course, you stupid halfwit. Who else?'

I looked at my watch. It was a few minutes after eleven. I could hear Larry and Sue Lander chatting in the kitchen and water being run. I must have dozed off on the sofa. I stood up.

'Ok Katie, just calm down a minute and tell me what's happened.'

She started to sob. 'She should have been home by ten. It's rehearsals night for the drama group tonight and Rosie's mother was due to pick them up to bring them home. Only when she got to the school, Rosie was there but not Alice. She'd not been to the rehearsals at all. You've got to come home. Now.'

'Katie, I can't. I've been drinking. And there are no trains at this time of night. You've tried her new mobile, I guess?'

'Yes, of course I have, dozens of times. It just cuts into her voice-mail.'

'You've rung around other friends?'

'A few. I tried Beth, Anika, Liz. They said they thought she left school at the normal time. Liz said she thought Alice was waiting at a bus stop with a gang of lads from the boys' school. Oh my dear god, what's happened to my little girl?' Katie broke down again.

'I'll ring the police, Katie. But I expect she's got a boyfriend we don't know about. It'll be something as simple as that. Anyway, why didn't you collect her from rehearsals?'

'I was out.'

'Out? Where?'

'That's really none of your business.'

'In these circumstances, I think it is.'

'If you must know, I went out for a meal. With a friend. That's not against the law is it?'

'A male friend?'

'Oh, that's right, try to blame me, Tom. God, you're fucking useless, even when Alice needs you most. I'm going to drive around looking for her.'

'Katie, don't, there's no point, you need to be at home in case ....'

Before I had finished the sentence, she had hung up.

I rang the number for Blackheath Police Station and was transferred to Missing Persons at Westminster. A female sergeant took Alice's details and I emailed her my most recent photograph of my daughter. The sergeant asked about circumstances at home. When I told her, she told me not to worry. 'Girls of thirteen often go missing for twenty-four hours, sir.' It was not reassuring.

Sleep was not easy and when it did arrive, it was brief.

17

Six o'clock Thursday morning. I know it is that time because the wolf-whistle on my mobile phone has just announced the arrival of a text message. I had been asleep but it had been uneasy rest. I remember being awake at three o'clock and four o'clock, anxiety gnawing away, bad thoughts crowding in. As I tried to focus on the little screen, the ache behind my eyeballs told me that however much sleep I had got, it had been brief. I saw the time and then the alert: 'message from Ali'.

I fumbled with the tiny keys to put in my pass code, cursing as I twice touched the wrong number. Then I got it right, and relief flooded through me. She was alive and well.

'Hi Dad, I'm at Nan n Gramps. Mum not home last night. Dont no where she is. Ali xx'

Nan and Gramps were Ali's pet names for Katie's parents. They lived in a quiet cul-de-sac in Orpington, eight miles from the family home in Blackheath. She was obviously awake, so I rang.

'Ali, you're OK aren't you?'

'Of course, Dad. Why?'

'Only because your mother was having a pink fit last night when you didn't come home from rehearsals. What did you mean in your text when you said that Mum wasn't home?'

'I didn't go to the drama group, I've given it up. I went straight home from school and she wasn't there. When it got to about seven and she was still out, I decided to come to Nan and Gramps'.

'Mum wasn't there?'

'No. She was out again, she's always out. Probably with *him*.'

I did not want to know who *him* was.

'What did you tell Nan and Gramps?'

'A little lie. I hope you don't mind. I said that Mum was visiting her friend in Cardiff for a couple of days. I brought a bag of things with me and said she must have forgotten to tell them. They don't mind, they're lovely. Gramps is driving me to school this morning.'

My initial relief was being rapidly replaced by anger – anger at Katie, whose dalliances appeared to have driven our daughter away from her home.

'Dad.'

'Yes?'

'I don't want to go home again. And I want to leave *that* school. I hate it. I want to go to an ordinary school.'

'You've got to go home some time, darling. As for the school, that's something we'll have to talk about.'

'What about Mum?'

'Don't worry, I'll talk to her. Yes, I'll talk to her.'

I should have telephoned Katie next but I put it off. That small act of vindictiveness gave me a troubling amount of pleasure. Let her stew. Her sexual adventuring had caused this mess. I telephoned the contact number I had been given by Westminster police and spoke to a different sergeant. I told them Alice had turned up safe and well. He thanked me. Case closed.

The rest of the Lander household was still silent as I went downstairs and made myself a coffee after I had finally worked out how to get a pod inside the Nespresso machine. Half way down the reviving cup of strong black liquid, I decided to ring Katie.

'You didn't say you were out yesterday tea-time as well as in the evening.'

'Tom, have you heard something for Christ's sake?'

'About Ali? Oh yes, she's fine.'

'Oh thank God. Where is she? Not with you?'

'No. Not with me.'

'Where then?' She was beginning to shout, which made me pleased. I remained calm.

'You weren't there when she got home from school, so she's moved out for a couple of days.'

'What the fuck, Tom? I was out. OK? With a friend. But I was home by nine and Ali doesn't get back from play rehearsals until about ten.'

'She's quit drama. Didn't you know? She came home at the normal time. She wants to quit that school too, by the way.'

'Leave St Jeavons? She can't. Where did she spend the night?'

I was enjoying this. 'She also wants to leave home – your home. But I think I've talked her out of that one. For the time being.'

'I'm going mad here, Tom. Stop playing fucking games with me. I've been frantic all night, I must have driven all over south London, I've rung all of her friends. Where is she?' Katie screamed the last three words.

'You didn't try ringing your parents, then?'

'No. Why? I didn't want to worry them, they couldn't have helped anyway.'

'Only if you had have done, you could have spoken to Alice, who, by the way, covered for you and your night of lust.'

'She's in Orpington?'

'Yes. She told your folks you'd gone to see your friend Jilly in Cardiff for a couple of days. So don't worry, they don't know about your shagging habits just yet.'

'I've got to ring her.'

'Yes. You do that.'

We probably hung up simultaneously. Alice was safe, Katie was in a state and I knew what she did not want me to know about her private life. Oddly, it felt good.

'Useless.' I was not sure if Sergeant Hilary Hopps was referring to me or the memory stick she was handing back through a hatch in the glass screen at Normanden Police Station.

'Thank you for your time, sir, but DC Brooks has had a look at the photos and says they are of no use to Operation Syn.'

'Operation sin?'

'Syn, as in Dr Syn, our legendary smuggling hero in these parts. Not 'sin' as in three-in-a-bed. It's the name we have given to our investigation into the alleged smuggling of our Afghan friends. The photographs you supplied of vehicles and lights on the beach are too indistinct to tell us anything, and certainly could not be presented as evidence in court.'

I took the memory stick from her. 'And the sleeping bag. The other business about Jimmi Valgren?'

The sergeant avoided my eyes and started shuffling papers on her desk. 'Yes, that. Well, sir, there seems to have been something of a mix up.'

'Mix up?'

'Yes, mix up.' She was clearly reluctant to elaborate.

'Go on,' I said. 'Humour me.'

'Well, it seems that when the cleaners collected the dirty linen this morning from the cells and the canteen to send off to the laundry service, they mistakenly included the sleeping bag thinking that it belonged to some itinerant who was spending the night in a cell.'

'And now it's been laundered and is of no use as evidence of any kind?' I tried to sound as withering as possible.

'That's about it sir. Just human error. It happens. Look, we don't think there's anything in your concerns about Valgren's drowning, but a member of CID will speak to you about it. We'll be in touch but we are only a small station and are rather preoccupied with other matters right now.'

The closing of the hatch suggested that was also the closing of the conversation. I pocketed the memory stick and headed for town aware that my mobile phone had been merrily buzzing in my pocket announcing the arrival of messages or emails.

The Station Café was busy with shoppers getting their caffeine fix. I found a table in the corner and turned to the *Guardian* crossword while I waited for my large

Americano and bacon sandwich. Then I remembered the messages that had arrived on my mobile. There were three of them.

'Pls ring. Danny in hosp. Don't no what to do. Eve x'

'The job's yours if you want it. 35k pa, fringe benefits! Dinner? Call me. Jo xxx'

'Hi Tommy. Fancy a sibling dinner tonight? Sis x'

Three messages from three women all needing me for one reason or another. I felt alarmed, aroused and concerned all at the same time.

I wanted to ring Jo first but my head told my heart I should call Eve Hathaway. I assumed the Danny to whom she referred was Danny Lawton, her former boyfriend who had been jilted when Jimmi Valgren appeared on the scene.

The call cut straight into her voice-mail. I left a non-incriminating message just in case it should be heard by the wrong ears.

My coffee and bacon sandwich arrived. I had a feeling the tubby waitress, who reeked of cigarettes and cheap perfume, had been eavesdropping the call. On top of everything else, I was getting paranoid.

I tapped in the next number. Another voice-mail message.

'Jo. It's Tom. I accept … both the job offer and the dinner invite. Give me a call.'

I had better luck with Fleur, who, by the sound of the roar that almost drowned out her voice, was halfway up a cliff.

'Hi Tommy. How was the school visit and my favourite niece?'

'Oh, so-so on both counts, it's a long story and it sounds like not a good time to talk. Are you at the cliff project?'

'No, just walking along the top of Shakespeare Cliff, part business, part pleasure. It's gorgeous up here despite the windy weather. Fancy coming to my hotel for dinner? I'd like some different company to Dr Ntini and his team?'

I said I would be there that evening. My yearning to see Jo Etheridge again, to make sure I had not been a one-night stand, would have to wait for another twenty-four hours.

A second large Americano finally dealt with the previous night's lack of sleep and I was ready to face the day. Whatever the day had in store.

The *Guardian* crossword kick-started the grey matter: 12 Down: *Seaside resort beginning to be fashionable with hippies (8).*

The phone vibrated quietly on the table. I had switched it to silent mode. 'Hello, Kidd speaking.' I glanced around to see if the waitress was within earshot this time. She was, although she was serving another customer at the counter.

'Tom, it's Eve.' The voice at the other end came in a whisper.

'I can hardly hear you Eve. What's up? What's wrong with Danny?'

'I'm using the landline in the pub. Danny's been beaten up. Badly. He's in the Normanden Clinic but he thinks they may move him to Dover General.' She started sobbing. 'He has some head injuries as well as a few cracked ribs.'

'Christ. Is he able to talk?'

Eve said he was, and we arranged to meet at the clinic at midday.

I filled in the crossword clue: *Brighton*. I looked at my watch, drained my coffee and left. I had seen a town map on a board outside the railway station. That should tell me where the clinic was.

Eve was shivering in the porch to the single storey red-brick building on the edge of a modern housing development on the outskirts of town. It looked more like a library than a medical centre from the outside but the two ambulances parked nearby gave it away.

Eve was underdressed as usual in short skirt and crop top, but it was her face that caught the attention. Her left cheek had an angry red weal that she had tried to conceal with make up without great success. Her eyes were puffy, too.

'What happened to you?'

'Let's see Danny first.' Her voice was flat, the emotion wrung out of it. She turned towards the double doors that opened inwards automatically as she broke the invisible sensor beam.

Her steps did not falter at reception when the woman behind the counter looked up. Eve had obviously been here before and said she knew where Danny was. We turned into the Day Ward, which had four beds down each side, only three of which were occupied. Danny was in the far corner by a large picture window, lying back with a bandage around his head, earphones in and his eyes closed.

'Danny,' she whispered, touching his arm.

He sat up quickly and winced, bringing up a grazed right hand to his ribs.

'Keep forgetting about it 'til I move,' he said, pulling out the earphones and switching off his iPod. At least he was smiling, which was a good sign. 'The painkillers must be wearing off.'

Danny told his story. He had been jumped from behind in the car park at the Lucky Fisherman the previous evening, much the same way I had, although the damage to the boy was much more serious.

He thought there had been three of them. They had used fists and feet, not weapons, punching him to the ground and then kicking him, mainly in the ribs and crotch but also once to the head.

'It seemed to last forever but I guess it was all over in thirty seconds. I passed out for a while and then a young couple apparently saw me in the headlights of their car as they pulled in. They called an ambulance which first off took me to Dover General for a CT scan. That was all clear so they transferred me here first thing this morning.'

'Who was it?' I asked.

'Pretty sure it was the TA boys.'

'But when I saw you in there last week you seemed pretty friendly with them. You were playing pool or darts with them.'

'I was sucking up to them, trying to gain their trust. I'd heard they sold dope to people they trusted. Obviously they didn't trust me enough when I started asking questions.'

'Why were you doing that, Danny? You don't use it.'

said Eve, who had cupped his right hand in hers on the bed sheet.

'I was partly curious about that Jimmi character of yours who was dealing with them, but you also know how much I hate drugs. I didn't know what I was going to do really, but I had some idea of going to the police with some information and getting the fucking place busted.'

The boy's voice had turned hard. There was anger in his eyes.

'Have the police been to see you in here?'

'Yes, one came in this morning but said they were rather stretched at the moment. She took down some details and said she'd get back to me. The doctor wouldn't let her stay long, said I needed rest. I've got to have some more checks this afternoon, but the doctor says he's pretty confident there isn't any serious damage. He said I could be out in a couple of days.'

'Well, that's good news. Did you find out anything about Jimmi?' I asked.

Danny shook his head. 'They played dumb when I mentioned his name, but I reckon they knew something. I got much the same response when I hinted that I was looking to buy some dope for a party. The bastards. I think their course at Cheyne Camp ends this weekend, so they'll be going back to their boring little nine-to-five jobs. Hopefully I'll never see them again.'

'That might not be a bad thing. Stay clear, Danny. They're not worth it and neither is the Lucky Fisherman.'

We said our goodbyes. Eve wanted to hug Danny but he said it would hurt too much, so she restricted herself to a kiss on the cheek.

In the car park, we sat in the Ford Fiesta, the engine ticking over and the heater pathetically trying to churn out a modicum of warmth. We both had a lot of questions. Eve went first.

'I thought you'd buggered off?'

'I did. Sort of. I'm sorry, I misled you a bit, but I wanted the locals to think I'd dropped the case of Jimmi's drowning. It was all getting a bit heavy. I'm still trying to find out what happened, though – just doing it more discreetly.'

I turned to look at her more closely. 'And what happened to you?'

Her eyes turned to the floor. 'It was Dad. He gets angry sometimes.'

'He hit you?'

She nodded but there were no more tears. She was all out of them.

I let the silence hang to give her a chance to explain some more. She did.

'He gets on edge from time to time. If the horses don't come in or if he has to go to visit Turk at the Lucky Fisherman. He usually returns from there in a foul mood. Don't know why. They've got some business going on and I think sometimes it goes wrong.'

'Why do you put up with it? You're old enough to leave home.'

'If I did he'd only start on Mum again. While I'm there he takes it out on me and tends to leave Mum alone. I can put up with it – for a while at least.'

'Does he, you know … sexually interfere with you?'

Eve seemed shocked, almost affronted. 'Shit no. I wouldn't put up with that crap. He just lashes out occasionally but he's never tried any pervy stuff.'

'OK, next question: do you believe Danny's story about wanting to expose the drug dealing at the Lucky Fisherman? Why would a young bloke like that "hate" drugs?'

'Oh yes, he hates drugs all right. Always has done since his poor mother died in a car crash about five years ago when he was fifteen. The driver in the other car was high on something, lost control and ploughed into his mother's car while it was waiting at a level crossing. It was awful. She was shunted into the oncoming train.'

Eve turned to look at me: 'That's why Danny took against Jimmi so. I don't think it was jealousy, because we'd already more or less split up before I met Jimmi. We remained pals, but he couldn't get his head around me and Jimmi being together – and having the occasional spliff.'

'I can understand that.'

Silence fell between us. An ambulance pulled up outside the medical centre and a young boy in a wheelchair, no more than ten years old, was lowered on the lift at the back. There's always someone worse off, I thought, although Eve might not think so right now. She looked crushed by what the world had thrown at her.

'Let me know how things go with Danny. I'll stay in touch – and if I were you, I'd move away from your Dad. You and your mother.'

Driving out of Normanden I felt angry on behalf of both Danny and Eve, two young people caught up in something that was not of their doing, both stuck in the bleak backwater of Shoreness with no obvious way out; a place with a future as barren as its stony environment occupied by chancers, thugs, bent coppers and criminals.

As for me, I was going to walk away to a fresh start in a day or two. Or, at least, that was the intention.

Jo Etheridge had called back. She sounded genuinely disappointed that I already had a date that evening, albeit with my sister, but gave me the details of the job.

'The contract will be in the post as soon as you can give me a permanent address.'

I gave her the address of Fleur's flat and said I would be there in a couple of days. I was keen to get on with my life.

'There'll also be a medical, but that'll be a formality, I'm sure,' she said.

'I thought you gave me a medical the other night. Didn't I pass?'

She chuckled a deliciously dirty chuckle. We arranged to meet for dinner the next day. At the Lighthouse Inn.

I was about to push open the door of the Station Café when I recognised the thickset profile of the man standing at the counter talking to the overly-fragrant waitress. The customer was Romeo Turk. He looked agitated and banged his fist on the counter. I spun on my heel and walked back across the road, convinced I had not been seen by either of them.

What was Turk doing in town? I was pretty sure he was not about to visit Danny Lawton at the medical centre with a bunch of flowers and a get-well-soon card.

On the other hand, there had been another dust-up in his pub car park. Perhaps he was doing his duty as an upright citizen and helping the police catch the culprits. I doubted that option too. Perhaps he was looking for me, but that made little sense either. As far as Turk was concerned, I had left the area, never to be seen again.

I looked at my reflection in the window of the offices of the *South Coast Gazette.* I could see the Station Café behind me. Turk appeared in the doorway and headed towards the station. Time for some amateur detective work.

I crossed the road again and sauntered past the café trying to look as casual as possible. I briefly studied the menu in the window to give Turk time to get a safe distance ahead and then headed for the station along the approach flanked by the commuter car parks.

There was no sign of Turk. In front of the station building were six spaces for short-stay parking. Turk's unmistakable Toyota Rav4 with its personalised number plate – ROM 30 – was there. A shot of adrenalin alerted the senses and made my stomach feel loose. The front of the station and the car park appeared deserted. I took a few slow deep breaths and told myself not to be silly. I was in plain full sight, nothing could happen to me in such a public place.

By this time of day the ticket office was shut, the blinds pulled down. The few travellers heading up to London in the evening were expected to purchase their tickets from a vending machine by the side entrance to the platform, which was open. I went over to the machine and pushed a few buttons in case I was being watched.

The yellow electronic sign over Platform One announced that the next train due to depart for Charing Cross was in another thirty-five minutes. The stations it called at rolled across the bottom of the display. On Platform Two, the information sign read: 'The next train terminates here'. There was a footbridge to Platform Two. That should be a good vantage point.

Standing in the middle of the bridge, I could just see over the high sides if I stood on tiptoe. The twin lines that headed north across flat farmland were illuminated in the fading afternoon light by red signals that reflected off the six rails – four carrying the trains, two carrying 750 volts of electricity. Looking south, one track went into a siding, the other continued on a loop around Normanden's church towards the coast and Shoreness. Passenger services ended here but there was the freight service to the power station for its regular hazardous cargo of nuclear waste.

Behind Platform Two and its boundary wire was a stretch of rough ground dotted by large dirty puddles with ramshackle industrial units scattered around the perimeter. There was a scrapyard in one corner, a scaffolding firm along the side nearest the station, and on the far side a rank of lorries and containers.

One of the articulated vehicles had 'Dart-Line Transport – Intercontinental Hauliers' emblazoned in red italic letters on the grey tarpaulin down one side, and Turk was standing by the cab talking up at the driver. At the back of the lorry, a fork-lift truck was loading pallets swathed in clinging black plastic sheeting. The background check on Turk courtesy of two old media contacts had shown that his father-in-law ran a fleet of lorries out of Dartford. Was Dart-Line the family business?

The fork-lift driver tooted his horn and gave a thumbs up to Turk, who in turn stepped back and gave a thumbs up to the driver. The diesel engine fired into life and a plume of filthy smoke belched out of the silver exhaust pipe that rose above the cab. The long load started a slow turn of the waste ground splashing through the puddles towards an exit on the far side.

Turk started to march back towards the station. I ducked down in mild panic. Had I been seen? Surely not? I pulled up the collar of my North Face jacket and hurried down the steps from the bridge back towards Normanden High Street without looking back over my shoulder. As I arrived at the Station Café, a Toyota Rav4 thundered by, the driver seemingly intent on looking only at the road in front.

I turned to study the café menu again, just in case Turk should look in his rear-view mirror. I could hear my heart beating furiously. This was ridiculous.

Lander was scanning the front page of the latest edition of the *South Coast Gazette* with all the beaming pride of a father holding his new-born.

The headline announced: 'Smuggling ring smashed in dawn raid' and underneath was a photograph of two men, heads bowed, being hustled into Normanden Police Station.

The melodramatic report alongside did not name the Wilde brothers but said two local fishermen were helping police with inquiries and that the asylum-seekers had been found cold, hungry and living in squalid conditions in a windowless shack on Shoreness beach.

'Proper news, at last,' said Lander. 'Beats the hell out of our regular diet of planning protests, church restoration appeals and complaints about dog fouling on the school field.' We were sitting in his editor's office, a huge brown tea pot and two chipped mugs between us.

'Will the Wildes get done?'

'Almost certainly. The police are very confident. It's being handed over to the big boys from Dover CID but people smuggling is such a sensitive issue right now, and the politicians want the police and customs to be seen to be doing something positive.'

'And the Afghans?'

'They're the victims in all of this, and if the guy's story about being on the army payroll as a guide in Afghanistan is true, they'll almost certainly be allowed to stay, poor sods.'

'Poor sods because of their ordeal or because they might have to live in this country?'

'Both.'

Lander also had news of the assault in the car park of the Lucky Fisherman that put Danny Lawton in hospital. The Shoreness policeman, PC Trotter – aka Peter the Pig – had been asked to investigate and he had reported back to Normanden that the closed circuit television covering the pub car park had not been working. As there were no witnesses, he did not hold out much hope of a successful outcome to his investigations.

'Now why does that surprise me?'

Lander decided the pot had stood long enough and filled the two mugs with the dark, dense tea.

'Larry, the large piece of scruffy land beside the railway station that's used as a lorry park. Who owns it?'

'Genor-X. They purchased it from Network Rail a couple of years ago amid much local opposition. They plan to build their own rail depot there to bring in the material they need for the new nuclear power station they want to build alongside the current one.

The project has been held up because of planning protests and legal wrangling but they're still likely to get the green light. If they do, work will start there in about 2019, but in the meantime, as a gesture of goodwill to the local community, Genor-X let a few businesses use it for a peppercorn rent.'

Fleur's hotel – The Customs House – was on the old cobbled quay, its refurbished rooms offering views of the modern Dover Ferry Terminus that never slept. The restaurant was chic and busy. Fleur was at the bar deep in conversation with a man I recognised: Gideon Squires. Dressed in a dark suit instead of the tracksuit I had last seen him wearing, he looked every dapper inch the businessman.

'Hello you two.'

'Oh Hi, Tom, you know Gideon, don't you?'

We nodded and shook hands.

'Hello Tom, sorry you had to move out of the cottage earlier than planned – and sorry to hear about the intruders there. I don't know what Shoreness is coming to.'

'That's OK. Things have worked out.'

'Gideon's just passing through, been for a meeting with the Samphire Hoe project team this afternoon to see what precautions we are taking about the orchid raids.'

'It's a worrying business,' said Squires, looking at Fleur. 'I've told your little sister she shouldn't be exposing herself to any sort of risk with this round-the-clock watch they are keeping on the site.'

'I didn't know you and Kew were involved in this project.'

I looked at Squires. He picked up an olive, popped it into his mouth and shook his head.

'We are and we're not. This is Edinburgh's baby but I'm here to lend a bit of moral support – and expertise if it's wanted.' He looked at Fleur. 'And advice.'

'Stop worrying, Gideon, I'll be fine.'

'I hope so, Fleur.' He leaned across and pecked her on the cheek. 'I'd best be getting home. All the best, Tom. Enjoy dinner. It's good here.'

The grilled Dover sole – what else should one eat in Dover? – was perfect, as was just about everything else about the meal that Fleur insisted on paying for. Edinburgh Royal Botanic Garden could pick up the tab, she said, if I was going to help stop whoever was plundering the site at Shakespeare Cliff.

'I didn't know I was,' I said, reluctantly declining a second glass of Chablis.

'I'm sure you will, Tommy.'

Her faith in her older brother was touching.

She said that the initial fears that the Bat's Wing

Orchids growing at the chalky habitat had been almost wiped out were unfounded. The latest, less hysterical, estimate was that about ten per cent of the plants had been removed, and another ten per cent badly damaged by being trampled underfoot.

'The site on the cliff is about the size of two football pitches, so there are large areas untouched. However, that doesn't mean whoever did it won't be back.'

'How difficult would it be to stop thieves abseiling into the site. Surely some sort of fence could be erected higher up the cliff?'

'I don't think the thieves abseiled to it, after all,' said Fleur. 'When you phoned me earlier I was walking along the cliff top. There are no signs of staves having been hammered into the ground to attach ropes to. There's nothing solid up there to attach a rope to either. I think they climbed up from below.'

'Without being seen?'

'Possibly at night. Although the old walkers' path up the cliff is inaccessible to the public, there's little to stop a determined thief from scrambling up the rock once he has crossed the rail line and got over the wire mesh fence. It would be a precarious business but people will do anything if the rewards are great enough.'

'What do you make of Ntini, Sis? He strikes me as being a bit of a cold customer.'

'David? Aye, he is a bit. But I think he's just one of these scientists who's so obsessive about his work. He's not easy to get along with, I agree. He doesn't talk about anything other than the project, either. That's why I was keen to get away from the botanical world for an evening and talk to my lovely big brother.'

She was teasing again. I decided to ignore it.

'Did he tell you that we bumped into each other yesterday? At Samphire Hoe?'

'No.' She sounded surprised.

Well, this might surprise her even more: 'He as good as warned me off.'

'Warned you off. How d'you mean?'

'Told me I wouldn't be welcome at the scientific site again. Not a place for sightseers, he said.'

'Cheeky wee so-and-so. He might be the project manager down here, but I'm above him in the staff pecking order in Edinburgh. I can take whoever I like on to the site. But now you mention it, I must admit I did feel he wasn't happy with me for taking you there. I'll ask him about it. Subtly, of course. I'm due to take over from him at midnight.'

'Take over?'

'We're running a round-the-clock watch on the place now. There are four of us doing shifts there between six in the evening and eight in the morning when there are no staff actually working on the site. It's my turn for the midnight watch tonight.'

'And exactly what are you proposing to do if the raiders of the lost ark turn up again? Attack them with a rolled up copy of *Orchid Monthly*?'

'Good question, Tommy.' She laughed. 'Don't worry, I'll raise the alarm. The Eurotunnel air-conditioning plant has at least three security staff on duty at all times. We liaise regularly with them.'

All the same, I was not at all happy with the thought

of my little sister putting herself in harm's way for a nondescript plant that had decided to root itself half way up a precarious chalk face on the Kent coast.

18

I went back to the footpath that took me along the summit of Shakespeare Cliff. It was my first visit since the day I discovered the body of Jimmi Valgren almost two weeks earlier. The view across the English Channel at eight on a clear cold Friday March morning was breathtaking. It was easy to understand why people felt passionate and patriotic about these cliffs. They were at the edge of England rubbing shoulders with the country's sea-faring history.

Along the route of the North Downs Way were physical reminders of the last great conflict to affect this shoreline. Observation posts still kept watch over the stretch of grey water below. Concrete footings where guns once stood now provided a base for litter bins. Almost hidden behind the gorse and brambles was a brick gun battery cut into the hillside to help protect the strategic port of Dover in those uncertain war years when Europe, barely twenty miles away, was occupied. The artillery that pointed out towards the water was long gone and, judging by the graffiti inside the battery, love not war was now made in the dank recesses.

I left the footpath and edged towards the cliff edge to look down on Samphire Hoe. I had never liked heights. I got down on all fours to peer over the ledge. The 300-foot drop down the side of the chalk cliff seemed to be sucking me down while at the same time the wind was pushing me back.

The botanists from Edinburgh, their safety harnesses attached to climbing ropes, moved around their 'site of special scientific interest'. Dr Ntini was scraping at the stony ground but there was no sign of Fleur. She was probably off that morning having done the nightwatchman's duties last night.

From this precarious vantage point, I also noticed the distinct contours of a zig-zag path that appeared to originate from the back of what had been Shakespeare Halt beside the railway at the foot of the cliff. The path could not be seen from sea level at the Hoe, but its route was clear from above. In places it had broken away into chalky scree and looked impassable, but much of it was still there, making its way backwards and forwards up the cliff towards where I was kneeling. Near the top, it disappeared again into the crumbling chalk face.

Had Jimmi Valgren used this path to get better photographs of the sea birds that nested on the cliffs? He could have easily slipped and fallen to his death. But that did not explain how he ended up in the sea naked.

'Breathtaking, isn't it?'

I lurched forwards momentarily before scrambling backwards and on to my feet.

'Wouldn't go too near the edge, though, if I were you. It can be very crumbly, particularly after the rain we've had.' The dog walker was in her mid-twenties. Wearing a Barbour coat and expensive Hunter boots, her long dark hair trailed behind her in the wind like a sail. An excited collie tugged at his leather lead.

I wondered if she thought I was a jumper. 'I wasn't, you know – thinking of ….' I pointed down.

'Oh no, I didn't think you were.' She seemed embarrassed at my suggestion. The collie was beginning to eye me suspiciously. He tugged her backwards again.

'I come up here most days, rain or shine.' She took a deep breath through her nose and closed her eyes for a moment. 'It's lovely. It just feels so exhilarating. I'm not sure Bertie thinks so, though – I have to keep him on the lead because of the edge,' she said nodding at the dog, who was barking at a herring gull pecking at a plastic bag ensnared on a clump of gorse.

'It's only my second visit but, yes, it's lovely. I just noticed – there's an old path zig-zagging up the cliff from the railway line. Is it used much?'

'That's not been used in years I think. It was cut out for the soldiers who were based at the wartime camp here. They used the station down below. But the path has never been open in my time here and I'm sure it's extremely dangerous. The limestone is very crumbly, chunks are always breaking away. That's why the railway line has to be protected by the wire mesh fence.'

The gull took off squawking having discarded the blue and white striped supermarket bag in disgust. Bertie strained at his leash barking.

'I'd best go, he needs a run but I can't let him off here. Nice to meet you.'

'You too. And Bertie.'

I turned to head back to the car park at the foot of the rise but stopped. 'By the way, do people use this path much at night?'

'Not so much, but you do get joggers along here in the evening, and, of course, the young couples looking for a bit of romance.'

Larry Lander had done some more digging with his police contacts. Dart-Line Transport was a haulage firm based in Dartford on an industrial estate literally in the shadow of the Queen Elizabeth II Bridge that carried London's orbital road over the Thames.

Dart-Line's registered owners were Jeff and Monica Stammers, the parents of Charmaine, now married to Shoreness publican Romeo Turk. The haulage firm specialised in taking containers from nearby Tilbury Docks to destinations in the Midlands and Glasgow. They also took fresh produce from Kent to the Continent, returning with top-end laminated flooring made in Belgium. It was, so it seemed, all above board.

The email from Lander said the police had recorded two occasions of a Dart-Line vehicle being stopped at Dover and found to be carrying would-be illegal immigrants who had strapped themselves to the chassis under the trailer. On both occasions the driver was believed to have been oblivious to the presence of his extra cargo and was not charged.

On three other occasions, Her Majesty's Customs had been tipped off that Dart-Line vehicles were carrying contraband including stolen cases of Martell XO Cordon Bleu Cognac and Moroccan Rif Mountain hashish, but each time the stop-and-search at the docks had found nothing more incriminating than wine gums and the driver's packet of Marlboro.

The worst offences the police records on the hauliers had thrown up were a few non-payments of toll charges in France and a broken tail light or two.

'Thanks for not a lot, Larry,' I said, re-reading the email. 'It doesn't mean, though, that Stammers and Turk aren't rotten to the core,'

I was sitting in Lander's office reading my emails while he was on the other side of the desk tapping out a list of instructions for the coming week for his deputy editor. He was about to go on holiday to Scotland with Sue.

'You're on your own for the next week, Tom. Don't do anything daft. Like I told you, some people out at Shoreness are a law unto themselves.'

My mobile rang. It was Fleur.

'We've had another raid,' she said matter-of-factly. 'We reckon about twenty plants have gone, this time dug up much more expertly and without so much damage, which is a small blessing I guess.'

'But how? I thought your team was watching it twenty-four-seven.'

'We were … still are in fact. I don't know. It didn't happen on my watch thankfully. The Eurotunnel CCTV around the air-conditioning plant shows no activity through the road tunnel while I was on duty from midnight until six. A couple of night trains rolled through but they did not stop, a few foxes were spotted strolling about. That's it.' She sounded exasperated.

'So when?'

'It looks like it happened between dusk and when I went on duty – in fact, while we were having dinner in Dover,' she paused and then added pointedly: 'When Dr

Ntini was meant to be on watch.'

'What's the good doctor had to say about it?'

'He's at a loss to explain it. The CCTV recordings showed plenty of vehicular activity during his watch, but that's not uncommon in the early evening when visitors are leaving and the Eurotunnel security shifts are changing. But no cameras are trained on the side of the cliff so there's nothing to see.'

'Do you think the Bat's Wing Orchid is being stolen to order or is it just random plant collectors?'

There was a silence while she pondered the question. 'Must be to order, Tommy. A: not many people know about the Bat's Wing and its potential properties. B: it's too risky on the cliff for casual plant collectors. C: the thieves are targeting just the orchids, nothing else. They know exactly what they're after.'

She paused again. 'My guess is that the plants are destined for a very expensive private collection somewhere in the Far East or America, or, and this is less likely, for the lab of some scientist who's got wind that the plant may provide the cure for dementia that the world is waiting for.'

'Surely none of the big pharmaceutical companies would resort to illegal activities like that?'

'I agree it's unlikely, but you never know. They have research labs all round the world and won't be keeping tabs on all their scientists. It only takes one mad boffin out to make a name for himself. He or she could be after the plant.'

'I'll get over there as soon as I can.'

I decided it was time to tell Lander the background

story to what was happening on the cliff at Samphire Hoe where this precious orchid had been found growing in the unique microclimate.

'But whether this has anything whatsoever to do with Jimmi Valgren's death, I don't know. I guess it's possible.'

Lander instantly saw the journalistic possibilities of the story. It would be national news. No – international news. The sort of world exclusive that could make a journalist's name for life: his Woodward and Bernstein Watergate moment. I wondered if he was about to change his mind about the planned holiday, although I doubted Sue would be too understanding.

'Not a word, Larry. Not yet at least. I promise you'll get the story first but the work of the Royal Botanic Garden in Edinburgh is strictly off the record for now. If the general public thought there was a potential cure for dementia, the clamour could ruin the project according to Fleur. It might also spark a devastating Klondike-like rush to Socotra, where the orchid originates.'

Lander agreed to 'sit' on the story. That was good enough for me.

'Where's the well-upholstered Jasmine, by the way?'

Lander looked crestfallen. 'Had to let her go. By order of the boss indoors. Great shame, she was coming on well.'

'Bet she was. So is that spotty intern out front her replacement?'

'Looks like it. He's very keen – and he's the son of the print works manager.'

The waiting room in Normanden Clinic had bright

red chairs, potted plants and children's paintings of the staff taped around the walls, but it was still a place of foreboding. You were either here because you were ill or because a loved one was ill. Like schools, medical waiting rooms made me feel uncomfortable. The *Telegraph* crossword was a welcome distraction: 6 Across: *power failure at research centre for dogs (5,4).*

A female nurse in starchy blue rustled over breaking my train of thought on matters canine. 'Danny can see you now, but only ten minutes please. He's had a tiring morning.'

Danny was sitting up in bed looking worse than he had the previous day. The bruising was coming out, turning the right side of his face an ugly purple-brown. By contrast, his mood was chipper. The scans and follow up examinations had shown no serious damage and the pain killers were having the desired effect for the cracked ribs.

'I'll be out by Monday, they say. The giddy spells have stopped and I'm in the clear,' he said.

'That's great. Any news from the police?'

Danny shook his head. 'I'm not holding my breath and I don't really care. Being in here has given me time to think, Mr Kidd. When I get home I'm going to convince Dad to sell up the farm. He's had a few offers from other neighbouring farmers who could make a go of it as a bigger project, but on its own, it's too small to be profitable.'

'What'll you do?'

'Part of my agricultural college course has included tree work. There's money to be had in arboriculture – tree surgery to me and you – and there's always a demand. With what we could get for the farm, Dad and I could set up a small business. I want to get away from this place. Shoreness is a fucking hole.'

'You said it. Tell me: the TA squaddies, who almost certainly did this to you and who were probably the ones who jumped me in the pub car park too – do you think they are capable of worse?'

'What do you mean? Jimmi?'

I nodded.

'No, don't think so. They're just low-life thugs, but not murderers. Anyway, it wasn't them who attacked you.'

'Oh really? Explain.'

'I was with them quite a while around that time trying to find out about the drug scene at the Lucky Fisherman and I heard them talking about you. Apparently you caught two of them having a joint in the bog, didn't you?'

'Yes. Go on'

'Well, they were talking about that and laughing that someone else had done their dirty work for them and given you a good kicking.'

'So who?'

'They didn't say. But my guess is it was the Wilde brothers. They're at the beck and call of Turk, and if he thought you were sniffing around his business, he might have given them the nod. Anyway, they're inside now. I hear they've been charged with people smuggling.'

'They have.'

The nurse reappeared and headed in our direction carrying a small pill pot and a beaker of water. I took my cue. I told Danny to stay in touch. Danny told me to be careful. I most certainly would.

There was still one person I was expecting to see at the clinic but she had not turned up as arranged. I sat in the waiting room again hoping Eve would show. She was late and had not sent a text to explain her non-appearance.

I opened the paper to the crossword and filled in 6 across: *black labs*. The rest of the answers came easily and I finished the word quiz. I looked at my watch again.

Twenty minutes later, with three sudokus also completed, I left. I had another date for which to get ready.

I had been putting it off but it had to be done. So I dialled Katie's number. I had no idea what sort of mood she would be in. We had not spoken since yesterday morning when our *missing* daughter turned up safe and well at her grandparents. I had tried to make my wife feel guilty about our daughter's absence. After all, she was the wayward parent with a lover, but I knew deep down it was the fault of both of us. At thirteen, our daughter was coming to terms with the breakdown of her parents' marriage. The Landers were out, the house was quiet, I was composed. It was a good time to call.

'Have you heard from Alice, today?' I decided on a non-confrontational question to start.

'I met her at lunch time, we had a sandwich out. She's coming home from my parents this evening.'

'Well, that's good, at least.'

'What do you mean, "at least"'?

'Nothing, in particular. It's good she's coming home.'

'It's not good, Tom. She's giving up on clubs at school,

her work is suffering and she's got this crazy idea about leaving St Jeavons.'

'I don't think it's such a bad idea, in fact.'

'What? Don't be so bloody stupid, Tom. She's not going to that Prospectus Academy down the road – have you seen the sort that go there?'

'They don't look that different to me. Just ordinary kids from different backgrounds. I didn't see too many with two heads wielding knives.'

'Oh that's right, go on, make your stupid socialist point, why don't you? You never wanted her to go to St Jeavons in the first place. It's only because my parents offered to stump up half the fees that you agreed.'

'It wasn't that and you know it. I've never thought that rarefied snobby place was right for her. She'd be far better off mixing with normal kids who have normal parents.'

'Fuck you, Tom.'

'You're not. You're fucking someone else. That's part of Alice's problem, Katie.' I was enjoying this. 'No, I agree with her changing school, and she ought to do it this summer before she gets too stuck into her GCSEs.'

'Well, it's not up to you, thank God. My answer's no.' She was shouting again.

'You'll drive her away, Katie. She'll want to come and live with me. In fact, that's not a bad idea. Think about it, my love.' I hung up.

Something was wrong. I was early, as usual, and Jo Etheridge's Volvo was not there yet, but that was not unexpected. I switched off the Fiesta's dim headlights, silenced Meat Loaf in mid-bellow and then realised: the

Lighthouse Inn was in darkness. I checked my watch – it was ten to seven. No light at all came from the sprawling ugly pub. Neither was there another soul nor vehicle in sight.

A bright flash caught the corner of my vision. It was the beam from the lighthouse, now strafing the black sea. I could hear my heartbeat pounding in my ears.

I closed the car door as silently as I could and walked slowly towards the building. All I could hear was the distant soft clatter of stones being tumbled up and down the beach by the waves, and the deep soft hum of the power-station generators. And my thumping heart.

I reached the conservatory and cupped a hand to the window. The curtains had been left open and the tables were laid up, with cutlery stacked in wicker trays on each one. Salt and pepper pots, vinegar and sauce bottles were standing to attention, napkins were in stainless steel clips and menus were piled on a table by the door awaiting the evening's customers. I tried the door expecting it to be locked. It was.

It was impossible to walk silently on the loose stones but there appeared to be no-one here to hear. Around the side of the building, the large picture window gave a view inside the bar. In one corner, a fruit machine blinked gaudy colours and gave the room an eerie neon glow. The pool table was set up with balls stacked in a neat triangle, two cues laid across the cushion at the opposite end. A red light blinked over it on the ceiling. Behind the bar, another red light blinked. Another smoke alarm or security camera. It was as deserted as the *Mary Celeste*, but outside I was not alone.

The crunch of stones under tyres and two beams of light panning around the car park fired adrenalin into my system. I peered around the corner of the building. The vehicle pulled up next to the Fiesta and the engine was killed. It was Jo's Volvo.

'I think dinner's off,' I said emerging from the shadows. 'Place is shut up. Not a soul.'

'That's odd. When I booked the table yesterday they didn't say anything about it being closed. What a desolate dump this is.' She looked around and shivered.

'What do you want to do?'

'Well I don't really fancy dining at my little hotel in Normanden,' she said. 'There are some other company people there and I'd rather they didn't start gossiping just yet. How about the other pub in Shoreness?'

I really did not want to go back to the Lucky Fisherman just yet but decided it should be safe enough if I had company, particularly now that the Wilde brothers were under lock and key at Dover Police Station.

'Yes, why not. Follow me. I know it well.'

We drove in convoy along the beach road past the holiday cottage where I had spent my first week in Shoreness and past the fishermen's shacks where I imagined the Afghan refugees had been incarcerated. The car park at the Lucky Fisherman was almost empty.

'Hello squire, long time, no see,' said Turk casting an all-too admiring eye over Jo Etheridge, who was dressed in a tight cashmere sweater and jeans. 'Still waiting to see that review in the local rag.'

Turk was still happy to play along. Either that or he was a fool, and I doubted the latter.

'Should be next week,' I said over my shoulder, steering Jo by the arm to a table in the corner as far away from the bar as possible. 'I'll explain in a minute,' I whispered to her.

I returned to the bar. 'Are we OK for a meal?'

'Of course. Fish special tonight is sea bass, panfried, or roasted turbot. Both fresh in today.'

Armed with two menus, two glasses and a bottle of chilled pinot gris, I returned to the table.

'So, go on – explain,' she said after sipping the wine.

'When I was here last week nosing around about Jimmi's disappearance, I did it under the guise of being a food critic for the local rag. I don't think anyone believed me – and for my pains I was jumped in the car park.'

'What the – ?'

'It was nothing too serious, a bit of a warning off I think.'

'Who?'

'Two of the landlord's henchmen, I think, but I don't know. Anyway, it's over and gone. Don't let it spoil the evening,'

It didn't. The food was better than good, and the conversation flowed as smoothly as the wine I had chosen. We talked briefly about the job-to-be with Genor-X but really she wanted to know about journalism, the sports men and women I had got to know, and my failed marriage. It was Desert Island Discs without the music.

I had even started to forget my misgivings about returning to the Lucky Fisherman when Turk wandered over beaming.

'Enjoy your dinner, miss?' he said, flashing his pearly

teeth. 'Can I show you the dessert menu?'

'It was lovely thanks, but not for me.'

'Afters for you, sir?' I thought I detected a mucky man-to-man innuendo in the question.

'No thanks. Just coffee please.'

When Turk returned with a large plunger of coffee and two cups, he seemed keen on lingering.

'I thought you'd left these parts,' he looked at me expressionless.

'Well, I did. Now I'm back. Job hunting in fact, at the power station.'

'Good for you, perhaps we'll be seeing more of you in that case.'

'You may well be, especially if the Lighthouse Inn has closed down. Do you know what's happened to it?'

Turk's bravado switched off like a light switch had been flicked. 'No idea'

'No idea at all?

'Only rumours, and there's always plenty of them.'

I waited for him to fill the silence.

He turned to walk away and then swung back and lent across the table.

'If you were friends with the daughter – Eve – as I hear you were, it's her I should be worrying about. Poor kid's gone missing.'

19

Jo looked at me as we stood in the pub car park. 'What did he mean by "poor kid"'?

'I don't know, Jo. I really don't know. She said her father occasionally lashed out, but ….' I let the terrible thoughts that had started to crowd in go unspoken.

Jo slipped her arms inside my jacket and hugged tightly. I felt her warmth and softness against me. She looked up and we kissed tenderly. Then she pulled away.

'Perhaps it would not be a good idea tonight.'

I knew what she meant by 'it' and nodded.

'You're probably right. Soon though?'

'Yes. Soon,' She kissed me again, this time her tongue probing and teasing before she ended the embrace. 'Now go home and get a good night's sleep. This business with Eve can wait until the morning – I also have the uncomfortable feeling we're being watched.' She looked over my shoulder towards the Lucky Fisherman's brightly lit windows.

'Knowing this bloody place, we probably are. How much sleep I'm going to get though, I don't know. I'm seriously worried about her, Jo. I really am. She seems a good kid who's stuck in this backwater – her boyfriend's dead, she has an abusive father. She seemed lost when I last spoke to her. Unable to see anything good in her future.'

Jo put her index finger on my lips, then buried her head in my chest again and hugged me hard.

'Go home. We'll talk tomorrow,' she said.

When I got back, Larry Lander was still up watching the late local news.

'You look like you've seen a ghost. Dr Syn hold you up, did he?' Lander was slumped in the leather sofa, feet tucked underneath him, a tumbler of something strong in his hand.

'I could do with one of those.' I nodded at the golden liquid.

'Edradour ten-year-old single malt coming up. No ice I take it?' Lander walked over to a fitted book shelf where Hemingway, Fleming and Rankin shared their space with a collection of Scottish malts, and he flipped the top off the nearest bottle. 'What's wrong? You don't often touch the hard stuff.'

'I heard some worrying news about thirty minutes ago. Eve Hathaway, the young publican's daughter at the Lighthouse Inn ....'

'I remember her all right, all tits and tee shirt,' Lander butted in, quickly checking over his shoulder to make sure his wife Sue was not within hearing range.

'She's gone missing Larry, and the Lighthouse Inn is closed up. Not a soul there.'

'Well, there could be a hundred and one possible explanations.'

'Yes, I know. One hundred of them probably quite innocent, but it's the one I don't want to think about. Her father's a nasty piece of work, really nasty. He lashed out at Eve a few days ago. She's been incredibly upset by this Valgren business too.'

I took the heavy cut tumbler that Lander was offering and swallowed the smooth strong contents in one, handing it back to my host. 'Refill please, Larry.'

Lander took the glass and at the same time pointed the remote control at the television and silenced it.

'There was a brief item at the end of the local news saying a woman's body had been found at Beachy Head, but they gave no name,' he said. 'You don't suppose?'

'Oh God, Larry. Please don't let that be the case.' I swallowed the second glass of whisky and went back to the bottle to help myself to a third.

The pneumatic drills thumping away in my right lobe and the sandpaper on the roof of my mouth reminded me of the night before.

I rolled over, pulled the duvet over my head and groaned. The fears for young Eve Hathaway had not been washed away in malt whisky. Surely she would not have taken her own life? But surely she would have been in contact having missed our arranged meeting to see Danny the previous afternoon?

I pushed the duvet away, feeling angry. Slowly the radio alarm clock came into focus. It was just after ten on a Saturday morning. Beside the clock was a mug of something. I guessed it was tea that Sue had brought in before her daily jog.

The liquid was strong and still surprisingly hot. Just what was needed, purging my mouth of last night's excesses. I picked up my mobile and resisted the temptation to call Eve's number. Instead I sent a text asking her to ring.

The walk to the bathroom was an unsteady one and I decided it was probably better not to look at the mirror. I stood under the shower, slowly turning up the heat as high as I could bear before slowly turning it down to as cold as I could bear. It was a tried and trusted method of sobering up and it nearly always seemed to work. It was also a useful method of self-chastisement for the stupidity of the night before.

By the time I wandered downstairs, coffee and bacon sandwiches were ready.

'Thought you could do with a little more than muesli to soak up the alcohol,' said Lander, pushing two doorsteps of white bread and half a pig across the kitchen table.

We ate in silence, browsing through the morning newspapers, both intuitively knowing there was no need for small talk.

Lander spoke first. 'Do you really think she could have done it?' he asked as he collected the empty plates and started stacking them in the dishwasher.

'I don't know Larry. She didn't seem the type to take her own life but who knows about people deep down? She was upset about Jimmi and, yes, she hated Shoreness. But she was a gutsy, bright girl. On the other hand, she's not been in touch. It doesn't make sense.'

'What doesn't?' Sue asked, breathing heavily as she walked into the kitchen, glowing with bright lycra and health.

Sue Lander had always been a voice of reason; a

perceptive advocate. She listened to my tale without a word of interruption until I finished with my list of unanswered questions.

'As worrying as Eve's disappearance is Tom, it really has nothing to do with you,' she said having perched herself on a kitchen stool, a bottle of mineral water in hand. 'And – no pun intended – don't jump to conclusions about the suicide at Beachy Head, sadly it's a monthly occurrence there. It could be anybody. If it's Eve, we'll soon hear, but from what you say, she doesn't sound as if she fits the profile of a jumper. As for Jimmi Valgren, you were looking into his death as a favour to Eve more than anything if I'm right?'

I nodded.

'Eve's disappearance rather negates your interest in Jimmi – unless you have some burning journalistic desire to get to the bottom of what we laughingly call a *good story*.'

I nodded again.

'So that leaves you with helping your sister out with the plant disappearances at Shakespeare Cliff, which, to be honest, is also none of your business and out of your league. It's a police matter, perhaps even a customs matter.'

She took a long glug from her bottle. I could tell my learned friend's summing up was over.

'You're right. Of course you are. Thanks Sue.' I looked at Lander. 'Where did you find such a brilliant wife, Larry?'

'What are you going to do?' he asked.

'Sort out my personal life, I guess. Find a new home,

start a new job, give my daughter the attention she deserves. Simples.'

'Well, one thing you don't have to worry about is moving on immediately,' said Sue.

'Oh. Holiday off?'

'No, far from it, but we had a chat yesterday and decided that it's pointless you moving out tomorrow just because we're not going to be here. While we're in Scotland, you can stay as long as you need. In fact, it'll be nice to have someone in the place while we're away.

You can drink as much of Larry's precious scotch as you like too, and when you move out, just leave the key where you found it: under the heron. Only one request – don't have a harem of women back here. I'm not sure the eighteenth-century beams are up to it.'

'Fat chance. If only. Thanks, I'll take you up on that.'

The hangover was beginning to subside enough after the third cup of coffee to make tackling the crossword feasible. 6 down: *Used snot could be facial jewellery? (4,4).* Charming.

The chef on the Saturday morning cookery show was stuffing a squid with something yellow. In the kitchen, Sue was doing something similar with peppers and aubergines.

Despite the culinary distractions, it was difficult to get my mind off Eve. What goes through someone's tortured mind as they stand on top of the cliff looking down at the rocks and sea below? What are those few seconds like after you have leapt and are falling conscious towards oblivion? Exhilaration? Fear? Freedom?

The mobile rang. I was disappointed to see Gerald Marler's name come up on the screen and not Eve's.

'Morning Gerry, any news?'

'About Jimmi? Not really. But there's some local gossip about the Lighthouse Inn.'

'And that is?'

'Word is that it's been sold to some overseas buyer and for a heck of a lot of money.'

'I didn't know it was for sale.'

'Neither did anyone else. Rumour is this buyer came in and made Hathaway an offer he couldn't refuse. Close to a million, apparently. He was probably glad to get rid too … the pub trade is on its uppers – and he had quite an overdraft at the bookies according to the postie, who seems to know everything.'

'Any idea where the family have gone? Including Eve.'

'No idea at all, Tom. Place is all shut up.'

'Is that what you were ringing about?'

'No, well, yes, partly that, and partly to see how you were getting on with your inquiries.'

'Nothing much to report. The workers at Samphire Hoe had seen Jimmi but knew nothing about his disappearance. The police didn't seem that interested in the sleeping bag we found. I'm not sure where I go from here.'

There was a pause at the other end.

'There must be something, Tom. You and I know Jimmi didn't just fall in the water and drown. Or go swimming and be swept away. There must be something we've missed.'

'If you're determined to carry on, there's one thing I thought of doing.'

'Yes, go on.'

'Well, along the top of Shakespeare Cliff, above where the Edinburgh scientists have their site, is the North Downs Way. It's used a lot by walkers and cyclists in the day, and in the evening, it's a popular spot for couples, I'm told. It might be worth going there asking if anyone has seen anything unusual in the last couple of weeks. It's a long shot, but you never know.'

'Will do. I'll report back tomorrow.'

I smiled for the first time that day. The phrase 'salt of the earth' was coined for people like retired Royal Navy Commander Gerald Marler.

I returned to the crossword and completed 6 down. *Nose stud.*

Now that was something of which the commander would disapprove.

The telephone rang again. This time it was Eve.

The wind was in a tearing rush to get across the Channel. It veered up the landside escarpment and incessantly pushed me towards the edge of the most famous drop in England. Beachy Head.

The phrase 'so loud you cannot hear yourself think' made total sense. The thunder of the wind in the ears scrambled the senses. It was quite disorientating – and Beachy Head was not the ideal spot to be disorientated. Eve hung on to my arm tightly. I am not sure who was reassuring whom.

The few leafless trees clinging to life on the cliff top were stunted and deformed, permanently bent over by the unforgiving wind like weary figures in a Lowry painting.

Out at sea, rays of sun broke through the dark clouds and created silver ponds of light on the battleship grey water. Two yachts, their sails down, ploughed through the waves heading east. Further out, a red-hulled tanker barely seemed to be moving at all.

The 500-foot drop was just ten paces away yet there was no protection. Nothing to stop us walking across the closely cropped grass to the chalky edge. On the most notorious cliff in England, you could inadvertently take a few steps off the footpath and plunge to your death. Eve's grip tightened.

'Wonderful, isn't it?' she shouted, her face alive with pleasure.

There were old flaking signs dotted randomly along the path edge warning of cliff erosion but there was nothing more than a few cowslips between us and oblivion. Here and there small sad wooden crosses had been planted in the ground with messages of love from the families of those who had taken the ultimate leap.

Eve laughed at the thrill of the danger like a teenage girl on a fairground ride as I edged towards the precipitous ledge, got down on my knees and peered over. Below was the red and white hooped Beachy Head lighthouse on its rocky promontory. The churning water turned a murky brown around the lighthouse base as the waves dredged up the seabed before tumbling over the white boulders of the shore. There was nothing between me and the rocks below to break a fall. The limestone cliff face was sheer. How many seconds did it take for a human being to fall 500 feet? It was so easy to jump and yet so hard.

'How can people do it?' I said quietly.

I crawled backwards a couple of yards before getting to my feet and turning my back on the sea. My legs felt weak yet they wanted to run away from the edge as I walked across the rolling grassland towards the main road. Eve followed talking excitedly, looking around.

'Isn't it exhilarating? So wild and natural. That's why Jimmi and I loved it here.'

'Did the pair of you come here often? It's a long way from Shoreness.'

'Exactly. No-one knew us here, no prying eyes, no nasty gossip. I could always get the van on Saturdays, and Dad thought I was off on a shopping trip with some girlfriends. Instead I was here with Jimmi. He'd have gone mad if he'd known.'

On the road that led back to the Beachy Head Inn and the car park where we had met, a black and yellow four-wheel drive with warning lights on the roof cruised slowly by. The sign on the side read: 'The Beachy Head Chaplaincy Team.' Waiting for Eve, earlier, I had read on a notice board in the car park that this volunteer group had had seventy-six call outs the previous month and rescued thirty-nine 'despondent' people, losing one. I stuffed a £20 note in the collection box thankful that Eve had not become one of their grim statistics.

I was relieved to get into the warmth and safety of the pub, which bleakly was known locally as 'The Last Stop Inn.' I shrugged off my coat and sat by the inglenook fire on a deep leather sofa while Eve went to the bar to order coffee for two. She had refused to tell me anything when we had first met an hour earlier, saying she wanted to walk first. I sat their waiting.

'Don't you love this place, Tom?' She sat opposite across the low polished oak table. There was no saucy tee-shirt today, just a baggy black hoody.

'It has its curious attraction, I s'pose. You know, Eve, I've been worried sick. I think I deserve some sort of explanation as to why you didn't show to see Danny yesterday, why I've not heard from you.'

'Sorry, Tom.' She paused as the barman put down the tray containing mugs and a large cafetiere. 'It's quite a long story.'

She told me that her father had been becoming increasingly edgy the previous week and had repeatedly disappeared during the afternoons. Then, on Wednesday evening, his mood had changed. Three men, dressed in suits, had visited the Inn, looked around, shared a bottle of the pub's most expensive red wine and shaken hands with Will Hathaway.

'The next day, Dad announced we had sold up and had to move out immediately. I hadn't even known the place was for sale,' she said.

'Who's bought it?'

'Don't know. To be honest, whoever they are, they're mugs. Trade has gone down the pan and Shoreness is only big enough for one pub, and the Lucky Fisherman does much better than us.'

'Someone told me whoever it was, paid a lot for it.'

'I don't know that either, but Dad seemed pretty happy. Mum too. I think she's pleased to get out of the trade.'

'So, where are they?'

'They've moved to a caravan on the Sunset Holiday

Park for the time being but I didn't want to go with them, so I went to a college friend's place in Brighton on Thursday. It was all such a rush, I forgot my phone charger and couldn't get back into the Lighthouse Inn to get it, which is why I've not been in touch. I finally bought a new one this morning. I also had no transport, so I couldn't get to see Danny yesterday.'

I asked Eve what she planned to do. She did not know. Her friend's sofa was comfortable enough for the time being, she said.

'You looked very emotional when I got off the bus today.'

'Well, I was worried about you, Eve. You know, you hear things about this place – you went missing … and a woman's body was found on the shore only yesterday.'

'You didn't think it might be me? Oh Tom, silly man.' She got up and sat on the sofa next to me and hugged me.

'I'd never do anything like that, not even because of what's happened to Jimmi. We only had a few months together but they were wonderful months and he opened my eyes to lots of opportunities. This was our favourite spot for sketching – if we could stop the paper blowing away.' She laughed and small tears ran down her chubby cheeks.

She wiped them away with the back of her hand. 'Don't worry, they're happy tears, Tom. That's why I wanted to meet you here today, to explain that I'm OK, my life has moved on but I'll never forget Jimmi.'

At last I felt relaxed enough to hug her back without it being misconstrued. We drank the coffee and chatted about Jimmi and my prospective job with Genor-X, but I had the feeling the subject of her parents was closed.

'Come on, I'll give you a lift back to Brighton.'

When we got in my courtesy car, Eve tuned the radio to a local station she said she liked. It was playing Joe Jackson's classic 'Different for Girls.' As I pulled out of the car park, we both started singing along.

After several wrong turns around Normanden's new estate of 'two and three bedroomed designer executive homes', I found what I was looking for: the rutted road that led to the expanse of wasteland that served as an industrial estate behind the railway station. The one I had seen from the footbridge where Romeo Turk had business.

Sue Lander had sounded convincing when she had said there was no point in carrying on investigating the death of Jimmi Valgren yet my journalist's instincts said otherwise. For better or for worse.

Being late on a Saturday afternoon, I was not sure what I would find at the industrial estate. The scrapyard appeared open, the hand-painted sign leaning against a plastic chair announcing that best prices were paid. The scaffolding firm was closed and although two lorries were parked up, they did not appear to be going anywhere soon, and neither of them were Dart-Line Haulage. There was, however, some activity in the far corner.

The remains of a boot fair was still doing business. Toys, books, CDs, and computer games were laid out on trestle tables. At the back of one van, a plastic sheet was spread on the ground and was covered with old garden tools, iron watering cans and wooden water butts. Another trader had trays of plants for sale while others appeared to just have a collection of junk beside their vehicles. There was also a mobile tea-wagon offering enticing smells that reminded me I had not eaten since breakfast. I ordered a bacon sandwich and a mug of tea from a large woman in a grubby apron who was flipping over sizzling rashers and burgers.

'No Dart-Line trucks in here today, luv?' I thought the 'luv' made me sound more authentic.

She glanced up and looked to the far side of the car park where two container trucks were parked.

'No, but then that ain't unusual. Wizzards and Llewellyns are our regular drivers. Don't know about Dart-Line. Oi, Benny.' She shouted the last two words in the direction of a man tinkering with a motorbike beside the snack wagon.

Benny looked up.

'Gent 'ere asking about Dart-Line, can you 'elp?'

Benny was in his twenties. Long clean hair tied back in a ponytail, creased leathers and oily hands, which he wiped on a rag draped across the handlebars of an immaculate Triumph Thunderbird 900.

'I've just moved into the area. I'm looking for work as a driver and someone mentioned Dart-Line to me.' I had prepared my story on the drive from Brighton after dropping off Eve.

'Dart-Line are here occasionally for the odd pick-up or drop-off, but between you and me, I wouldn't touch them.' Benny had a surprisingly soft accent that sounded as if it had been honed in an expensive public school.

'Why's that?'

'Just rumours. Look, you're not the law, are you?'

I shook my head. 'No. Like I said: just looking for work.'

Benny relaxed and offered his mug to the woman for a refill. He said he worked at the scrapyard during the week and kept an eye on the comings and goings at the site. He stirred two spoonfuls of sugar from a polystyrene cup on the counter into his refilled mug and took a sip before continuing.

'Dart-Line don't collect or drop stuff off for any of the local firms or farmers. When they do come here, which is about twice a week, stuff is unloaded into vans, or loaded from vans into the lorry. It tends to be done quickly and at quiet times – probably dodgy goods headed for the continent if you ask me. I'd keep my nose out if I were you.'

'Why do you say that?'

'I've had a run-in with them. One of their drivers was in a hurry turning round here and brought me off my bike. I wasn't hurt but the bike was a bit damaged. When I asked for the insurance details the driver was a bit evasive and gave me a number in Dartford to call. The Dartford people were the same, they didn't seem very keen on exchanging insurance details, but a couple of days later a cheque for £1000 came through the post. It more than covered the damage but I had a feeling they just wanted the incident forgotten. Nothing official, like. All a bit suspicious if you ask me.'

He sipped his tea and then nodded at a Portakabin by the far fence. 'Now Wizzards and Llewellyns – they both have a site office over there, but it'll be closed today. They transport a lot of furniture and white kitchen goods. And they both have good reputations. Try them on Monday.'

'Thanks, I will. Nice bike, by the way.'

Instead of heading directly back to the Landers' house, I decided to make a detour to take in Shoreness. Apart from the gulls and a dog sniffing around a black refuse bag beside the beach road, there was no sign of life. Smoke drifted out of the flues of some of the converted railway carriages but there was no one to be seen. Even the anglers had packed up for the day. The vast stony beach was lifeless. The Lighthouse Inn told the same story. The car park was empty. I pulled in and parked as close to the sprawling building as possible. The front door was locked and the lights were off. Dusk was closing in.

Around the side of the weatherboarded building was a pile of four recently painted green pallets and two black sacks neatly tied at the top. Wind chimes somewhere nearby were clanging tunelessly. A black-backed gull standing on a fence post was startled by my appearance, squawked indignantly and slowly flapped away. To the left was the dead end of the coastal road with a large turning circle. Beyond that was the perimeter fence of the nuclear power station and the towering walls of the plant itself that was covered in twinkling lights like an industrial Christmas tree. The new lighthouse was the only other building that overlooked this side of the pub and that was unmanned, its beam strafing the inn every few seconds like a solitary lazy disco light.

Convinced I was alone, I ventured around the back of

the building where a fence enclosed what was a large back yard on the stony soil. A row of aluminium beer barrels was stacked under a window that I guessed belonged to the kitchen. The backdoor had a cat-flap that rattled in the wind. A rotary washing line with three ragged towels pegged to it swung around gently but there was no sign of human life. The yard had a collection of plastic furniture that had seen better days, a large shed that was padlocked and beyond that a half-brick greenhouse that was relatively new. It looked well-tended although it was impossible to see inside because of the green gauze sheeting across the windows.

'What the … ?' I shouted, and then shook my head at my own nervousness. The cat-flap had crashed open and the pub's ginger tom came bounding towards me. It leapt onto the waist-high fence post where the seagull had been perched and started purring, looking up adoringly. The poor thing was probably starving.

'Sorry mate. Can't help unless you want an extra strong mint.' I tickled the mog under the chin. 'You'll have to go and catch yourself a fish.'

The cat followed as I walked to the shed and rattled the padlock just to ensure it had been fastened. It had. I switched on my mobile phone and shone the light into the greenhouse but could not see past the green sheeting that had been tacked around each window. Was that to keep the glare of the sun out, or to keep prying eyes out?

I headed towards the back door and looked in through the kitchen window, again using the phone as a feeble torch. If the Hathaways had left in a hurry, they had also left the place neat and tidy. The sink was empty and so too, in the middle of the floor, was the cat's bowl. Ginger jumped on to the window sill and purred hopefully.

'Looks like you're on your own, Ginge.'

20

'I can't take much more of that man,' said Fleur.

The man was Dr David Ntini, leader of the Samphire Hoe project but not her superior in the hierarchy of the Royal Botanic Garden in Edinburgh, where they were both employed. Fleur had very few superiors in Edinburgh. She had also never taken to men bossing her around very well. I decided it best not to interrupt her flow.

Ntini, she said, clearly saw himself as a young scientist heading for the top. The research work at Samphire Hoe was a prestige project that could make his name in the world of botanical research.

We were sitting in the Landers' kitchen enjoying a long, lazy Sunday breakfast. Larry and Sue had left at six that morning for their twelve-hour road trip to the Isle of Skye in the Inner Hebrides. I was no fisherman, but I had envied them their escape as I helped them pack the rods, waders and fishing paraphernalia into the back of their giant Subaru and set off for Scotland's west coast.

Fleur had borrowed an RBG Landrover and made the shorter journey from her Dover hotel to Normanden to get away from her frustrations.

'He seems to think this is his pet project and the rest of us are simply there at his beck and call. It's meant to be a collaboration, that's how it works in science. It's not a vanity trip to win him some Nobel Prize. Bloody man.'

'I thought you were meant to be going home this weekend.' I helped myself to another piece of toast and started buttering. I knew how to wind her up. 'I'm sure he'll manage just fine.'

'I was.' She glared at me. 'But Edinburgh are desperately worried about the raids on the cliff. The fact that we could have stumbled across the biggest medical breakthrough since penicillin has focused even the most befuddled old minds at the RBG.'

'I'm sure, Sis. But it's better to have a man at the helm in difficult times. Don't you agree?'

I was pushing my luck but she ignored me.

'I'm not going anywhere until this is resolved.'

'I'm still puzzled about how the raiders got up – or down – the cliff without being seen. The first time, I can understand. That caught you unawares, right?'

She nodded.

'But the second raid: that happened when you were staging round-the-clock watches. Right?'

She nodded again.

'So what happened? Why didn't anyone see or hear the second raid happening?'

'That's what Ntini can't explain although he was supposed to be the one on watch that evening.' Fleur shook her head. 'He gets irritated if the subject is raised. Says he's a scientist not a security guard. He's very touchy about it.'

'Do you think he could somehow be involved in the thefts?'

She paused in mid-chew and then shook her head.

'I can't see it.'

We fell silent as if waiting for the answer to appear in a blinding flash. I sipped my mug of coffee and looked around the Landers' kitchen. It was decorated with arty monochrome photographs that Larry had taken himself. He had always fancied himself with a camera. There were back-lit pictures of a young Sue, her hair blowing in the wind; sunset shots of hay bales and Kent oast houses; a lone deckchair blown inside out on a wintery promenade; a pile of higgledy-piggledy lobster pots on a quayside beside a weather-beaten fishing boat.

'Boat. What about a boat?'

Fleur shrugged. 'What about a boat?'

'We don't think our raiders of the lost orchid abseiled down the cliff, right? And we don't think they simply drove through the tunnel, the only road access to the Hoe, because that is closed by barriers at night and covered by CCTV, right?'

Fleur nodded but still looked bemused.

'But we've missed the most accessible way to get to Samphire Hoe: by boat. The thieves could have landed by boat, scaled the cliff for the plants and made their escape again by boat without ever being seen.'

'That's possible, I guess, but not easy,' said Fleur hesitantly. 'For a start, there's no jetty or mooring points along the sea wall.'

I wanted it to make sense. There were plenty of small boats in Dover, Sanctuary Bay and Shoreness and plenty of skilled sailors. It could not be that difficult to bring a boat in alongside the Hoe, or even run a small craft aground on the stony beach that ran the short distance from the Hoe's sea wall to the rocky western point.

'Even if the thieves came in by boat,' said Fleur. 'It doesn't explain why Ntini didn't see them when they were on the cliff. He was meant to be on watch. Bloody man.'

The Sunday morning politics show on television was a bore. Fleur was tapping away on her iPad, which was balanced on her knees. I returned to the *Sunday Independent* crossword I had started over the toast and Marmite that morning.

10 down. *High court official. (6,6).*

The mobile rang. It was Gerald Marler.

'Morning Gerry.'

'Tom, old man. Just reporting in from last night's recce. Bit of a palaver up there on the cliff top, I can tell you. Damn constabulary got hold of the wrong end of a mucky stick.'

'Constabulary? What's been going on?'

'Well, I suppose it's all rather funny now, but it wasn't at the time. I did as you asked: went up there yesterday evening to ask around to see if anyone had seen anything unusual going on.'

'And?'

'There were a few dog walkers and joggers, but no-one who said they'd seen anything, so I went back to the car park, which was much fuller than when I had arrived. This was about nine o'clock, it was dark of course. As far as I could tell, there were quite a few people still in their cars, so I tapped on a few windows to ask them the same question. The response I got was not very friendly, I can tell you. So I went back to my car, where I had a

Thermos. Then it happened.'

'When what happened?'

'The police turned up and the young bobby – a female at that – asked me to get into their vehicle. Wanted to know what I was up to, even accused me of dogging. They'd had a phone call from a couple at the car park complaining about me.'

I could not suppress my laughter.

'You may well laugh now, Tom, but it was pretty embarrassing at the time. I explained to them that I didn't have a dog, but they didn't see the funny side. They told me to stop trying to be smart and told me to follow them in my car to Dover police HQ to answer more questions.'

'Go on, Gerry. They didn't put you in the slammer?'

'No, fortunately. Thing is, Tom, it was all a bit awkward. I didn't want to tell them the full extent of our business.'

'So what did you tell them, Gerry?'

'Said I'd heard about some vandalism along the cliff top and in the old gun battery and wanted it stopped. Quick thinking, eh?' The commander began chuckling himself.

'The boys in blue are not the sharpest knives in the drawer. They fell for it and told me I could go but told me to keep away from the car park at night time.'

'Well, that's good, Gerry, but it doesn't get us any closer to finding out what happened to Jimmi, does it?'

'No it doesn't, does it?'

The commander's Shakespeare sortie was much ado about nothing, much like the politicians on the television.

I filled in the answer to 10 down. *Tennis umpire.*

The Gun House. Normanden's newest boutique hotel and eatery for Sunday lunch. Over starters, Fleur wept tears of laughter as I recounted the commander's brush with courting couples and the law. It was good to see her laugh again. She was being worn down by the Samphire Hoe affair and Dr Ntini. She had been also in regular touch with her partner Chris, and their plans to get hitched were in full swing. All that remained was to break the news to our parents that their daughter was in a same-sex relationship.

'They're probably more open-minded than we imagine,' I tried to reassure her without great conviction.

Being told that their only son's marriage was on the rocks and that their only daughter was about to marry another woman was certainly not what they had envisaged for the New Year when we had all last been together for the traditional Boxing Day celebrations at the family home a few months earlier.

'I'm heading back to London and your flat tomorrow, if that's still OK?' I said as we waited for the main course. 'I could stay at the Landers' for the rest of the week but I really don't see the point. I've got to return the courtesy car, and my contract with Genor-X will hopefully be waiting for me on your mat.'

'Fine Tommy. Stay there as long as you need. I'm thinking of selling it but there's no rush. What about the death of the artist? Giving up on that?'

'I think I am, sis. I've really no idea what happened to him. I suspect he tried to get too close to his birds and fell. Nothing more sinister than that. If he had ventured further along the cliff away from your plant site, there's a direct drop into the sea. Fall there and you are in the water.'

'But I thought he was naked when you found him in the sea?'

I nodded. 'He was .... I don't know. Perhaps the fall didn't kill him and perhaps he tried to take his clothes off in the water to make swimming easier but never made it back to shore. It's all supposition.'

The waiter delivered our Romney Marsh lamb cooked three ways with mint chutney.

'The point is,' I said, picking up the tiny trimmed chop with my fingers, 'the one person who really cared for him – apart from his parents, that is – is Eve, and she's moving on with her life now. I don't see much point in carrying on with it. Another white wine?'

She shook her head and put her hand over her empty glass. 'I'll stay on the water now, thanks. Work to do this afternoon, then I'm on watch at the site between six and midnight tonight. I'll never stay awake if I have any more.'

I was making sure I left the Landers' house how I had found it: spotless with everything in its rightful place, when Ali rang.

'Hi Dad.'

'Ali, you sound happier than the last time.'

'Yeah, guess I am. I'm back home with Mum. I know I've been a bit silly but it's OK, we've sorted it out.'

'Good. What about school?'

'Well, she's asked me to think again about leaving,

but there's nothing to think about really. I've had it at St Jeavons, I want to leave this summer and Mum knows that. She said she'd have to discuss it first with you, Dad.'

'She knows what I think, Ali. I'm happy for you to go to the local comp … but I do think you should stay living at home. No more escapades.'

'No. I know. Mum's around, she's upstairs. D'you want to speak to her?'

'Not right now, Ali. The divorce is going to happen, you'll have to accept that but it will work out OK for all of us. I promise.'

'That's what Mum said.'

'Good. Look, I'll be back at Auntie Fleur's flat this week, so we'll meet up. I'll pick you up from school on Tuesday if that's OK with your mother. Check first and let me know.'

'OK. Bye Dad.'

I emptied the dishwasher and eventually found the magnetic slab on the wall where the Sabatier knives were stored. I plumped up the cushions on the sofa and watered the aspidistras in their giant pots either side of the entrance hall. I wiped the glass rings off the walnut coffee table and put the newspapers in the recycle bin. I cleaned the loo and put my dirty laundry at the bottom of my case to prepare for an early start in the morning. I even wrote a thank you card I had bought and left it on the breakfast bar beside a bottle of Taittinger Champagne.

Satisfied, I settled down on the sofa with a coffee having put Jake Bugg on the Landers' fancy audio system. He was in 'Trouble Town' when the mobile rang again. The clock over the inglenook fireplace said it was 7.30.

Fleur's name came up on the screen.

'What's up Sis, bored watching the orchids ….'

She butted in with a frantic whisper I could barely hear above the roar in the background.

'Tommy, help me, he's after me …. Please. Please. *No* ….'

21

Fleur's desperate words kept replaying in my mind as I slammed the courtesy car through its gears on the twisting country lanes, my imagination racing as much as the 1.1 litre engine I was pushing to its limits.

'Tommy, help me, he's after me .... Please. Please. No ....'

The plea had come in a crescendo, rising in volume until the final shouted 'No'. Then? I wasn't sure what had happened and tried not to imagine. There had been a loud clatter; a rushing, crashing noise as if the phone had been thrown out of the window of a train. And then silence. I had been cut off. The line had gone dead.

The hedgerows that hugged the single-track road from the Landers' home to Normanden flashed by in the headlights, whipping the wing-mirrors with loud cracks to warn me I was getting too close. I just prayed nothing was coming the other way around the blind bends.

The two miles to Normanden seemed to be taking forever, not helped because I had to come to a skidding halt on the damp road and reverse into a gate entrance as a Range Rover dragging a horsebox came the other way.

'He's after me.' I could hear the panic in Fleur's voice. The Range Rover driver waved her thanks as she passed. The tyres of the Fiesta spun in the muddy gateway as I pulled out on to the road again.

Who was he? Was it Ntini? I had never liked the man with his aloof air and black-rimmed glasses. But why? It didn't make sense. The two were colleagues seemingly dedicated to everything botanical: plant-lovers, planet savers, environmentalists. Tree huggers, quite literally. Or did the moody Ntini have another agenda?

Perhaps the 'he' was just a generic 'he'. Some random unknown nutter after my sister, who happened to be in the wrong place at the wrong time. She was due to be on the evening watch at the Bat's Wing site, but there should have been very few people around Samphire Hoe this time on a Sunday evening in March. The Countryside Project walks were closed to the public at dusk, the barriers on the road tunnel, the sole entrance to the Hoe, should have come down. There was, though, the possibility of stragglers hanging on beyond the official closing time, as Jimmi Valgren used to do before he met his watery end. Visitors could always get in or out via the long walkway that went through the tunnel. Pedestrians could easily duck under the single road barrier at both entrances to the tunnel and walk through. Then there was the possibility of landing a boat at the Hoe. The fears crowded in.

At last: the main road at Normanden. Barely slowing at the give way lines, a sharp swing to the right pointed the Fiesta eastwards towards Dover. Thankfully the roads were quiet. At seventy miles per hour, the courtesy car had just about reached its limit as the tyres tried desperately to stay in contact with the tarmac on the corners. I wished I had the Audi.

'Tommy, help me ....'

And who was Fleur talking to when she pleaded 'Please . . . Please'? Was she still talking to me, urging me to come to her aid, or was she imploring her assailant not to do whatever he was threatening to do?

There were, possibly, other men on site at Samphire Hoe at this time in the evening. The countryside volunteer rangers who helped visitors, looked after the sheep and cattle, and emptied the litter and dog-waste bins, might be there. There were also staff at the Eurotunnel air-conditioning plant, which was constantly manned with at least three security personnel.

For a shocking moment, I failed to notice the red-flashing lights and the barrier that barred my way. I stamped on the brake pedal, bringing the little car to a juddering halt, its bonnet just inches short of the level crossing barrier. The wait felt like an eternity. There was no sign of a train on the single track in either direction.

I thumped the steering wheel in frustration. Torment gripped my stomach. Tears squeezed out of my eyes. 'Hang on Fleur, just hang on.' I shouted at the dark night. For some bizarre reason I started thinking about a family camping holiday we had had with our parents in Normandy. How she had screamed with mock fear at the top of the water flumes in the aqua-park as I grabbed her and made her slide down the longest chute with me into the pool at the bottom.

My mind then fast-forwarded to a week before and our night out in Leith when she had proudly introduced the woman in her life, Chris. The pair had talked excitedly about their plans together, moving in with each other. Possibly starting a family. Where was all that now?

I took my phone out of my inside pocket and tried Fleur's number again. It cut straight into her answering service: 'Hi. I'm either up a mountain or looking down a microscope. Please leave a message.'

Another tear rolled down my cheek. I punched the steering wheel in anger again, making the car horn blare as the freight train rumbled steadily by, its cargo being a single flat-bed truck carrying a sinister grey flask heading towards the Shoreness nuclear plant.

I gunned the engine as the barriers rose and the little car lurched over the uneven rail lines towards the A20. The sky was starless and the rain grew harder, lashing into the headlights and overwhelming the wipers' slow pass across the greasy windscreen. At last the neon road lights lit up the dual carriageway announcing the outskirts of Dover, their yellow glare bouncing off the wet road. The back of the Fiesta slewed alarmingly as I threw the car around the roundabout just outside Dover docks to head back towards London on the dual carriageway and the slip road to Samphire Hoe.

The traffic lights near the tunnel entrance glared red, the sign underneath informing drivers that the average waiting time was three minutes. Beside the lights running into the darkness there was a large lay-by made of loose stones where drivers of long vehicles were instructed to park and to ring ahead from the control booth to get permission to proceed.

I was vaguely aware of a vehicle parked in the gloom as I sped towards the red light and the tunnel beyond. I had no intention of stopping, but the Fiesta had other ideas.

Several times on the approach to Dover, the engine had coughed and spluttered but picked up again. I had assumed it was just the damp. But now it sounded terminal. The engine coughed one more time and just died. I looked at fuel gauge. The needle was in the red. I had paid it no heed. The Audi gave its driver a fifty-mile warning when fuel got low. Either the courtesy car had no such device or, more likely, it was not working.

'Not now, not now,' I screamed at dials. 'Please.'

The Fiesta rolled silently through the red lights and came to a halt as its lights picked out the dark mouth of the tunnel about two hundred yards away. I turned the key one more time in hope rather than expectation but there was not a flicker of life from under the bonnet. There was nothing for it but to leg it. The gloomy tunnel was lit with half-hearted security lights high up in its arched roof. Bats swooped silently in and out grazing on the wing on the insects attracted to the lights. I decided to use the walkway just in case a vehicle came the other way. It was dusty and draughty, the Channel wind rushing through the concrete tube under the cliffs making my progress tougher, but at least it was downhill as the tunnel dipped towards the sea.

My lungs were beginning to burn as my legs pumped but the adrenalin in my system refused to let me slow down. At the end of the slope, the path emerged into the open and flattened out beside the walls of the Eurotunnel air-conditioning plant. As I moved alongside the wall, a motion-sensitive security light clicked on and flooded the area with brilliance. I momentarily froze like a rabbit caught in headlights and then ducked into the shadows tight against the wall. The rain was still sheeting down, bouncing off the road. Had I been seen by security staff inside the plant? I doubted it. They were probably tucked up in their warm fuggy cabin playing cards or watching Dave instead of the closed circuit television monitors. Even if they had noticed the light come on, I hoped they assumed it was caused by a passing animal. If they were alerted, I feared they would not believe my story and simply hold me for questioning.

Up to the right was the looming dark mass of Shakespeare Cliff. Straight ahead was the Samphire Hoe car park and the visitors' centre. The sea murmured and splashed against the wall beyond that. The gulls were silent, for a change.

I hugged the wall to the entrance gates to the air-conditioning plant, then made a dash into the open space of Samphire Hoe. The car park was empty, the centre in darkness. The small hut selling guide books and refreshments was also boarded up. There was not a soul in sight but that did not mean the place was deserted.

I looked up at the ominous black cliff. I could just about make out the harsh shape of rocks and mounds but could hear nothing but the wind and the sea, churning resolutely behind me.

I started to feel helpless. Panic gnawed deep inside. I had assumed Fleur had called from the Hoe because she was due to be doing that evening's security watch, but she had not said that she was here when she made her desperate call.

The best way to the site was via the old unstable footpath that weaved up the rockface. Fleur had taken me that way on my previous visit. But the only access to the path was via a back gate in the air-conditioning plant, and to get there I would first have to rouse the security staff and then convince them my story was legit.

Looking back at the forbidding wall that surrounded the Eurotunnel plant, I noticed two Landrovers tucked up against it in what was a private delivery and parking area. I guessed one had been driven here by Fleur for her evening shift. But the other?

I ran towards the vehicles not sure what I was going to do. Both vehicles had the Edinburgh RBG logo on the side. The doors were all locked. On the passenger seat of one was a ring-binder folder and the Ian Rankin detective novel Fleur had been reading. Through the rear window of the other vehicle behind the back seat was a pair of Wellington boots and trainers, a high-viz jacket and several gardening tools. There was a name badge on the jacket.

One flash of the camera on the mobile phone was worth the risk. It would hardly be noticed anyway, as the vehicles were in a corner that was out of sight from the rest of the Hoe and most of the cliff face. I took the picture through the Landrover's window and studied it. It was hazy but it might do. I enlarged it using thumb and forefinger and although the close up image was blurred, I could read the name on the label pinned to the jacket. 'Dr D Ntini'.

Any brief satisfaction with my own detective work was interrupted by what I was sure was a shout followed by a scream. The shout sounded male and guttural. The scream was definitely female and filled with terror. It came from somewhere on high as a rumble started from somewhere on low.

The 19.42 stopping service from Dover Priory to London Charing Cross burst out of the tunnel in the hillside and charged along the line at the foot of the cliffs, its silhouette illuminated dramatically by a flash of brilliant white light and a crackle as 750 volts of electricity arced between the live line and the train's conductor pads. Another spark went off. This one in my brain.

The train raced by the disused Shakespeare Halt and the dilapidated workman's hut that Jimmi Valgren had used to doss down on his bird-watching expeditions. More significantly, I remembered looking down on the halt from the cliff top and seeing the outline of the long-neglected path zig-zagging from the halt up the chalk face that had been used by soldiers stationed at the camp on top of the cliff during the Second World War.

I ran towards the railway line looking up at the cliff straining to see if I could spot anything, or anybody. The wind swept stinging little pellets of rain into my eyes. If there was anyone up there – and I was sure there was – they would not be easy to find. And then they were. A small but distinct beam of light was moving in a sweeping motion across the rocky surface. It disappeared as quickly as it had appeared. It was a torch, and it gave me an area of the cliffs to aim for.

I stepped over the two live rails near Shakespeare Halt with exaggerated care. The tunnels into the cliffs on the Dover side were about fifty yards away. The tunnel at the westerly end which took the tracks back through the cliff was almost a mile away. At the Dover end of the old crumbling Halt platform was Jimmi's hut, and a break in the wire mesh fence erected to protect trains from rock falls. I looked up again, straining to see movement against the ink black cloudy sky. There was not even moonlight to give me much idea of what lay ahead.

Once through the fence, I followed it along the side of the railway towards the cavernous black mouths of the twin tunnels heading towards Dover. They were shaped like giant chapel windows: narrow and tall with their curved tops coming together in a point. I was sure I would find the old soldiers' footpath this way.

But first I found a body. My heart thundered in my ears. The dark still shape was huddled up against the fence, the unmistakable Royal Botanic Garden jacket ripped and partially covered with stones and chalky dust.

'Oh no, please God,' I mouthed the words silently, kneeling down and rolling the body onto its back.

It was Dr David Ntini. Not Fleur.

Blood had started to congeal around a head wound, his right leg lay at a sickening angle and his thick-rimmed glasses were shattered alongside him. But he was alive.

'Help us, please,' he said weakly, lifting a ripped hand towards my face.

'Us?'

'My colleague ... she's up there with him.' The battered hand tried to point. Ntini was in no state to recognise who I was, with or without his glasses. I lowered my mouth to the doctor's ear.

'I'm Fleur's brother. Tom. Who's up there with her?'

'I've no idea. He's desperate though. He's after the Bat's Wing.'

Ntini coughed and groaned. He closed his eyes and slumped back into the gravel, the rain gently washing the bloody gash on his forehead. His breathing was steady although he was starting to shiver.

'I'll be back. Just stay still and quiet. I'm going for Fleur.'

I had no idea if he heard or understood me and I didn't really care.

Any thoughts of stealth were forgotten. I set off scrambling over the rough ground, grasping at clumps of vegetation, a stream of loose stones tumbling down behind me as I clawed my way upwards, not daring to think about the ever-increasing drop below.

I suddenly realised that the ground under my feet had flattened out into a smooth ledge a couple of feet wide. By chance, I had found the long-disused soldiers' path. It gave even my inadequate leather shoes a chance to find some purchase. I paused for breath, chest heaving with the effort, while the adrenalin pushed me on. I needed to get my bearings. As I looked up, the moon poured its eerie light through a gap in the clouds scudding across the Channel and illuminated the hillside and the silver rail tracks a frighteningly long way below.

The path snaked on up ahead. To the right and off the path I could make out the rough rectangle of the cliff sectioned off with flapping tape by the scientists from Edinburgh. In the pale moonlight, the vegetation behind the tape looked no different to the small, scrubby vegetation hanging on for life elsewhere in this harsh environment, but to those in the know, it was the difference between gold dust and chalk dust.

There. Movement inside the taped off area higher up the rock face. It was a large figure leaning against the slope of the cliff, flashing a torch around as if he was looking for something. I ducked down flattening against the rocks certain it was not Fleur. The torch light went off and the figure moved stealthily and steadily away from me to where the cliff ran around directly over the entrances to the rail tunnels.

'Gotcha, little missy.'

The words were spat out with satisfaction. I recognised the voice from somewhere. The torch beam came on again piercing the rain-flecked darkness and shining on to another slight figure scrambling across the rocky ground. Fleur.

A mixture of fear and anger gripped deep inside, squeezing and twisting my gut. All I cared about was Fleur's safety. I forgot about trying to stay out of sight and hearing, and surged upwards, frantically gripping at vegetation and trying to dig my soft shoes into the stony soil. The torch beam arced around the cliff, sweeping over me. I paused hugging the wet ground trying to flatten myself on the rock. Had I been seen? Of course, I had. The bright light veered back towards me and was shining blindingly into my eyes.

'Who the fuck?' The voice sounded alarmed as well as angry.

If I had his attention, perhaps Fleur could put distance between herself and her pursuer. The light went out. I heard a grunt and a clatter of small stones tumbled down the cliff nearby. I sensed he was closing in. I had to move. I edged to my left, away from where I had last seen

Fleur. At least that would help her. Where was he? I could sense his bulk moving but I could see nothing except the dark rocks a few inches from my face. The memory of Ntini's crumpled body at the foot of the cliff sent a shudder down my spine. Was the same fate awaiting me? I grabbed at a thorny piece of vegetation ignoring the stab of pain in my left hand, and shuffled crablike along the cliff face. My left foot slipped, my grasp tightened and then it happened. The clump of vegetation came free from its shallow anchorage and I toppled backwards into the dark oblivion.

My right hand swung instinctively around to the cliff face as I spun outwards and grabbed at the ground, the stones tearing at my fingernails as I fell. I was now facing out towards the Channel, my back to the rocks as I dropped. Bouncing. Tumbling. Screaming.

It seemed an eternity.

Screaming.

It was probably no more than two seconds.

Screaming. Then I hit solid ground. The back of my head made contact with something surprisingly soft but my back and legs were not so lucky. Hot searing pain stabbed through my legs into my back. I had not hit the bottom of the cliff but landed again on the soldiers' path that zig-zagged back on itself. It had given me a ledge that broke my short fall and almost certainly saved my life.

I looked up feeling tears mingling with the soft rain. The torch beam was sweeping the rocks above me. I pressed myself flat against the sloping ground, bit my lip to defy the pain in my legs, squeezed my eyes shut and told my heart to beat as silently as possible. It ignored me, pounding furiously, trying to escape my chest. I buried my face in the damp vegetation that curiously smelled of marzipan.

'Who the fuck's there,' snarled the voice, which I could now put a name to. It belonged to William Hathaway, the now ex-landlord of the Lighthouse Inn. A man with an expensive taste in clothes and a gambling habit who liked to hit out at his kith and kin.

'Is that you, the interfering so-called author?' mocked Hathaway.

I opened my eyes and was looking directly into piercing white light. I guessed he was about fifty feet above me and to my right.

'You'll regret sticking your nose into other people's business just like that fucking hippie photographer did.'

So Jimmi Valgren's death had been no accident after all, just as Eve had feared.

The light was extinguished. I had a few seconds. I felt sure my hunter would expect his prey to move away so I decided to do the opposite and move towards Hathaway, but hopefully keeping below him. The problem with that strategy hit me after one step: my left ankle sent another shard of pain shooting up into the base of my spine the moment I put my weight on it.

I cried in agony. I could not stop myself. I had suffered some serious damage in the fall, and my whole left leg was now throbbing in protest.

I could hear and feel Hathaway heading downwards, more small stones tumbling down the cliff a few feet away. The stones clattered into the rail fence below. They must be landing close to where Ntini was laying. Had he been another victim of Hathaway? Almost certainly.

Run Fleur. Please run.

I had to try to move although my body was telling me to curl up in a ball. Nausea and pain came in alternate waves, washing away my resolve. I squatted on my backside and, with my useless left leg dragging in front of me, I levered myself along backwards using my right leg and arms. It was slow and every effort sent another stiletto of pain through me. But it was progress and it was silent.

Another train, this one bound for Dover, emerged from the western tunnel on Samphire Hoe and broke the tension. For a few seconds, illogically, I did not feel so isolated. Nor so helpless. Surely at least a few of those people sitting by the window seats in their brightly illuminated carriages would look out and see what was happening?

Pull the communication cord. Stop the train. Jump out and come to my rescue. Fleur's rescue.

'You're becoming delirious, Tom. Come on.' I softly scolded myself as the red tail light on the four-carriage train disappeared into the east tunnel.

Hathaway was not far away. That much I could sense. The pain in my leg was now a deep throbbing ache. My fingers were raw, fear rather than cold was making me shiver violently. Weaknesses was urging me to close my eyes and rest. Instincts were telling me to cling on. Literally. I had to keep moving, however slowly. I had come off the soldiers' path and was inside the botanical research area. I had not noticed that I had dragged myself under the tape that flapped around the blessed Bat's Wing plot but I knew I had made it that far because of the heat. The ducts from the Channel Tunnel air-conditioning plant were wafting warm air up the hillside and, even on a cold wet March night, the outflow was turning one tiny corner of this English coastline into a Mediterranean paradise. If only the circumstances were different.

Willpower and strength were nearing the red zone. I huddled into what felt like a large crevice and wondered if I could sit it out – at least for a short while. Gather thoughts, regain some strength. Hide long enough and Hathaway might give up.

Fat chance.

The torch came back on but its beam was much less powerful. Like me, its batteries were fading.

Hathaway seemed further away than I had expected. He was higher too. The beam of torch light swept around the rockface, backwards and forwards. The vertiginous slope with its hummocks of vegetation and outcrops of white stone looked curiously benign as the light passed over them. Hathaway was looking in the wrong area. Had the dark, the rain and the wind all combined to disorientate his senses too? Perhaps. Or had he turned his attention to Fleur again?

I clung to my rocky refuge. It was so warm despite the rain. The stone was cool and damp to my face. A small tufted plant tickled my nose. Was this a Bat's Wing Orchid close up and personal; the cause of all this trouble mocking me in my last moments? I closed my eyes and tried to ignore the blaze raging inside my left shoe, breathing as quietly as I could.

Little stones tumbled down, bouncing off my back. Hathaway was above and moving. Time to look down and make a decision. The moon reappeared through the scudding clouds, casting its silver light on the train lines below. We were directly over the rail tunnels that disappeared into the hillside. One slip here, and there was not even a fence to break your fall.

Out in the Channel, the Varne Lightship blinked its warning in the middle of the world's busiest shipping lane. The light swept around glinting off the black sea and flashed in my eyes before disappearing for a second or two. It was almost mesmeric. In the warmth of the outflow from the giant fans below, I felt consciousness slipping away. It was almost a relief. At least the pain would go away.

Fight it. Fight it.

If I did not care about my own fate, I was still there for Fleur. Wherever she was. I had not seen nor heard her since the moment Hathaway turned his attentions away from my sister and on to me. She could have got off the cliff safely. She had had time. She may right now be alerting the security team at the Eurotunnel plant. If they were coming, it had better be soon.

Hathaway stood above me triumphantly. Panting, perspiring heavily, red-faced, he looked like a man with only evil intent in mind.

'Found you, you bastard.' He said the words slowly and deliberately through clenched teeth. His short black hair was plastered to his head. The knuckles of his right hand were bloodied, both knees of his black jeans were torn.

'Why couldn't you just keep your fucking nose out?'

He did not want, nor expect, an answer to the question. Hathaway's eyes were wild and angry. He looked a desperate man, and desperate men were dangerous.

I levered myself up to protect myself the best way I could but my left leg was useless and numb. As I tried to stand, it gave way. I toppled backwards and was falling uncontrollably into the void for a second time. Hitting the rocks, crying out in fear, heading into darkness. It must have been only a tiny moment in time, but as I fell, I glimpsed the grinning face above me. My head hit something hard. Senses reeled, stars exploded behind my eyelids. And suddenly I stopped, slumped in a heap. Pain gouging through my legs and up my spine. I had come to a halt on the old walkers' path I had used with Fleur when she first brought me to see the Bat's Wing Orchid site.

I had put about thirty feet between me and my pursuer. It would be only the briefest of respites. Hathaway looked left and right trying to work out his best way down. He was not about to take the same torrid route as I had. He took two paces left, then turned to face the rock and clambered down like a man picking his way down a wobbling ladder.

He was now on the same path a few short paces away. He turned to face me, breathing heavily, running his tongue over his lips, the spittle glistening in the moonlight. I lay propped up by whatever had broken my fall. No more fight left in me. No more options.

'You're going over, pal. Say cheerio,' said Hathaway with a leering grin as he moved forward.

I tried to shuffle backwards thinking I might be able to slide further down the rock face but something hard and straight wedged in my back. It shifted a little under my weight. I made one last desperate move. What had stopped my tumble down the cliff was one of the rusted metal posts that had once carried a fence protecting the old walkway. The wires between the posts were long gone but the sturdy poles remained, hammered into the limestone. That was what was propping me up. I reached over my right shoulder with both wet hands, dredged up what feeble strength I had left and yanked.

The post came free.

Laying on the ground, I wheeled around, screamed and swung the metal bar at knee-height. It made delicious damaging contact with Hathaway's left leg, which caved inwards at the most unnatural of angles.

Shock then anger and finally agony burned in his eyes in a split second as if he had realised what had happened too late. A deep guttural unnatural howl came out of his mouth. His angular frame crumpled like a snapped twig and toppled towards the abyss. Our eyes met as he flailed at thin air with windmilling arms trying to reach for me. Fingers grasping at nothing – like those of Jimmi Valgren when I had seen him floating face down in the sea two weeks earlier. It was as if Hathaway was reaching out in a gesture of rapprochement.

'No chance. Pal,' I screamed.

Hathaway's tumbling body bounced twice off the rocks before it fell over the lip of the west-bound tunnel and thudded across the rail line and electricity conductor line below. Grotesquely, it arced up into the air again, propelled by 750 volts that sparked and crackled violently, throwing him back on to the tracks like a dancing manikin before the 20.28 from Dover Priory to Charing Cross thundered out of the tunnel and finished the grisly job.

22

Her close encounter with death had not made Fleur a more circumspect driver. The RBG Landrover, its suspension unforgiving at the best of times, hopped rather than cruised around the succession of roundabouts on the A1. Door grips had to be gripped, one good leg braced, and buttocks clenched.

We were heading north on Britain's historic artery from London to Edinburgh although thankfully we were not completing the journey in one hike. Each lurch around a roundabout reminded me that my left ankle was not connected to the rest of my body as it should have been. Broken in two places and encased in a surgical boot, it dangled at the end of the leg, the dull throbbing ache accentuated by the vehicle's rock hard springs and Fleur's delusions of being a rally driver.

'Take it easy, Sis. Patient on board, remember.'

'You'll live, my hero,' she laughed as Cambridgeshire's flat countryside flashed by.

It had been five days since Will Hathaway had fallen to his death at Samphire Hoe. For several hours the transport police had searched for his body parts, and even then he was not complete when the undertaker's private ambulance staff had boxed up what they could find and taken him to the morgue. The 20.28 from Dover Priory had done a very thorough job. The search for Hathaway's remains had been good for one person: Dr David Ntini, who was found curled up and barely conscious beside the wire mesh fence not far from part of Hathaway's right leg. Ntini's rapid departure to hospital came before hypothermia set in.

The police, who had been alerted by the train driver, were convinced Hathaway was dead before the train had hit him, killed, if not by the fall, then by the 750 volts that had turned his body into a contorted Jack-in-the-box after it had landed on the lines below Shakespeare Cliff.

As for me, I was eventually slid down the cliff strapped into an orange stretcher by the Dover coastguard team after Fleur, who had scrambled to safety, had told the police I was up there, somewhere in the dark.

All of Monday and part of Tuesday had been taken up with 'helping the police with their inquiries' from my hospital bed.

Initially, they had seemed suspicious of my hazy version of events and my reason for being half way up the cliff on a wet and windy Sunday night. But by the time Fleur, Gerald Marler, Larry Lander and David Ntini, who had also been interviewed in his hospital bed, had told their stories, the police accepted that I was little more than an innocent do-gooder concerned about his sister.

Ntini had suffered concussion, a cracked vertebra and a broken leg but he was on the mend. He told Fleur that he had been at Samphire Hoe that night for a variety of reasons: the main one being that he had felt guilty about falling asleep on his watch on the evening the scientific site had been raided a second time. This was his prestige project. He was desperate to put matters right – but he had other reasons for being there during Fleur's shift of watching guard over the orchids.

'Turns out you were right – he'd taken a fancy to me,' Fleur told me. 'I'd never have guessed it. He had a funny way of showing it by being rude to you and pretty prickly with me. Anyway, I've gently let him down by explaining that our chemistry would never have worked. Poor wee man.' She giggled.

Ntini told the police that he had arrived at Samphire Hoe after Fleur had started her watch. She had been sitting in her RBG Landrover when he had pulled up alongside her. They had walked along the seawall together, enjoying the bracing wind and talking about the project to grow the Bat's Wing Orchid on a commercial scale. As they turned to walk back towards their vehicles, he had seen a flash of light on the cliff above them.

It had taken them more than ten minutes to rouse the security staff on the entrance intercom to the Eurotunnel air-conditioning site, and when one did turn up, his English was as bad as their French, and another ten minutes elapsed before they could make their way to the back entrance of the site and the gate that gave access to the old footpath that led up the rock face.

'Didn't you think of calling the police at that stage?' I had asked Fleur.

'It was hardly a police matter we felt. And, anyway, when your overriding concern is to safeguard your plants, you just get on with it. We're a bit like protective parents with a child, I suppose. Act now, think later.'

Ntini, she said, had tried to persuade her to leave it to

him but she was having none of it. They had clambered up the cliff without trying to keep their presence secret, and that was their first and almost fatal mistake. Hathaway had heard them and then seen them, and lay in wait behind an outcrop. As they passed, he had stepped out and simply pushed Ntini over the edge, expecting the drop to do the rest of his deadly work, and then he had made a grab at Fleur. She had been too quick for him, and scrambled up the rocks.

'I kept going for about ten minutes and found a crevice,' she said. 'I couldn't have gone much further. I was totally pooped. That was when I called you. He must have seen the light of my phone because he was there just as I got through to you. He grabbed at me and I dropped the phone. I think that distracted him because I kicked him where it hurts most and got free again. He was very strong but he was not very mobile after that. Serves the bastard right ....'

Guiltily, she had let the sentence trail off, realising she was talking about a man who had met a particularly shocking end in every respect.

Fleur said she had clambered higher up the cliff to escape her assailant in a game of deadly cat and mouse. At one stage, she thought Hathaway had given up looking for her as he had returned to the taped-off site on the cliff, swung his backpack off his shoulders and gone down on his hands and knees. When the moonlight broke through, she could see him clearly. He was digging at the stony soil with a small tool, putting specimens in plastic bags and stuffing them in his backpack.

His work seemingly done, he had stood up and

stretched. He fastened the back-pack and pushed it under some vegetation checking it was secure. He then clicked on his torch and sent the beam over the face of the cliff.

'That was when you arrived. I saw the security light come on down by their air-con plant – and Hathaway did too. He switched off his torch and watched you come across the railway lines and start climbing. Stupidly, I called out. You didn't hear me, there was probably no chance you would what with the noise of the wind and the waves – but Hathaway did and came for me again. Thank goodness my knight in shining armour made it just in time.'

The police had recovered Hathaway's backpack from the hillside. It contained thirty Bat's Wing Orchid plants. He had known exactly what he had been looking for even if his method of collection had been crude, the root system on half the plants being damaged to such an extent that they would almost certainly not survive.

The police had also arrested Hathaway's accomplice in crime: Susan Hathaway, his wife – the woman who Eve had said suffered in silence from domestic violence at the hands of her husband. Susan Hathaway had been found sitting in a vehicle parked in the gloom of the long loads lay-by on the Dover side of the entrance tunnel to Samphire Hoe. The same vehicle I had been aware of but had forgotten in my frantic race to help Fleur.

Hathaway had confessed to dropping off her husband near the tunnel entrance and waiting for him there. She claimed to not know what he was doing. On two previous visits, Will Hathaway had disappeared along the pedestrian path through the tunnel and re-emerged a couple of hours later with muddy boots and hands, and a heavy back-pack, she told police.

'But her hands were as dirty as his,' Lander had told me.

Larry Lander had cut short his fishing holiday in the Scottish islands after I had phoned him and said to expect a call from the police. With such drama happening on his patch, he could not bear to be away anyway. He flew back with Sue's blessing while she drove home. She knew the *South Coast Gazette* would never carry a more important story.

Lander's contact at Normanden police, Sergeant Hopps, had filled him in with the details. Back at the Lighthouse Inn, a search of the premises had discovered Sue Hathaway's involvement may not have been so unwitting. In the locked greenhouse and shed behind the pub were plastic trays planted up with Bat's Wing Orchids. Susan Hathaway's DNA was evident in all the trays.

'The pair of them didn't know how deep they were in or what they were doing,' said Lander when he visited me in Dover General. 'They were being used by a much bigger organisation with links in Beijing, Paris and Santiago. Will Hathaway was a small time crook, he dabbled in a bit of smuggling with his mucker at the Lucky Fisherman, Romeo Turk, but unlike Turk, he was stupid with his money. He was in debt up to his neck, apparently. The Lighthouse Inn was losing money but it was his gambling debts that were crippling him. There are tales that he owed more than fifty grand to various bookies, who were running out of patience.'

'Were they the men in suits Eve saw visiting the pub last week?'

'No, the police don't think they were heavies from the bookies because on Wednesday of last week £750,000 was transferred to the Hathaways' joint account, supposedly for the sale of the pub – although it's barely worth half that.'

'So, who were they, Larry?'

'Representatives of agents acting on behalf of a pharmaceutical company called Sino Seine Solutions. Never heard of them? Nor had I, but I'm told they're big players on the medical drugs scene. Based in various locations in deepest China but with glossy presentable offices in Beijing and Paris and an above-board research lab in Chile.'

Lander said that when she was presented with the facts, Sue Hathaway had confessed all she knew. Her husband's introduction to Sino Seine's men and money had come from a local property owner called Gideon Squires.

'My God, I know him. Not well, but I know him.'

'You what?' Lander was incredulous.

'He is the owner of Lighthouse View Cottage. A colleague of my sister, except he works at Kew not Edinburgh. He's an expert in orchids. It's beginning to make sense. He knew how important the Samphire Hoe project was, by all accounts he was pretty pissed off with the direction his career was headed at Kew, and he knew Hathaway – a small-time crook who could do the dirty work.'

In her confession, Sue Hathaway confirmed that her husband had been briefed about the plants that Squires wanted but had not been told why. Squires had provided an exact description of the orchid, a ground plan of where they were planted and details of the duty rota for keeping watch at the site overnight.

Hathaway had done the first raid to prove he could get the orchids. The second and the third had earned him the hefty payment into the couple's bank account. The plants were to be stored at the Inn – now the property of a shell company in Gibraltar – while the Hathaways planned to make their future in an apartment in northern Spain, for which they had already paid a deposit.

Lander said: 'The paper trail will never lead back to the supposedly respectable Sino Seine Solutions either. The money paid to the Hathaways came via other shell companies in the Channel Islands and Panama. As for Jimmi Valgren, Hathaway couldn't be linked conclusively to his death, but the police have little doubt that he had a hand in the drowning.'

'I already knew that, Larry. Hathaway told me as much in a cliffside confessional on Sunday. My guess is that Jimmi was halfway up the cliff photographing his birds and saw Hathaway up to no good, collecting the orchids. Whether he challenged Hathaway or not, or whether Hathaway saw Jimmi first, we'll never know. You can be certain it wasn't an even contest, whoever started it. Jimmi would have been no match for him, and Hathaway didn't strike me as the sort to take prisoners.'

'So why was Jimmi's body naked?'

'Your guess is as good as mine, Larry – but stripping Jimmi to make it look like an accident or suicide and dumping him over the sea wall before disposing of the clothes would have taken little effort on Hathaway's part.'

Fleur pulled into the services just south of Grantham. The Landrover needed diesel, I needed Americano and painkillers.

'Won't be long, Ginge. Just a quick comfort break.' Fleur leaned over to the back seat and tickled the purring moggy through the mesh of the cat basket. When I had told her about the abandoned cat at the Lighthouse Inn, she had taken pity on him. 'You're going to love it in Edinburgh. Lots of fat Scottish mice to catch in the greenhouses.'

Our first destination, however, was Derbyshire, where our parents lived in a small village in the Dales. They knew I had broken my ankle in an accident, but nothing more about the drama of the last three weeks. That could wait. First they had to digest the news that their daughter had fallen in love and was about to embark on a same-sex marriage.

'You know, Tom. I was going to invite Gideon Squires to be one of the witnesses at the ceremony. I thought we were good mates but clearly I didn't know him at all.'

She cupped her coffee mug in front of her chin and her eyes shone with moisture.

'I don't know whether to be upset or angry. I was such a fool. He was clearly using me that day last week when he came to meet me in Dover and talk about the security plans we'd put in place. I knew he was disillusioned with life at Kew but I didn't know he'd stoop that low … to become a common criminal and risk the whole Bat's Wing project. He was the brains behind it all.'

'Well, he won't be doing any more harm, Fleur. He's in custody, and I suspect the only plants he's going to see for a while will be on the prison allotment.'

'He had a brilliant career ahead of him, too. I sort of feel sorry for him.'

'Don't.' I reached across the table and squeezed her hand. 'Look, he was ruthless. He planned Sunday's raid by Hathaway alright, and he knew you'd be the one on watch that night. He probably reckoned you'd cause much less bother than one of you male colleagues. I doubt whether he could've cared less about what happened to you up on that cliff.'

We were sitting on a quiet corner sofa in the unusually smart service station. Fleur shook her head vigorously as if to shake out the debris.

'You're right. Sod Squires, sod the whole damn project. Let's talk about this wedding – and how you reckon I should break the news to Mum and Dad about Chris.'

I laughed 'They're more broad-minded than you think. Lesbianism did exist in their time too, you know.'

'Don't call it that,' gently scolded Fleur. 'It makes it sound so butch.'

'You and Chris are certainly not that. I promise you, they'll be happy for you.'

'I do hope so, I really do.'

'More to the point, Sis, I've got to get my story straight about this.' I pointed to the blue plastic surgical boot on my plastered left ankle.

We had agreed to tell our parents that I had slipped climbing to see the Bat's Wing Orchid site at Shakespeare Cliff, which was, to all intents and purposes, true. For now, at least, we intended to leave out the details of the circumstances – and how close we had come to tragedy ourselves.

The police had started looking into the activities of Romeo Turk. He was in the clear over the death of Jimmi Valgren. The break-in at the boy's Dormobile at the nature reserve had been the handiwork of Gary and Bronx Wilde, the fishermen brothers about to stand trial for smuggling asylum-seekers into the country. The Wildes had feared that Valgren had seen too much from his vantage point in the Danish Hide, from where he had been taking pictures of the water fowl and the shoreline beyond. Valgren had unwisely inquired about 'lights on the beach at night' when he had visited the Lucky Fisherman to buy cannabis. Word had quickly got back to the Wilde brothers. The Ness was a small place.

Turk was little more than a small-time smuggler. I was convinced it was Turk who had given the Wilde brothers the nod to give me a warning off in the car park of his pub after my first evening at the Lucky Fisherman. I had asked too much and the folk of Shoreness did not take kindly to nosy incomers

It had also been the Wildes who had ransacked and soiled my holiday cottage at the behest of Turk. Getting in had been no bother for them as the cleaner at the Lucky Fisherman also gave Lighthouse View Cottage a weekly once-over whenever visitors stayed. She had the front door key – and she was the Wildes' younger sister.

Using his father-in-law's Dartford haulage company, Turk had been bringing cases of stolen vintage brandy, Armagnac and Champagne in from France, a trade in which Hathaway was a partner. Going the other way on the trucks were small quantities of cannabis resin and E tablets produced locally and hidden in pallets carrying speciality gearing for wind farms in northern France.

It was a business to which the local bobby, Peter Trotter, had turned a blind eye on the understanding that a percentage of the profit went into his retirement pot – a retirement pot to which he would no longer be entitled as he faced a stretch behind bars. It had been a very cosy community affair in Shoreness.

The next time I went back the Shoreness, it would be as an employee of Genor-X. We had interrupted our journey north from Kent to stop in south London and collect the mail from Fleur's flat. As Jo Etheridge had promised, the job offer and contract from the power company was there in a large white envelope. I had read and signed the contract as Fleur battled through the London traffic heading north towards the M11.

'I never thought I'd turn my back on journalism and be signing up to be a PR man Fleur, but, you know what? I'm quite excited about it.'

'Perhaps that has something to do with your immediate boss. From what you tell me, this Jo Etheridge is pretty accommodating.'

'Stop it, Fleur. Just stop it.' I drained my second coffee. 'Time to hit the road, Sis,'

'Loo, first. Won't be long.' She headed towards the busy concourse.

I picked up the newspaper I had been working on in the Landrover. Just one clue to complete to finish today's crossword.

20 down. *Confused copper birdie ends up in a steamy story (6,6).*

I filled in the letters. My novel was under way at last: *Bodice Ripper.*

End

About the Author

Colin J. Bateman has spent his working life as a newspaper journalist, first in the West Country and then on the national press based in London. He has also dabbled in magazine, radio and television work. He has written two other books but this is his first venture into fiction. He and his wife live in Kent.